Owning Regina
Diary of my unexpected passion for another woman

LORELEI ELSTROM

Sebastopol Bay Press, LLC

Copyright 2014 Lorelei Elstrom
Manufactured in the United States of America. All rights reserved. No part of this book may be reproduced in any form or by any electronic or mechanical means including information storage and retrieval systems without permission in writing from publisher, except by a reviewer, who may quote brief passages in a review.

Published by Sebastopol Bay Press, LLC.

Library of Congress Cataloging-in-Publication Data
Lorelei Elstrom

Owning Regina: Diary of my unexpected passion for another woman

ISBN NUMBER: 978-1499362190

Proofreading by Marianne Haynes
Additional details: www.elstrombooks.com

The author or publisher does not have any control over and does not assume any responsibility for any content of this book on third-party websites or distribution platforms.

This diary has been fictionalized in order to protect the privacy of certain individuals. Though it may bear many striking similarities to real life situations, people and relationships, any such depictions are purely coincidental. Many punctuation, spelling, and grammatical errors have been preserved to illustrate the spirit of the original work.

--- THURSDAY MARCH 1, 12:01am --- It's all about me.

My boyfriend is an ass!

Hello Diary! I've always wanted to keep a journal, but never had enough motivation to actually do it. I should have gone to you a lot sooner, but I usually just bitch a while about things until I calm down, then change course until some other episode arises. But today is different. My boyfriend's an ass. Did I make that clear? Ass Ass Ass Ass Ass dickwad fuckface. Ass.

Let's see, how long have we been dating? Um, about one and a half years. And how many times does he initiate ANYTHING with me? Umm, about zero. He takes me for granted. When I was a kid, I used to think it was "take me for granite." Ha. I wish I were granite. That way I would never be the one to make the first move. I would just sit there as a rock. If boyfriend Stephen would want to do anything with me, then he would have to come over and say… hey Rock, wanna go to a movie? Or wanna make out? It's like this song by Eleni Mandell, "I'm Soulful" where she sings, "Treat Me Like I'm Heavy". What a great frickin' song. I want to mean something to Stephen. But I mean jack to him. Dick! Did I mention he is an ass?

When we first met, he fawned on me. "You're beautiful! You are amazing. I've never seen a grown up with dimples. It's so childlike and magnetic. I love how smart you are. Not many girls I know are as outgoing and charismatic as you! You are absolutely my dream woman. I can never imagine anyone sexier than you. Your dark red hair glistens. Your body is amazing, always looking like you could be teaching a yoga class or appear in a Broadway dance show. You are amazing! Blah blah blah blah blah blah blah." Yeah, right. He's so full of it. Yeah, I'm so great.

But I swear, nothing would ever happen unless I made the first move. Did he think to go to the movies on Friday? No. Did he think to sneak the chocolate and drinks into the theater? No. Did he call me to ask if I wanted to take a trip up to Sonoma this weekend? He never does shit. If I'm so hot and sexy and beautiful and smart and dimply, then why does he never initiate anything? Even with sex, it's always me. It's supposed to be the opposite with dudes. They are supposed to be the horny ones.

So is Stephen gay? Far from it. I caught him with porn a few times and it was exotic women… Indonesian, Egyptian, Mediterranean, all exotic with long, skinny legs and bony everything. So he definitely likes the copper colored women. Oh, and flat too. They were all flat. I don't blame him for the porn, but I blame him for faking that he was attracted to me and my boobs. Why would he want to be with me and pretend he's attracted? Is it because he is too checked out to be real? Is it because his friends always tell him I'm a catch?

I've been keeping score for the past couple weeks to see if he would ever initiate a single thing with me. Nada. During the whole two weeks, he only called me twice. Both times he wanted to share something about work or whatever. I think he was sensing that I was testing him and wanted to make a showing. There is only one reason I have stayed with him: It was better than being alone. Better than being with someone strange. At least with Stephen, I know his flaws and being with him is harmless. Well, if you want to be in a lame relationship, it's harmless.

Besides, he's extremely good-looking and it feels good when we go out. People think we are the couple that has it all. In public, he hangs all over me, as if to show me off. That feels great. But in private, I may as well be a sofa. I've never seen him pop a spontaneous erection over me.

There's never been passion. From day one it was really difficult to get him in the mood. Whenever he finally would get an erection and we would start messing around, it would only take about 5 minutes until he was not present and the passion would turn cold. Then, as soon as he was gone, I would have to play with myself in my dark little fantasies of being used as a sexual object. The few times when I had tried to get kinky with Stephen, he would close down faster than anything. I tried to explain to him that I want to explore dark and dangerous sex, but he just poo-pooed me every time. He has no clue what turns me on.

Me, on the other hand, I know him well. I know he likes me to give him a hand job while we are kissing. That's his thing. Cool. But that's the extent of it. He has a very narrow sexual appetite. Very narrow. If I want to get him off, I just start kissing and doing the hand thing. Two minutes later, he's done. Does he like oral anything? No. Does he get turned on by my breasts that other men have described as "large and perfect"? No. Does he ever want to stick his cock up my ass while I offer my yoga butt to him doggie style? Not in a million years.

Back to testing him about initiating things: Last week I called him and said that today I really want to drive up the coast to Petaluma. It was supposed to be foggy and Pete (from work) told me about this awesome restaurant near the water. So when today came, I called Stephen to see if he still wanted to drive up there with me. He said, "Sure." I was really excited. I played all these fantasies in my head about how today would be the day he really appreciated me. I put on my olive sweater dress with a thick brown belt and wore my brand new really tall cognac colored boots.

I have the biggest boot fetish. Boots always look strong and powerful and sexy. And brown boots have this earthy, yet commanding feel to them. These particular boots have a 4" stacked heel (kind of blocky) and a rounded toe that is absolutely classic!! Last night, crazy as this sounds, I slept in them!! I swear to God. I was trying on outfits for today, and then sat in bed to watch a news story for a minute and before I knew it, it was morning and I still had my boots on. I was surprised when I woke up to see them on me. But they looked pretty hot, I must say. I started pretending that a beautiful 42-year-old woman was sitting across the room, staring at me… as I was naked with just my high brown boots. I was imagining she was getting secretly turned on.

I don't know why I was thinking about a woman, but it felt nice. In fact, I started slowly playing with myself as she watched. She seemed to be encouraging me with her eyes to keep going. I kept looking at my high heels digging into the sheets and then back at her. She seemed to be leaning in and getting very interested. I kept going with myself. The woman (dressed in a fresh white blouse, tweed wool skirt and high maroon pumps) was calmly drinking a glass of water as she watched. I love the way the leather looked against my legs. Finally, I exploded! It was fireworks. Right then, the woman had vanished.

So I showed up at Stephen's in those same boots and my dress. I felt so alive and sexy and excited to be heading up the coast with him. Just the word "Sonoma" sounds sophisticated and romantic!

But when I got Stephen's, he gave me a retarded excuse about not being able to take the trip. He had to move the crap in his storage unit and didn't realize it was the last day of the special they were offering to upgrade to a bigger space. So he dissed me. And when I was walking away, really hurt and pissed at the same time, he said, "You sure look great. Sorry I can't go. By the way, that outfit would look way better on you without those boots. Too overbearing."

I shot him a look and took off. AAAAAASSSSSSSS!!! I resolved myself to give him until midnight to make amends and get back to me about missing the day up north. He didn't call me after 4pm, when he would have supposedly been done with his storage thing. He didn't call me at 6pm. He didn't call me at 8pm. Not at 8:05. Not at 9:00. Not at 11:15. It was 11:59. The fuckface never got in touch with me during the whole day. But when there was still one minute left before midnight, I thought… maybe… maybe. Maybe it was all a blunder on his part and he would call to profusely apologize and get us back on track. Oooops! The clock just flipped to 12:01. Nice year and a half wasted. I will never contact him again. … I can't remember his name… What was his name again?!!

Happy birthday, Meg! I had taken the whole day off work for

absolutely nothing! Happy Birthday, Meg Curtis. It only comes once a year, and this one just passed with no acknowledgement whatsoever... Not even a candle on a cupcake!

--- FRIDAY MARCH 2 --- Burn sucker

Ok. Now it's Friday and I'm at work. Boyfriend X called me at 10:30am. I didn't answer and he didn't leave a message I was hoping for such as, "Oh shit!!! I feel like a jerk!! I totally forgot your birthday! Let me take you to Santa Barbara for a weekend trip to make it up to you!!" But he left no message at all. At 12:15 BX (Boyfriend X) called again and left a message "Hey. How's it going? Haven't heard from you today." At 2:15 he called again. But this time I was ready for him. Pete, the coolest guy I know (too bad he's gay) picked up my phone and said "She's done with you. Never contact her again." Burn BX. Burn. I wondered what would happen after that. Will he call me 20 times in a row in desperation to make amends? Turns out he got the message loud and clear and never called again. He was probably relieved. He can go suck on the toes of his exotic brown girls. Ciao, BX.

--- SATURDAY MARCH 3 --- Stewing versus lamenting

Don't know what to say. Kind of pissed, but kind of don't care about BX. Didn't really do much but lie around and channel surf.

--- MONDAY MARCH 5 --- Not big with strangers

A guy hit on me today at Starbucks. He seemed really cool and had some charm. He was about thirty, 4 years older than me. But something told me to blow him off. I think my intuition is always right. Besides, I have rebound goggles on and every guy looks like my savior. Then again, part of me just wants to have a one-night stand to shake off BX.

But as much as it sounds exciting, I'm embarrassed to say that a real life one-nighter is not really for me. I'm the type of girl that needs to warm up to a person... for like a month. After that, there are no depths of passion I won't explore.

It was that way with BX at first. But for whatever reason, his passion faucet turned off and he left me high and dry. X is the best part of his name. I'm going to call my best friend Victoria to celebrate my belated 26th birthday with some margaritas. Whenever I see her, my mood lightens up. She's a hoot! She's got one of those big "let's talk to strangers" personalities and has no trouble getting guys. The funny thing is, she is pretty curvy. But guys still go crazy for her because she is so fun and willing to do anything in the name of bringing up a room. She's a bombastic class clown with a giant potty mouth, a super beautiful face and a seductive smile when she works it. See ya.

--- TUESDAY MARCH 6 --- Big meets little

Had a great time with Victoria. But then, sure enough, she had a few too many drinks and bailed with a short guy in a big BMW. HOLD ON --- She's calling.
Ok, I got the low down. She had a great time and the guy was really nice. They didn't end up doing anything other than kissing a lot while he fondled her boobs. Then she was too tired and split. Shorty was cool with it.

He drove her home… during which time she learned that he doesn't even live here. He lives in Baltimore but was just renting a condo in the city for a week for some biz thing. It's funny that San Francisco has so few single men who aren't gay and one of them just left to diminish Victoria's odds.

--- WEDNESDAY MARCH 7 --- Rocking the job

I really like my job. Takes my mind off BX and guys in general. When I started this job, I never realized what a good fit it is for me. It's a boutique commercial production company. We have made some of the top ads in the world. We have a director that earns at least $120,000 per commercial. Fucking guy is so loaded! Whatever. It would take me a year to earn less than half of what he makes on a single commercial.

But I'm not complaining. I get all kinds of perks. And without me, one of the sharpest production coordinators in the business (I must say), that company would earn way less money. I have single-handedly saved the company millions of dollars because of my ruthless negotiations with vendors and talent.

People think of me as really friendly and accommodating. But I always get what I want. I don't have an asshole style, so people tend to acquiesce when I want something. It's a talent I guess. My boss says I can talk anybody into anything. You get more with honey than with vinegar. Also, I always try to help anyone I can with favors. I like helping people. I get good Karma, but mostly I just like the feeling of helping. It also magically translates into dollars.

On a side note, I think I look really good today. Been getting a lot of compliments. I wore my cognac boots, no wonder.

--- FRIDAY MARCH 9 --- Dinner at my sister, Jenna's

I had dinner at my sister Jenna's. She is my only sibling. Even though we are only 18 months apart, it's clear that she's older… in more ways than one. She started a family right away. I haven't found the need yet. She was always the pleaser; I was the mouthy rebel. She got A's in school. So did I, but only in classes I cared about, psychology, for example. But I always got D's in classes like biology and Algebra. I just didn't care about that crap and knew I was never going to be working in a physics lab. My parents were always exasperated with my 2.5 GPA throughout my whole school career. If you take the average of a bunch of D's and a few A's, it pretty much rounds to a C.

Anyway, Jenna's "happily" married and has two kids. Truth is, she and her family are perfect. Nothing's ever wrong. Everything is fine. Her job's fine. His job's fine. The kids are fine. Even when we go to the movies, I say "how'd you like the movie?" and she always responds, "It was pretty good." Really? Even when it's a piece-of-junk annoying movie? It's always "pretty good". Me, on the other hand… I'm the first one to say it was terrible. I never hold back on having an opinion. I feel like I'm more real than my sister. I'm not afraid to be vocal. I keep waiting for the other shoe to drop with Jenna. All that "pretty good" has got to be a cover for something.

In fact, I know one thing that is not "pretty good" with them. She and Mark probably never have sex. They never touch each other. They are so pleasant and happy, but there is never raw passion. Doesn't Jenna ever just want to get fucked in a gutter somewhere? Doesn't she ever fantasize about being chained to a floor and having some guy ram her until she can't take it any more? No. Jenna would freak at that kind of a thought.

I'm telling you, we are all complex people and have complex personalities and sexual needs. I love a good back rub or cuddling as much as the next girl. I can be silly and playful. I can have fun just kissing. But I need the full range of expression and feelings. Some times I need to fuck and sometimes I need to cuddle. Sometimes I need to have road rage and some times I need to be a good Samaritan. How could anyone mask her emotional diversity like Jenna does?

And then there is the judgment. I always feel like she judges me for being so colorful and unabashed, no matter what my mood. I can be pissy or sweet. I can be a raving bitch or an adorable angel that everyone loves. I love contrast. Contrast is what makes us whole.

Jenna and Mark could live in San Francisco where they both work. It's a city with culture and wealth and poverty and lots of contrast. The ocean meets the skyscrapers. But instead, Jenna and Mark live in Burlingame, a boring suburb where nothing happens. There is no contrast there of any kind. "Pretty good" I guess.

Come to think of it, that's what was going on with Boyfriend X. For a year and a half I couldn't figure him out. Why was he so attracted to me, yet so distant at the same time? But I think he's like Jenna. He is afraid to let it rip. He's afraid to show more colors than tepid grey. I think he was super attracted to my sweet and pleasant aspects. That's what he wanted me to be all the time. But then, when my burning passion for something would show up, he would withdraw. I could never really be myself. I sensed it. And, trying to make it work, I would curb my wild self. But after about a year, it was getting to me. I felt like I wasn't living a truthful life. I was a closeted mood swinger and thinker. I was always tempered and contained.

Finally, after many vocalized observations from Victoria over cocktails, I discovered that I was, in fact, not living my true personality. So I started to be more of myself. And the more I stepped out, the more BX couldn't roll with it. He started pulling away. Sex was ridiculous. There was no passion at all. The more I pushed, the more reserved his sex was.

But the thing is, my natural sexual orientation is kinky. People are born gay, straight, or… kinky. I've always craved wild and dangerous sex. It sounds like a fake cliché, but it's real. I literally can't get turned on without thinking of being tied up or doing it in some shady back alley. The missionary position does nothing for me. When I was a little girl, I remember playing cowboys and indians with the neighbor kid. I always tied him up and would think of ways to torture him. One time, I humiliated him by bringing my littler girlfriend over to see him tied up. But I think he was kinky too because he kept coming over to play the game. More than a few times, I saw that he had a "stiffy". Ha. That's what we called it.

After having been to a lot of therapy on my own accord as a grown-up to try to figure out this dark side, my awesome therapist, Melissa, helped me see that it really doesn't matter how I got here. It's me now. I'm this person. So it can only bring shame and aggravation to try to un-kink myself or to judge my sexuality. In therapy it became crystal clear that I have no inklings of any type of abuse in my past. I was just a regular little girl.

In the "nature versus nurture argument" about what could have contributed to my desire for dark sex, I will tell you this: In my household, it was like *Leave it To Beaver*. There was never any room for any emotions other than bright and cheery smiles. There were never fights of any kind.

By contrast, whenever I would visit the home of my little friend Gianna Mastrogiavani (coolest name ever!), her family would have rip-roaring fights at the dinner table. Someone would end up crying. It scared me at first. But eventually I figured out that by the end of dinner, everyone had made up and they were laughing and hugging and having boisterous conversation together. Then, they may fight again, then back to the laughter. Even as a little girl, I found that to be more realistic. They were letting the emotions flow. They were having a range of feelings. I always wanted to be a Mastrogiavanni. I wanted to express the wild range of emotions that were never allowed in my Clever home.

Then there was "sex" in the Clever home. Well, actually not. The very idea of sex was verboten. It wasn't that sex was bad; it's just that it was non-existent, never spoken about. It was like sex was not real. My mom and dad would only peck kiss. They would give a formal hug upon greeting after work. That was the extent of human contact, just like with Jenna and Mark. But my parents sure had smiles all the time. So I guess if I was abused, it was abuse by happy facades.

When I was ten years old, I persuaded Jenna to pool her allowance with mine to buy my mom a 1 hour massage for Mother's day. When she opened the card and saw the gift certificate, she seemed so happy. She served up several comments about how great that would be and how nice we were to think of her.

But with each passing weekend, I would say "Mom, maybe you could get your massage this Saturday?" But invariably, she was always "too busy" and would have to try another time. It wasn't until I was about 16 that I overheard her boasting to a friend: "I would never have a massage. The idea of a stranger touching me is really creepy. Besides, I would worry about which gender was touching me. If it were a man, it would feel completely inappropriate because that kind of touching is reserved for marriage. If it were a woman touching me, that would present its own problems." The Mother's day massage coupon expired forever with her.

Here's one for you, my entire childhood, I was never allowed in my parents' bedroom. Never! It wasn't until I grew up and found out that other kids would jump on their parents' beds, open the Easter basket in there, get sick and go to the parents' bed for love and comfort, sleep or watch TV in the parent's bed when the other spouse was away on a trip. I know people now who tell me they would sit on their parents' beds for any old reason, just like it was a sofa. But for me, it was this sterile place that was off limits. We could play hide and seek in the house, but the bedroom was way out of bounds.

It's easy to see my parents' bedroom as a perfect metaphor for the idea of sex. It doesn't exist. Out of sight, out of mind. I had no role model for sex. At the Mastrogiavanni's, I saw people hugging and kissing all the time. Sometimes a young couple would be there kissing and playing at the table and everyone would riff on it with jokes or push them to snuggle closer. Teenagers would smooch on the couch or "disappear" for a while and return later with that telltale satisfied look and a smirk to boot. The dad would playfully spank the mom on the butt with a wooden spoon while everyone laughed. I wanted to be a Mastrogiavanni.

But unlike my family, I have always found big pleasure in physical contact and my sexuality. I've always liked extreme sex. The funny thing is, most of it has always been in my own mind… with myself. For as kinky as I am, I need a solid relationship in order to share that side of me. So without any one-night-stands or quickie relationships, I've always had the most pleasure with myself.

Even my boot fetish is big part of my sexuality. They are always there for me like a teddy bear. Maybe they are my security blanket. It may sound crazy, but ever since I was little, I was drawn to boots. I always had boots. Every kind. To me, boots, especially high ones, are as sexy as lingerie. To feel super sexy and sexual, I would rather go boot shopping than lingerie shopping. I love the contrast of soft skin against coarse leather. Light skin against dark leather.

But BX didn't get it, far from it. He always made me feel shame about wanting to wear boots: "A woman's leg's are her best feature and it makes no sense to cover them up". What the hell? That's like saying a

French, lacey bra isn't sexy because it covers up part of the boobs. And trust me, self, you will not find a single pair of boots in Jenna's closet. I don't even need to check. She would never own a pair because they can carry such a sexual charge. Why do you think hookers always wear boots? But saying tall boots are only for hookers is like saying guys on Wall Street should never wear suits because pimps wear them; the difference is huge, quality of fabric, accessories, attitude, and colors.

Prissy clothes are fine too. I wear prissy sometimes. The right shoe for the right mood. Jenna can never switch it up. She's all about the safety robot voice: "Must – protect – emotions - at - all - times. Passion – does – not - compute." Every woman, every person has to reconcile their childhood issues with their sexuality somehow. Some women do this by extremely punishing workouts, running marathons, etc. Other people over eat. Some take to substance. We all have to cope. The thing about me is that I feel super content with my sexuality. It feels healthy. Maybe it's dark. Maybe it's compartmentalized and a little different. But I own it.

Jenna wasn't so lucky. As the big sister, she somehow was too overcome with the smiley environment to ever see another perspective. It's living in a fishbowl, all your life and not knowing there is anything beyond the glass. But my own fish bowl was placed on the windowsill looking over the San Francisco Bay. There was an exciting world out there… and it wasn't all smiles. Like my emotions, some days were cloudy. Some were bright. I learned to embrace each one for its best qualities. I love rain and fog and nasty thunderstorms. I love summer heat.

My sister only likes cheery days. I feel like repressing expression and appreciation of life's peaks and valleys will take its toll later in life in some form or another. It's the Dutch boy and the dyke. You can hold back some water with your finger plugging a hole, but that only creates more pressure to do damage elsewhere. My family, and especially Jenna, has repressed their sexuality forever. It's going to either blow or rot in them some how.

Jenna would be mortified if she heard any of this! Doesn't she ever get horny? Geez. I have to masturbate at least once each day!! I bet Jenna doesn't even own a vibrator. It would scare the crap out of her. In the old movies, I used to hear the word "frigid." I never really knew what it meant. But seeing Jenna and Mark, it's pretty frigid all right.

Wow, after just re-reading this entry, it seems like I'm way more judgmental then her. I don't mean to be that way. I guess it's just a reaction to always feeling shut down whenever I let my real self shine, good, bad, or crazy. Sorry, Jen. I don't mean to judge you.

--- MONDAY MARCH 12 --- Star power

My boss let me drive Nicole Kidman to the commercial shoot today. She was really nice. Everybody thought we were best buds or something because, even after arriving, she kind of leaned on me for stuff and felt comfortable hanging out with me during the shoot. We get celebs from time to time, but this was the best. Gotta love her!

I'm starting to like writing this diary. I guess I'm secretly writing it for eventual release into the public. Maybe when I die, someone will find it in my nightstand and publish it. It will be like Franz Kafka who wasn't famous until he died when they found his writings. Only when they find mine, they'll be like… "Breaking news: Nicole Kidman once had a secret lesbian affair with production coordinator from a shoot she was on."

--- TUESDAY MARCH 13 --- Prospect number one

There was a cute guy eyeing me at the farmers' market this morning. He had this amazing swimmer's body and could pass for a model. We had immediate chemistry. After he bumped into me and knocked my smoothie over, I flirted with him. Joking around, I told him that I would have to punish him for that. And he flirted back with "Or I'll have to punish you for being so adorable." He gave me his email address. Who knows, this entry could be the first of many in a bright future with him. We'll see. I'll wait a couple days before emailing.

--- WEDNESDAY MARCH 14 --- Yoga class

I love yoga! It always makes me feel so connected. Even today when I'm starting my period, it helps ease my cramps. When my body feels yoga, I get really optimistic about life and start eating healthily. Then when I get away from it for too long, I start eating worse and getting blue. Oh, and when I go to yoga for a long stretch in a row, I seem to get a bigger libido, which for me, is like saying I go from a high level to a stratospheric level. I've been going there regularly for about 6 weeks now and I love it.

There was this woman there that I see some times. She has a bright energy and looks in her late 30's. She started talking with me and we had an easy time in conversation. You know how with some people it's really hard to click? It wasn't like there with her. She invited me to coffee after class next time. It would be nice to have a friend besides Victoria. I mean, I love Victoria, but this girl just seemed nice too… and not as flighty.

--- FRIDAY MARCH 16 --- Maybe a new friend

Had another awesome yoga class. After class, I went to coffee with the woman in class who seemed really cool. Regina. That's her name. It's kind of a cool name and it matches her. She's super skinny and has a great vibe. She's 38, the kind of girl who sundresses are made for. Her brown hair was up today, but usually, she wears it down. It looks like a loose perm, but it's natural. She's really healthy-looking and is a vegetarian. She has a spirit that feels light, but there is something very intense within her. She is the opposite of Jenna. Regina clearly has stuff going on besides a joyous facade. I like that. I like the idea that people can have contrast... and depth.

We went to coffee and it was actually awkward. It was like I didn't want to say the wrong thing and have her reject me. Not that it mattered, but I wanted to be liked by her. Stupid as it sounds, it felt like going on a job interview to find a new friend. I was so nervous. I even refrained from my usual potty speak and tried to be a somewhat flatter version of myself. But she saw right though it. She busted me with "You can be yourself with me." And we both laughed because she totally called me on my facade. Fine.

So I proceeded to grill her about her life's details in hopes of finding common ground for a friendship. She really intrigued me. Turns out that the dark intensity I saw mixed in with her bright chi was accurate.

Two years ago, she had a nasty divorce and has been a single mom since then. Well, kind of single. The dad, Alex, fought for 50-50 custody and the judge granted it. Alex is a trust-fund guy who doesn't have to work for a living. He's a Scorpio and really erratic. Regina and Alex have a 9-year-old boy named Tucker, who lives with her Monday through Wednesday and every other weekend. She showed me a few photos; He's adorable.

She said she lives a tale of two lives. When she's with Tucker, she is mommy of the year and throws herself at him. She's the super mom, bringing cupcakes to school, volunteering at the fundraisers when she can, and making home baked meals. He is her everything.

When Tucker is away at the dad's, she is lost. She does yoga, gardens, and works as a 5th grade teacher. She has worked in the same school for years. She loves San Francisco and uses it to full advantage. She says guys always try to hit on her, but she is not in the frame of mind to engage. There is something very substantial about her. When she smiles, a soul comes through.

Anyway, I bring all of this up because she hit me out of the blue with: "So why do you always wear boots?" -- piercing into me with a knowing twinkle in her eye. "Huh?" I feigned. "Most people wear flip-flops or clogs to yoga. You always wear high boots and then change into your yoga pants in the bathroom once you get there." Then I figured (even though it was my very first time with this stranger, Regina), if I wasn't going to be honest, I wasn't going to ever develop a friendship worth having. So I came clean with: "You know what? My whole life I have been fascinated by boots. (I actually started to blush). In fact, I have a really strong fetish for boots. I feel sexy in them. I'm always secretly hoping some guy will see me somewhere and think the same thing."

"What size shoe are you?" she asked. When I told her I'm a seven, she continued, "Hey, me too! Can I try yours on?" she asked very bluntly. My eyes widened. I felt naked. From my view, it felt as personal as asking if she could try on my bra. "You mean, right now?" I stammered. "Sure" she said in a steady, matter-of-fact tone. It was a really an odd request. I mean, has that ever happened to anyone on the planet? But Regina made it seem like "pass the salt."

So I unzipped my boots and passed them over to her. She slipped off her cool, chunky, leather clogs, then pulled on my boots, zipping them over her dark tights. These particular boots were black riding boots with a 3-inch wedged heel. She got up from the table and did a deliberate strut around the cafe, giggling and showing off. A few of the other customers watched her but didn't seem to think anything of it.

Now I saw why I always loved boots. She looked fantastic!!!!! They literally transformed her energy to this more sexual vibe. Anybody, fetish or not, would say she looked spectacularly alluring.

Good thing I'm not into women or I would have jumped on that thing.

After her little tour du cafe, she sat back down and leaned into me. "I don't own a single pair of boots. Unless wellies count," she said. "I'm going to buy some!" But then something fucked up happened. Somehow, some strange force took over my mouth and made me blurt out in a dry tone, "Wear them home tonight."

You would have thought I had given Regina a ten thousand dollar bill. She was stunned. She lit up like a spotlight was inside her. "You know what…" and she thought for a moment. "I will." She was beaming. "And you have to wear my clogs."

The whole thing had the strangest energy to it. It was like some kind of sexual metaphor innuendo. Or whatever. I don't know what it was. All I know is that she kept my boots on when we got up to leave. As we walked out, I said goodbye and watched her walk to her car in my boots. For whatever reason, I was oddly turned on. And she had this playful, sexy energy thing going. I was wearing her shoes! Crazy. I'm still wearing them!! I'm so not into girls, but I must get my vibrator. But first, I'm going to email the farmers market guy now to get that ball rolling.

--- SATURDAY MARCH 17 --- The dating game

Too bad there is no yoga tonight!

The farmer's market guy wrote back last night within a half hour. His name is Marcel. He works as a sales guy for high-end wine. He seemed really cool. But, my inner naysayer says the luster usually wears off with a second encounter. We're going to meet for a drink at 8pm. I told him I only have 30 minutes, so that I can bail if I have to.

--- Later ---

Ok. I met Marcel. He's an incredible catch. There's just one thing… Me, in my usual blunt self… pushed him on a couple comments he made once the alcohol had kicked in a little. Turns out, he is amazing and, by the way, he likes to cross dress. So that's pretty kinky. I could go with that. It's kind of perverted and cool. NOT! This sucks that I am so judgmental, but nothing turns me off more than a cross-dressing guy. I don't know why I have such a visceral reaction to it. But it's really strong.

It's ironic that I judge cross-dressing, but hate my own sexual kink being judged. I don't know what to say about that other than… I don't judge him, but just don't want that in a relationship. It would be the same as if he smoked. I'm not judging the smoking, I just don't need that in my life. I admire him for coming clean early on and not playing games until he hooks me on his best qualities. But still, I just can't go there. Oh, and guess what I wore to the date? Regina's clogs!

--- MONDAY MARCH 19 --- Yoga Friend

How stupid is this? I was actually excited to go to yoga tonight, not because of the yoga itself, but to see my new friend. But by the time class started, Regina wasn't there. And like some 7 year old, I kept checking the clock every 5 minutes and then checking the door. My mind wasn't on yoga at all.

She never came. Then I remembered that it was Monday night. She must be on mommy duty with her kid, Tucker. What's funny is I don't even have any contact info for her, just the yoga class. Guess I gotta wait until Wednesday when she shows up again. I feel dumb for being so excited for a friendship.

--- TUESDAY MARCH 20 --- Lunch with my parents

Met my parents for lunch. They are really proud of me for landing and keeping such a great job. They looked good, but sure are getting older. For the first time, my dad, who was a career pilot with perfect vision, finally has to have reading glasses for the menu. My mom put on some weight. Not much, but just enough to show me that I want to always workout and stay healthy my whole life. We only get one body. We need to use it or lose it.

I've always gotten along great with my parents. They're great, even though they were always smiling in the house and nothing was ever wrong. It could have been worse. They could have been assholes. Between full time smiles or assholes, I guess I would have to pick the smiles. The truth is, our house was pretty sterile, but my parents did the best they could, despite always covering true emotions. Victoria wonders how I got so kinky when I was never abused or molested. I tell her I was born that way. I always like a dark side: Yin and Yang. It's all a balance. I'm wired differently than cheerleaders or librarians or my family.

--- WEDNESDAY MARCH 21 --- After yoga

Today was the day I expected Regina back at yoga. But she didn't come. Just like the last time. I kept watching the clock, etc. We finished class and she never showed. Just then, she came in as everyone was filing out. "Meg!" she called out. I turned to see her standing there... with Tucker. "I couldn't make class tonight (making secret eye gesture to indicate it was because of Tucker). "Tucker, this is my new friend Meg," she said. I shook the 9-year-old's hand. He was really sweet.

"I wanted to get these to you and felt bad that I kept them so long", she said, handing over a Macy's bag containing my boots. "Oh, you didn't have to do that. I could have waited. But thanks" I said, somewhat disappointed. Then I slipped out of her clogs and swapped them for my boots in the bag. For some reason, I was really deflated. It was like swapping shoes was over with her; the magic had passed. I put my boots on. Suddenly, she delighted and said, "They look better on you. (She paused out of not really knowing where to take this next). "Do you want to go out to ice cream with us?"

Tucker looked hopefully interested in my response. But I felt pissy and passive-aggressively wanted to punish her for standing me up all week. Even though it is completely unfair and immature to be put off by something that wasn't personal against me at all, I just felt like being a pouty little martyr. So I told them "No thanks. I gotta get back right away."

Poor Regina's face visibly dropped right in front of me. "No worries, there will be other times," she dejectedly responded, "right?" as she urged with a loaded stare. I answered her with a gentle nod, and then ended by, "It sure was nice to meet you, Tucker. You guys have fun at ice cream." Regina gave me one last tug with her eyes. I could tell this martyrdom wasn't really going to fly next time. They headed off.

As I was rolling up my yoga mat, Tucker came running up to me. He handed me Regina's contact info on a slip of paper. I warmed and smiled at him with a "Thank you so much." He ran off. When I was walking away, I heard my heels tapping on the hard floor. To me, that sounds so sexy! I started thinking how Regina's feet had been in my boots before. For some reason, I liked that.

--- THURSDAY MARCH 22 --- Chemistry works both ways

At work, I could hardly focus. Never had an acquaintance affected me so much. We hardly knew each other. I didn't even know her last name until Tucker handed it over last night: Regina Baker.

But you know how chemistry is chemistry? That's what it was. There was this connection between us. I never had a friend with that much instant chemistry. I sure hope it doesn't bomb out and turn ugly. Usually, when things go too fast, they either peter out or crash and burn. That's happened lots of times in the past with "friends".

One time I had this fast and furious friendship with a girl at work. I thought we were going to be best buds and I would finally have someone to hang out with besides Victoria. But when push came to shove over an incident at the office, she fucking lied and blamed me. So the sparks of chemistry flew even stronger in reverse. It was war!! In a no holds barred attack, I played the game just right so the bitch got fired in front of the whole office. You can do a lot of things, but you can never fuck me. I fight back… smarter!!

The point is, I hope the chemistry I have with Regina doesn't show its flip side. I really don't want to have an intense reversal. But somehow, Regina feels different. Our connection feels more sincere and deep… for all the two hours I have known her! Regina Baker, I'm going to call you right now!

Crap. She didn't answer. Bitch! (just kidding). Still, hearing her voice on the voicemail was satisfying. I left the message: "Thanks for taking the trouble to come by the yoga studio. Tucker seems like a great kid. So sorry I couldn't make it to ice cream. I look forward to seeing you again." But what I really wanted to say was "Sorry I didn't want to go to ice cream, but you are fucking with my head and I don't want to seem like I desperately need a friend that bad… and I was pissed at you for being away from yoga."

--- FRIDAY MARCH 23 --- A walk in the park

After work, I had a load of laundry in my arms when my phone rang. When I saw the caller I.D. my heart raced. I leapt for the phone… but didn't answer. I didn't want Regina to think that I was enthusiastically awaiting contact from her. Even though there is absolutely no basis for my interest in her, I never remember wanting a friend as much as I wanted it with Regina.

A few seconds later, the phone indicated a voice message had been left. Of course I listened to it right away: "Meg, this is Regina. I'm all clear from Tucker and I need to speak to you in person as soon as you are available. Please call back." What the hell did she want? I couldn't read her tone. Was she going to burn me? Was she going to ask for a favor? What's with all the urgency? What's wrong with me? Why am I acting like such an idiot?

I didn't want to call her so I texted her to meet me at South Park, this cool little park south of Market St. that actually feels like a slice of Paris. She texted right back and said she'd see me there in a half hour. I thought, "This ought to be interesting." I wore tennis shoes and a baggy sweatshirt to make it seem like I didn't make a fuss about seeing her again. I really wasn't looking forward to some kind of reverse chemistry dismissal.

I arrived at the park first. About two minutes later, I see Regina pulling right up on an electric Vespa. I could tell right away it was electric. There is no sound. Duh.

But more importantly, what most people don't know about me is that I have a very strong mechanical mind. Growing up, my dad would be home for two weeks, then away for two weeks flying his trips. But when he was home, he used to teach me everything about tools and equipment. Together we rebuilt his beat-up old Triumph TR-4 from the ground up. We turned it into a showpiece over the course of two years. I learned everything about cars. We used to have to go to the junkyard all the time to hunt for parts and remove them ourselves.

So, it only took me about a second to see that Regina's Vespa was electric. My first thought was, "that is so cool." My second thought was, "Of course, what else would a vegetarian drive besides an electric Vespa." She looked really great on it and it fit her.

She pulled up right into this shaft of light, parked, and then pulled off her helmet. Her hair spilled out like root beer and she radiated in the backlighting like she was in a commercial!

After getting off her bike, we did a little hug and I gestured for us to take a stroll. As we walked around the tiny park, the conversation basically went like this:

> **ME**
> *So what's going on that you had to meet right away?*
>
> **REGINA**
> *You're going to think I'm crazy. But I swear I have never done this before in my life! I have never taken a liking to someone so instantly with such a strong connection as with you.*
>
> **ME**
> (Playing it cool)
> *Yeah, It seems like we really click. I've always wanted a friendship to be easy and mutual. But frankly, I have this fear that we might hate each other in a couple weeks.*
> (We both laugh)
> *So, why are we meeting? What did you want to say?*

Regina turned really deep.

> **REGINA**
> (Embarrassed)
> *I... want to do something with you.*
>
> **ME**
> (Trying to grasp it)

"Do something with me?" Like what?

REGINA
I don't know.

ME
Well you must have some idea? I mean, we could go for tea, go shopping together, go to see Les Misérables, or I could just throw you in the back of my trunk and drive around for no reason. What did you have in mind?

REGINA
Anything. I would want to do anything.

ME
Ok. The trunk it is!

An odd look rushed over her face that meant she thought I was serious. I quickly let out my laugh to reassure her that it was pun. She laughed along with me for a beat and then the conversation continued:

REGINA
Do you want the same thing?

ME
To do something with you? Sure. I really think you are amazing; I'm intrigued by you. It's strange. If you added up all the time we have shared with each other, it would only total a few hours in yoga class together. Not to be blunt, but you're not asking me on a "date" are you? Because I'm...

REGINA

You're not gay.

ME
Right.

REGINA
Me neither!!! . I have never dated a woman or even thought about it. Like I said, I have never done this or felt this way. I don't know what came over me. But yeah, I guess I'm maybe thinking of... a date... just for fun.

Then this whole range of feelings came over me. First off, I was flattered. Everybody wants to be loved. It felt good. Then, I was frustrated and a little angry. I didn't want to be put on the spot and I also saw our new "friendship" collapsing at that very second forever. It fit with my idea of "too fast, too fragile".

ME
I'm totally straight. Besides, what would be the point? We are in different stages of our lives. I'm 26 and in career mode. You are a full 12 years older than me and have a kid to be concerned with. So even if we went on a date, it would be a dead end. How about we just do something fun together and see where the friendship goes?

REGINA
I can't believe myself. You must think I'm a psycho!

ME
It was a tad unexpected. We're total strangers. But I must admit, you are the most stunning 38 year old I have ever seen. You're beautiful! The thing is, I can't just

change my sexual orientation like flipping a switch. Sorry.

Regina looked crushed. I started feeling like the bad guy and didn't like it.

ME
(Escalating resentment)
I'm sorry. I really want to "like" you, but I'm not wired that way. And that's another thing, I'm not even wired straight the right way. My relationships have always fizzled. I'm wired differently. My sexuality is twisted. That's how I'm wired.

REGINA
(Coming out of her dejection a bit)
What does that mean, "twisted?"

ME
Never mind. I gotta go.
(Then I made the mistake of shooting her some solid eye contact)

REGINA
(Awkward pause)
Wait. There's something dark about you; I have it too. Don't you feel it?

ME
(I grabbed her helmet and put it on her head)
The best thing you can do is get out of here before any damage happens to our new friendship.

REGINA
You do feel it! Busted!

ME
(I started blushing at the truth of it!)
We don't even know each other.

REGINA
C'mon. What do I have to do to make this "date" happen? It will be totally platonic. It's not going to kill you. No harm, no foul. I'll do anything! Anything. I'll take you shopping or to the movies. I'll wash your dishes. Anything.

ME
My dishes? Now you're talking! But seriously, we'd better keep it at yoga and coffee.

And I turned and walked away. After a moment, I saw her drive off on her vegetarian Vespa. I knew that things were going too fast to be real. Fuck.

But then about a minute later when I was unlocking my car, she came speeding back up. She looked me square in the eye with a troubled expression and said, "I've never worn another woman's boots before." And she sped off. I must admit, if any parting shot had the force to reach me, it would be that exact line! I played poker face and pretended not to be affected in the least. Fuck her. She is clearly unstable!

It's really awkward now. I don't know how to be around her.

Later on, I skipped yoga class. I wasn't in the head space to deal with her. I figured I would have to change to an entirely different yoga studio. It pissed me off because everything was great and I loved that class. Why should I be the one that has to change my life when she was the one who blew it? Whatever. I really needed a little breather. She might have skipped it too for all I know. Who cares?

--- SATURDAY MARCH 24 --- The most intense day of my life

Just when you think you have yourself all figured out, some joker comes along and turns everything on its head. Thanks, Regina.

Victoria called today. She wanted to go out for drinks. But I wasn't in the mood. She'd be fine. I'd catch up with her another time.

Now what was I supposed to do today? I felt lazy and unmotivated. I tried watching a movie on Netflix, but after scrolling through the list for 20 minutes back and forth, I finally gave up on the idea. None of the films sounded any good or I had already seen them. What a waste of a Saturday.

So I started vacuuming. That's always therapeutic for some reason. I like the way it looks afterward with the indentation lines in the carpet. When I was putting the vacuum away, I noticed my pile of dishes in the sink. It only took about two seconds until I heard Regina's voice in my head saying, "I'll wash your dishes." Really? Fine. Let's put her to the test.

Against my better judgment, like putting out a fire with gasoline, I picked up the phone and called Regina. I was literally shaking out of nerves. But I stiffened up when she answered. She answered in a sweet voice, as if the whole park incident had never happened. Masking my emotions, I put it out there, "Are you really serious about washing my dishes?" She melted in her tone. "If you're serious, I'll prove to you I don't want anything from you other than your company. I can be there in an hour." "Fine," I said matter-of-factly. "But you are literally only going to wash my dishes." She eagerly snapped, "That's all I want to do. I'll wash them and you can just relax visit with me... or read a book!" And that was that. Why was I setting myself up for insane and unnecessary drama?

When she hung up, I wondered why it would take her an hour to get here when her house is only 10 minutes away. I was nervous that she would take that time to primp so she could impress me. But she would be beautiful wearing a burlap sack. She's one of those women with a natural glow, no matter what.

One hour later came a knock at the door. I was a nervous wreck. There was this odd tension in my soul. It was really strange and unexpected for someone who has always been straight to be suddenly nervous about having a female guest over. Was she really going to wash my dishes or just try to engage me in persuasive conversation about developing a relationship? What have I gotten myself into? Shit.

When I opened the door. She stuck out her hand to shake mine. She was already wearing blue rubber dish gloves!! "Good afternoon, Ma'am. I'm here to wash your dishes." she cheerily played. I looked at her and tried not to laugh, playing along and pointing her to the kitchen without saying a single word. She marched right over there and started right in on the dishes like she was a trained professional house cleaner. She was washing my dishes! Not knowing whether or not to make small talk, I decided to just ignore her. I watched her for a bit in amazement, then left the kitchen to get away from the awkwardness. But occasionally, I would sneak back and peek at her.

Sure enough, there she was washing the dishes. She was very thorough. The whole mood was professional, but she was clearly enjoying it and very committed. She must be fucking crazy.

But if I had been the type to like women, she certainly had the figure for it. Her yoga body was really appealing from the back. She never said a word or asked for anything. When the dishes were spotless and she was putting the last one away, I walked up to her from behind and, for some reason that felt like it was outside of me, grabbed her chin and turned her face directly toward mine. And in a cold voice that also didn't sound like myself, I told her, "Thank you for doing the dishes. Next, I need you to clean out the entire fridge."

I guess I was sort of testing her to see what her limits were and if doing chores would grow old really fast. But she warmed and said, "I'd love to clean the fridge. I'll do the best I can." Then I walked away, not really sure what the hell was going on there. But heck, she said she wanted to wash the dishes and that's exactly what she did. Then, jumping on to her next task, she started the fridge.

I sat across the kitchen on a bar stool watching in amazement. She had no trouble making executive decisions about which stuff to throw away and which to keep. She pretended to ignore the fact that I was sitting right there in the kitchen watching her. She just did her business like I was invisible. I think she was somehow turned on by it all. I watched her for a full 38 minutes. This was so trippy. But it was affecting me too. It's insane, but I was starting to get a little turned on watching her bend up and down, cleaning the fridge in silence under my stare. And the more I watched, the more I found myself getting excited. Some strange woman was in my house doing chores and ignoring me.

Finally, I couldn't take it and I had an idea… again, outside of my normal realm of personality. In that same unemotional voice, I told her "That's enough of cleaning the fridge. Now wash your hands and come up stairs." She shot me a look like "I will give you anything". I went upstairs to my bedroom and sat on my bed against a big pillow. A moment later, Regina entered.

Some other person that I didn't know was channeling my mind and body. This has never happened to me before! I told her to kneel on the floor at the foot of the bed. She quietly sat down in a kneeling position with her back perfectly straight, a testament to her yoga practice. She looked at me with deep eyes. But it all seemed too strange. "Stay there," I said firmly. I jumped off the bed and went to the dresser where I pulled out a black scarf. Then I came up behind her and tied it tightly around her eyes to blindfold her. She complied without a word. She wanted it. She was beyond turned on as she kneeled there with her perfectly straight back. I looked at her and suddenly all thoughts of straight vs. gay just became non-thoughts. She was an absolutely gorgeous woman and she was kneeling at my bed. As I studied her, she sat there blindfolded in silence without moving a muscle.

Then, I had this urge to go to my closet at grab a belt to tie her hands. How was this all happening so naturally? She allowed me to strap her hands behind her back with my belt, which I tied really tightly. I lied back down on the bed and looked at her. I loved the look of her tied hands! She couldn't see me. I was super turned on and began to slowly caress myself. But then I had to get up one more time. I went to my closet and found the same boots that I had loaned her that time. I lied back down on the bed and quietly put my boots on. As I slowly zipped them up, I sensed that she heard it. She became ultra attentive. Even a single feather touching her would have set her off.

The room was still. After settling in, I lied back and watched her, sitting perfectly erect on her knees, blindfolded, eager, and silent. Along with the sight of her, my boots were in my field of vision as I lied on the bed, an aesthetic turn-on to the highest degree. The light was hitting her hair. I began playing with myself… slowly at first. But in a matter of a minute, I was coming. I refrained from making a peep. I really didn't want her to hear me. It would have been embarrassing. So as difficult as it was, I climaxed in total silence. Then I relaxed for about 10 minutes. She sat obediently in giant anticipation.

I quietly removed my boots and walked over to the closet to put them away. I could tell she was still insanely turned on. I untied her hands. Then I came around in front of her and knelt down so we were face to face. I could feel her breath on my face. And I know she could feel mine because she seemed to be enraptured with each breath that hit her. I took off her blindfold and she opened her eyes slowly as she took in the sight of my face so close. Still in a monotone voice, I dismissed her: "Thank you for doing the dishes. Your services are no longer needed. Please make your way out."

Processing it all, she collected herself and departed without uttering a single word. Even though there were no "goodbyes" or fuzzy hugs, I knew in my heart that she got everything she ever dreamed of. When I heard the door close downstairs as she left, I got really cocky and said to myself out loud "And you'd better do a better job cleaning next time." Then I grabbed my vibrator and went crazy and loud for a good 15 minutes. Holy shit. That was the best climax in my life! I kept visualizing her slender neck and perfect upright posture. I kept thinking of her tied hands. I was the boss!! She did my dishes.

--- SUNDAY MARCH 25 --- What is it?

I woke up this morning with a new perspective. It was like that magic of an early romance. Did I say "romance"? I sure did. I felt passionately in lust. I don't know how else to describe it. I'm not a lesbian, so it's hard to say I'm in "love". Then again, I might as well dispense with the labels. Whatever it was, it was fun and it was the purest energy I have felt in my life. Maybe it was my kinky side finally getting what it wanted. This could have never happened with anyone but Regina. She was a bridge to some emotions I had never felt. It was kind of scary, exciting, and magic all at the same time. It was flat out bizarre.

After breakfast and a shower, I really wanted to check in with her. It didn't seem finished. I felt a little ashamed and nervous for making her leave without any conversation or even salutations. I made another cup of coffee in my French press and then went out on the veranda with the phone. I really didn't know if I should talk about what went down or if I should ignore it and talk about the weather. But I really wanted to hear her voice.

Slowly, I dialed. I feared. I waited for the answer on the other end. She picked up! It went like this:

> **REGINA**
> *Hello?*
>
> **ME**
> *Hi Regina.*
>
> **REGINA**
> *Hi.*
>
> **ME**
> *I'm smiling right now. Can you feel it?*
>
> **REGINA**

I'm smiling too.

And there was silence. More silence. Maybe 30 seconds of silence.

ME
Was I too mean to you?

REGINA
No. I'm still smiling.

ME
Are you sure?

REGINA
I've never felt anything like that.

ME
Me neither. We weren't our daily selves. Well, I'll speak for myself. But it was out of this world. It was a dreamworld. It felt like playing dressup when I was a little girl.

REGINA
For me too. It was like a game.

ME
Yes, let's call it "The Game"

REGINA
Ok. "The Game." We need to play it more.

ME
This is all so fast and crazy.

REGINA
I want you to own me!!

ME

> *Own you?*
>
> **REGINA**
> *I know. This is all seems outrageous! I want to be your object. You can do anything to me. Boss me. Hurt me. I just want to serve you. Don't you feel it too?*

Wow. This was really messing with my head. I don't know how this works because there are no templates from my past. It's scary territory. I don't want to screw this up. I want to develop a real friendship with Regina, but I also love that she wants to wash my dishes. Is this all for real? The conversation continued:

> **ME**
> *I do want the same thing. I want to toy with you. But I also want to explore you as a friend and develop that.*
>
> **REGINA**
> *Me too.*
>
> **ME**
> *Fuck. This is so gay!*

We both started laughing.

> **REGINA**
> *Well, if it's a game, we must have rules.*
>
> **ME**
> *Like what?*
>
> **REGINA**
> *Like we should have a secret code word to start it and end.*
>
> **ME**
> *Really, James Bond?*
>
> **REGINA**

33

No really. Like when you say the code, that means we are playing. And the rest of the time we are our normal selves.

ME
Ok. You think of the code.

REGINA
How about "Can you believe how blue the sky is today?"

ME
Mmmmmkay. What if it's cloudy?

REGINA
Then it's sarcastic.

ME
And how do we stop the game?

REGINA
We say, "That was some kind of crazy day I had"

ME
(Laughing, then...)
Any more rules?

REGINA
Yes. Absolutely no other people ever. And we always have to use the exact sentence of the code. The exact words are "Can you believe how blue the sky is today?" and "That was some kind of crazy day". Any other variations will not count.

ME
Agreed. It's freaky enough as is. Bringing anyone else into this is beyond my comprehension. It will just be our private thing.

REGINA

Oh, and the most important rule-- I have no limits except when it comes to Tucker. I always have to be free to be his mommy. If you use the code when I'm with him, I can just terminate by saying "That was some kind of crazy day" and you will know that I'm on mommy duty.

ME
This is so C.I.A. You're crazy.

REGINA
You're crazy
 (Turns to sexy voice)
And you own me.

ME
Can you believe how blue the sky is?

REGINA
(Flustered)
Ok. um. Ok.

ME
You need to come here right now.

REGINA
Yes Ma'am.

I hung up the phone and checked the clock. Sure enough, she was at my place inside of 15 minutes. She looked so cute in a super casual spaghetti strap asparagus green dress with little frill lace accents. But that wasn't all. She wore some brand new very tall brick red boots with a 4-inch wood heel. The leather was coarse and gave the boots a casual but strong feel. They looked like a strong accent to her dress. The opposite of dominatrixy. It was a real contrast to my bare feet.

I told her that I was impressed that she made it so quickly. The tone was serious between us. If this was a game, nobody was smiling. I took out a black scarf that I had standing by and blindfolded her. I held her face firm and the conversation went like this:

> **ME**
> *Listen, I own you. You are my object. Do you understand?*

She nodded "yes." Then I squeezed her face firmly:

> **ME**
> *I didn't hear you.*
>
> **REGINA**
> (Eager to please)
> *Yes, Ma'am! I'm your object!*
>
> **ME**
> *And from now on, you'll address me as "Mistress". Understood?*
>
> **REGINA**
> *Yes, Mistress.*

I released her face, then took her hand and told her to follow me. I guided her along as she was blindfolded. Holding her hand was incredible. Touching her hand elicited so many emotions. Her hand was warm and she squeezed back. As small as it was, the connection of holding her hand meant more than almost any contact I had with any other human. It was real. Our game was fake. But her hand was real. I knew Regina was in there. She was playing my object, but I knew she was in there… with me.

And maybe the game wasn't so fake either. It was real to us. For example, if you point a fake gun at someone and say they are going to die, they would think it's real. There would be a huge physical and emotional response from increased heart rate to shortness of breath and panic. Even though the gun is not real, the thought creates all the effects of a real event.

I led her to the kitchen area next to a vertical support post at the edge of the room, telling her to stand there and not move. I went to the garage and got a heavy chain that my dad had left behind after working on a car once. I wrapped the chain three times about the post and her neck together. I thought she was going to orgasm as I was doing it. Then I took out a padlock and locked it firmly.

So there she was, spaghetti strap dress, blindfolded, chained at the neck to a post in brand new, high boots. I loved looking at her like that. Remember when I wanted Boyfriend X to treat me heavy? Like the Eleni Mandell song? Well, that's what I was doing to Regina. She's heavy. She was starting to mean something to me. She's beautiful… and heavy.

But I wasn't done with her. I quickly dashed upstairs to get my belt, then came back down and tied her hands behind her back. For some reason, that really works for me. The image makes her look so vulnerable! I grabbed a wooden spoon from the counter and some strong cotton rope (formerly a clothesline) from the junk drawer. I wedged the handle of the spoon between her lips like a bit on a horse and snugged it all the way back as far as it would go against the corners of her mouth. Then I took the rope and secured the spoon tightly by tying it to each side of the spoon handle and going around the back of her head. I cinched it tight… and there she was with a stiff gag in place. When I was pulling it tight, she was making gentle moans, like the kind when the massage therapist hits the golden spot.

But I couldn't take it. I tiptoed away in my bare feet so she wouldn't know where I was. I went upstairs to take a shower. I needed to take a freezing cold shower to calm the hell down. But instead, I just let the warm water sprinkle over my face as I meditated in bliss. When I felt the urge to touch myself, I tried to shift my focus; I wasn't ready to satisfy myself and miss what might else be coming later with Regina.

To calm down my id, I tried to think of her as Regina… in yoga class, having coffee, pulling up on her electric Vespa. I like thinking of her as a woman who was my friend. She exudes poise and grace and charm and fun and smarts. She's silly too. One time during yoga, she was making these crazy faces when the teacher wasn't looking to mock how hard the poses were. It was like we were in 5th grade and doing shenanigans. One time I actually busted out with a laugh in the dead quiet yoga room. The whole class turned to me as if to say, "Shut up, we're trying to be important here!" Isn't it possible to do yoga and laugh at Regina's faces at the same time? Sheeesh.

After I calmed down with my shower, I was rubbing on some moisturizer and thinking how crazy it was that I had a beautiful woman tied up in my kitchen… just stuck there at my mercy. Was this really me? Am I really this person? Do I really want this? I guess I really *am* twisted. But for whatever reason, I felt true. It all felt organic and comfortable. We were two friends playing a game and having a good time. We were indulging ourselves by just letting it flow. It was warm and true. I believed it was natural and fulfilling for both of us.

I had no idea where it was going. I still had this feeling that strong chemistry works in both directions like the "War of The Roses." Two people can be wildly in love and then breakup and fight with an equal level of hatred. But I just had to trust and go with it. I could have never been this vulnerable with anybody else in the world except for Regina, even though it was entirely new. There was some kind of unlikely fit we had for each other. It was an impossible match. But I was self-conscious about the lesbian aspect. It just didn't seem like me.

That's why I haven't wanted to kiss her. I'm trying to get used to the gender thing and it scares me. You know when you profess to everyone your values and then have to eat your words? That's how it felt emotionally to me. I had taken a firm stand about being straight. My straight sexuality was a form that I thought I understood and could use powerfully when I needed to. But now I am suddenly at a loss about who I am as a sexual person.

But then again, this has only happened with Regina. I seriously doubt I could feel this free with any other human, male or female. Talk about a whirlwind. It's some kind of crazy REM dream, all happening so fast with blinding wind whipping my hair. I feel like we are driving down the highway at a million miles an hour with the top down. Thelma and

Louise. It's a spinning rush. It is levels of my heart being awakened that I never knew were in there. It's Regina.

I went downstairs in my bathrobe to check on my little toy. There she was. She was struggling a bit against the chain on her neck. I think she was pretty uncomfortable and trying to adjust to relieve some tension somehow. Plus, she was stuck there in those high heels. Probably didn't feel so great on her feet. As I was looking at her, DING DONG, the fucking doorbell rang. I could tell we both jumped with a start and we both got instantly tense, wondering what to do. It was something I never even conceived of happening in my blind lust. I was going to ignore the door until… DING DONG… it rang again. Shit. I figured I had better answer it and get rid of the person.

I opened the door to discover Victoria standing there. In her exuberance, she started making her way inside with "Hey, Stranger. What's going on?" I literally had to block the door in sort of an "I Love Lucy" move. "Hi, Victoria. You can't come in right now. I'm in the middle of something," I told her. "Oh, really!" she brightened as she gestured to the robe I was wearing. "Good for you, Girl, " she congratulated. "How come I never knew about this guy?" I responded, "I don't know; It just kind of came up. I'm sorry, but you can't be here right now." She backed off, "I getcha. But we have to get together soon so I can hear all the details." She headed out with "Don't go too fast! And always trust your intuition."

I closed the door and sighed to compose myself. Then, I went over to Regina, who was really struggling in discomfort. To calm her, I pressed my body against hers, kind of like a hug with out using arms. I sensed that she was relishing the contact in a major way. The wooden spoon gag in her mouth was producing a lot of drool. In any other situation, it would have been hugely embarrassing to her and I'm sure she would have been very self-conscious about it. But we were going with this thing. We were all in.

She was drooling and I was thinking she was the most beautiful creature I ever saw. I pressed my body against hers even more. But then something completely surprising happened. She started whimpering in sadness. I studied her, while continuing to press against her figure. But she got worse. Her whimpering turned in to crying. I wasn't sure what to do. And after a moment, she was bawling severally. It really freaked me out. I quickly removed her gag and said, " Hey, what's wrong?" But she kept crying. I pleaded with her to tell me what was going on, but she would only cry. I rubbed her back in a motherly way and talked sweetly to her in hopes of calming her. Nothing.

Finally, in desperation, I said, "That was some kind of crazy day I had." Boom!! Like snapping someone out of hypnosis, her whole demeanor changed and she seemed like regular Regina. Our secret code for stopping the game had worked. Then I raced with: "Hey, what's happening? Are you ok? Are you too uncomfortable? Please tell me what's wrong! Are you mad at me?" Words came from deep inside her heart: "I'm so happy. I never knew it, but I wanted this my whole life. I never knew it, but I wanted you so much! I'm in heaven. I never want this to end. Please don't leave me. I never want to lose you."

Needless to say, this was hitting my core. Even though it was the world's fastest romance, she was in love with me. She radiated it. She trusted me. Even though she never said the three magic words, I knew exactly what she felt. Turning back to the practical matter at hand, I said, "Here, let me unchain you so you can relax." But then she snapped back in a forceful tone: "Can you believe how blue the sky is today?"

I was broadsided. What? I was never expecting this. Especially since she was just exposing every ounce of herself to me. And now she wants to play the game again? She looked like she was so uncomfortable, if not miserable. But I guessed she needed more. Sheeeesh. Fine!! We'll play all right!! I took the wooden spoon and started swatting her bottom hard. "How dare you scare me so much. How dare you!" And I continued to hit her ass as hard as I could. It was starting to get through to her and she began agonizing with vocal moans. It seemed so sexual. But it was just a good spanking. I was thinking she would actually climax! So I stopped.

Then I went right up to her blindfolded face and put my hand gently on her cheek. I told her softly, "You can trust me. I want this too." And then I drifted into my very first kiss with her. It wasn't even from me. It wasn't an action. It was a melding. It was from the cosmos. We kissed without any care in the world. It was guided by the moment and not by a person. It was sublime. It was tender and deep. It was Regina.

And by the same means, my hand was guided to rest between her legs. She lit up as she felt the contact. Slowly, the focus narrowed and my hand was sending her to places that were impossible to feel in any other situation. She exploded in a giant vocalization of release! She relished the orgasm and worked it for a long time. Finally, when she was ready for the proverbial cigarette, I said, "That was some kind of crazy day I had."

And again, like a light switch, she was someone else, her old self. She started laughing and her laughter was building, like the reverse ramp up of the crying. Between her big smiley laugh, she said, "Wow, this power thing might just go to your head. You're crazy!!" And in the bright mood, I unchained her neck and untied her hands. "That was really fucking uncomfortable!" she said while giggling. "You don't have to be so mean!" Concerned, I quickly asked, "Are you serious?" "Haha. Just kidding. I wouldn't have it any other way," she reassured me. Then we fell into a great hug that felt like eating hot French bread. We kissed a little. I still can't believe I would ever be kissing a girl! But it didn't feel like that. It just felt like a part of me.

Regina looked pretty spent. I made her a smoothie and she seemed delighted, first that I made it for her, and second that it was so cold and refreshing after what she went through. She delicately asked if it would be ok for her to lie down for a bit. It was all so new and neither of us had an emotional road map.

So we both went up stairs to the bed. We cuddled in close. Within a couple minutes, she was fast asleep. And I was in her arms. What a feeling. I wasn't able to sleep. I kept going over everything in my mind. What a blizzard of feelings in such a short time! It was like nothing I would ever believe or expect to be true. We hardly knew each other in the least. Yet we knew each other like old friends. After about 20 minutes of taking it all in, I carefully slipped out of her arms to go downstairs. Even asleep, she looked pure. She was still in her boots. I wish my eye were a camera. I would blow that shot up to a poster and hang it on my wall.

Downstairs, I drank a glass of wine and listened to some classic Jack Johnson in my earbuds. I floated around doing nothing. A couple hours went by and Regina was still sleeping. It made me feel so happy that she felt comfortable enough to take a nice nap in my bed… in my home. It felt very loving. I decided to make dinner. But since she would be waking up, I thought I should make breakfast for dinner. I always loved that growing up. So I made some Belgian waffles and a Greek omelet. Once the table was all set, I went up to wake her. I sat down softly beside her and said, "Sweetie, I made you some breakfast." But before she answered, I surprised myself: Did I just call her "Sweetie?" This is crazy. I'm nuts! What about my filters and boundaries? What has happened to me?

She started stirring. "Breakfast?" she wondered aloud, "Is it morning? I gotta be at work!" And she started to hop up. But I quickly assured her it was still the same day, "just breakfast for dinner." She laughed.

At dinner, she told me all about her past marriage - all about how it went down and how Tucker had to go through some really crappy stuff during the process. In the case of her marriage, it really was "War of the Roses," you know… two people are wildly in love and then end up hating each other's guts. And since war is hell, Tucker ended up getting some collateral damage from being on the sidelines. Regina tried so hard to always keep him out of it, but sometimes it would be impossible to protect him because she only had control over her half of the equation. One time, her X grumbled to Tucker, "Nice haircut your mom got for you. The kids are going to laugh at you at school." Disgusting. That is the kind of stuff that Regina couldn't shield Tucker from. You get enough of those things in a kid's head, and it can start to cause real harm.

Even though they had split custody, Tucker always gravitated to

Regina (WHO WOULDN'T?) and she said they have always enjoyed an honest and special relationship. And I must say, Tucker seems like a super great kid. He could always turn out to be a serial killer from repressed damage, but I feel that his mom is a great role model for how to be a positive energy in the world.

Regina had to deal with her husband Alex's crazy threats and hassles for years. He has a substance problem. That was the root of the demise. Once he beat her and she called the cops. Tucker was there. It killed her inside. But she is doing everything she can to heal Tucker now. Because she is a teacher, she only has to work until 3pm everyday so she can pick him up from school. She tries really hard to always spend quality time with him. He's gonna be ok. I can just tell. She never badmouths Alex in front of Tucker. She said Alex is the greatest dad and an all around good guy... until he starts drinking again. Then it's a cycle of damage and rebuilding, then damage again. But he has been sober for a long time now, so things are calm.

After breakfast-for-dinner, Regina said she had to get back. Neither of us would dare suggest she spend the night. Not only did we both have work in the morning, but also I'm sure we both felt like things were moving fast enough already.

We needed to keep a deliberate, steady pace so as not to get ahead of ourselves with a big crash and burn. There I go again. I don't know why I keep thinking the other shoe is going to drop. I should let the goodness flow. I should trust.

She was going to be with Tucker for the next three days. I wouldn't see her again until yoga on Wednesday night. I walked her to her electric Vespa. The funny thing was when she was ready to leave for home, neither of us had an inclination to kiss. It would have been forced, not like the kind of kissing earlier in the day that was drawn magically from somewhere in the ether. But even though it was merely a hug goodbye, I could tell we both were clinging to the goodness of the day. We both wanted more. We both trusted in being connected. She joked as she sat on the motorcycle seat, "Ouch! You really did a number on my tush." I joked back, "It wasn't me. It was that mean Mistress of yours." She laughed and drove off… very, very, quietly on her electric vegi-bike.

--- MONDAY MARCH 26 --- Back at work

I woke up and still smelled her on my pillow the next day. Usually on Mondays, I'm kind of blue. It seems everyone is like that. It's a real thing. But today, I was different. I was more introspective. I was rerunning the whole weekend on a loop in my head. It was mind-numbing to think how fast things went. In a single weekend, I went from totally straight and into guys to a full-steam relationship with a girl. My intellect told me that the new relationship isn't me. I've never been interested in women… ever. It must have been some emotionally drunken rebound from Boyfriend X. It was some kind of exploration or whatever. Everyone I have known my whole life has heard me go on about boys and sex with boys. I like boys. I've always liked boys. That was my intellect.

But my heart tells me something opposite. My heart tells me that Regina is it! Look no further. It's a mind and heart tug-o-war. It's the little angel and devil on my shoulders trying to pull me to their side. It's really confusing. Regina, at dinner last night told me pretty much the same thing about herself. She would have never considered anything remotely close to what is going on with us. She said I was special somehow and drew her into my own personal gravity field.

But to fight with the devil for a second, there could also be a strong case that I have always been kinky my whole life and was sexually oriented toward dark sex. And dark sex doesn't necessarily have to adhere to any one gender. So in that sense, being with Regina is not about changing my orientation. I've always oriented toward kink. I've always wanted and needed that. So I'm still the same person and fulfilling my same sexual fantasies.

I wondered if Regina was having any sort of buyer's remorse. Was this just a wild little tryst for her? Was it just something new and exciting to shake the stress and doldrums of single mommyhood and thankless work as a teacher? Was she seriously kinky? Are we really a fit? Maybe she just let her guard down for a moment. After reality sets in, maybe she'll think I'm too dark. Maybe she'll burn out on being my toy.

On the other hand, I've read a fair amount about S&M relationships. Some go on for a lifetime. Some people find joy in kink forever. I'm not saying this is true S&M. That whole scene has always seemed cliché to me. I've been to a few dungeon/dance clubs with Victoria. We went there for kicks to check it out. It always felt false to me. It felt like straight people in costumes. Well, or gay people in costumes too. It was always showy and cinematic. I didn't believe that scene. Everyone wore the cliché black leather and studs. Boring. Fake. Then some dominatrix would be whipping some fat guy on a rack in the back of the room. The crowd would watch with their martinis and act like they really understood kink. Please. It actually pissed me off.

Kink isn't a costume. It's not an act. It's not flogging some stranger. That's all bullshit. I feel kink as the guiding rudder of my sexuality. It's me. It's not something you try at a club where you play with "danger" for show.

When I had Regina chained at the neck to that post, it touched my core. It ignited real passion in me that I have been shamed into keeping at bay for my whole life. So the only real question is, does Regina have the same wiring? Is it in her core? What if we start down this path and three months later, she turns vanilla on me and is repulsed by the idea of being my object. I would feel one inch tall.

All this doubt was swirling around my head. So I thought I'd better check it out with her. I texted her and arranged to call on her lunch break. When the time came, I called her from my car while driving to lunch. The conversation went like this.

        REGINA
        Meg!

        ME

Are you ok?

REGINA
I don't know. Are you?

ME
Are you feeling scared like me?

REGINA
Yeah. I'm kind of scared.

ME
Because you made a mistake or because you think it might end?

REGINA
I'm scared because I showed you my soul this weekend. I'm scared you will go away.

ME
That's the same thing I'm afraid of.

REGINA
Do you think this is real?

ME
Do you?

REGINA
I want it to be real. I want to love you.

ME
Me too.
(Long pause)

ME
Ok. I think we're good.

> **REGINA**
> *Ok. Me too.*

We both chuckled nervously for a moment.

> **ME**
> *Can you believe how blue the sky is today?*

> **REGINA**
> *What!! I'm at work.*

> **ME**
> *Can you believe how blue the sky is today?*

> **REGINA**
> (Whispering into the phone)
> *Yes it is, Mistress.*

> **ME**
> *You are my object. Do you understand me?*

> **REGINA**
> (Super eager)
> *Yes, Mistress. Yes!*

> **ME**
> *I need you to masturbate in the bathroom.*
> *Then email me and tell me that you did it.*

> **REGINA**
> *Yes, Mistress.*

And I hung up on her. About 15 minutes later, she wrote me and said that she had done it and was profusely thanking me for the command. I wrote her back a single line email with no subject: "That was some kind of crazy day I had"

An hour later, some flowers appeared at my work. There was a note attached, *"In spite of what the weather may be doing, I really appreciate our developing friendship. Fondly, Regina."*

This was particularly funny because I had sent her flowers about the same time and the school receptionist was probably signing for them at the same moment. My note wasn't as poetic. It just said, *"Regina, I've never shared my true heart like I have with you. Thanks for not judging me. You're beautiful. - I'm yours, Meg."*

Of course, my whole office teased me about who was sending flowers. Pete, in particular, commented that I looked different. He made the intuitive observation that something major has shifted in my life. He knew it was a relationship. He said he's never seen me like that, brooding, pensive, and daydreaming. And he was right. I'd never seen me like that either.

That evening I briefly called Regina to wish her goodnight and to tell her to enjoy loving Tucker. She was sweet and wished me well too. I must say, immature as it is, I was a little jealous that Tucker got to be with her. I skipped dinner and went to bed, sleeping all the way until morning.

--- TUESDAY MARCH 27 ---   No playing games

Tick Tock. Tick Tock. I have never felt time move so slowly. I felt like I was in stuck in a giant jar of molasses on a winter day. I really wanted to make it through the day without texting or calling Regina. I didn't want to seem too needy or desperate. It wasn't even lunchtime yet. I struggled to occupy myself with my job, trying everything to avoid calling. It was torture.

And of course, with each minute that went by, I had this running dialog with myself: "Maybe she misses me and is struggling hard not to call me too. Maybe she was getting angry with me that I wasn't contacting her. Maybe she thought I was playing games with her to see who would call first. Or maybe, she was just going along in the trappings of her day and has me on the back burner of her mind." But the way we connected told me that she wasn't likely to play games.

Also, from the way she was crying during our little session (for lack of a better word), I'm sure she was thinking about me, touched by the sudden and extreme emotional changes.

Ding-a-ling! The caller I.D. on my office phone showed that Regina was calling. My emotions started racing. I quickly picked up:

> **ME**
> *Hi Regina!*
>
> **REGINA**
> *Hi.*
>
> **ME**
> *I'm so glad you called. I was on the fence about calling you. I didn't want to bug you or seem desperate.*
>
> **REGINA**
> *I had the exact same thoughts. I felt like calling but wanted to play it cool.*
>
> **ME**
> *Regina, let's agree on one thing.*
>
> **REGINA**
> *Ok, what?*
>
> **ME**
> *Let's agree that we will always keep our relationship healthy by not playing any games.*
>
> **REGINA**
> *You mean like calculating to call or not call?*

ME

Right. We should just always operate out of honesty. If we feel like calling, we call. If we feel hurt, we say it. If we feel jealous or put off or slighted, we say it. I think that will help us stay on course with each other.

REGINA

Agreed. That's how I normally operate anyway. But with something as delicate and precious as what we are developing, I might have tended to cover some feelings in hopes of not pushing you away. But you're right. There is no place for that with us. The only games we can play are the games about the weather.

ME

(I chuckled)
Sounds good. Like right now... I don't know if you said that... in hopes of getting me to talk about the sky... or if you just said it for fun.

REGINA

I was just joking. If I really want to talk about the sky with you, you will know it. You will see me yearn. You will be able to read me. You will see my eyes begging for your control. You will know when to talk about the sky.

ME

Great. So in the same spirit of honesty and not playing games, I will tell you that I am crazy in love with you. I know it doesn't seem possible yet, but this has never happened to me!

REGINA
I feel the same way.

I can't wait until yoga to see you.

ME
I got an idea. I have to location scout tomorrow for a couple hours. I was going to go in the morning, but if you like, I can go at 4pm and take you and Tucker along.

REGINA
Really? You wouldn't mind if Tucker came?

ME
Normally, it is super bad to have kids meet all the various dates that a girl has. You're supposed to wait until something is more solid so that the child isn't jerked along with a string of new faces and drama. But this feels different. Am I high?

REGINA
No. It feels solid. (Pause) *Let's just be friends in front of Tucker. He will love you. I'll tell him you are my new friend.*

ME
Ok. The location scouting should be fun for him. We have to check out six giant stylized warehouses for a commercial shoot. They are all vacant. He can bring some roller blades or a little bike and have a blast in the big spaces! There's also one place that is on the 6th floor. We can throw paper airplanes off the overlook. I bet they will fly

forever.

REGINA
It sounds like so much fun.
(Thoughtful pause)
I want to touch you.

ME
Me too. But that will have to wait. It will be more fun that way. Forbidden love!

REGINA
I wish I could see you right now!

ME
See you tomorrow at 4. I'll pick you up.

Then there was a long pause as neither of us wanted the call to end. Finally, I hear a gentle kiss sound come over the phone. Then it hung up. It was only an audio kiss, but it may as well have been a full, physical kiss on the lips. The way she delivered it, it was. I could feel it like she was right in front of me. I could taste it. I could feel her breath in the kiss.

A while later, I went online to buy a few items for our new game. Before I knew it, I had racked up $438! But it wasn't like I did this all the time. I even refrained from paying the expedited shipping charges. When I was shopping, Regina's face and body kept popping up in my head and I fantasized about playing our game again. This was so fun! I never got excited like this with any guys ever!

--- WEDNESDAY MARCH 28 --- Inside her secret world

When I woke up, I felt alive! I was so excited to be seeing Regina. But I was also really looking forward to being with Tucker. See, it wasn't just that Tucker is a cool kid. It is that Regina would be letting me into her very personal world. It was a whole other half of her life. So now, instead of sharing half of who she is, it would be sharing all of her. It was a magnificent show of trust. It was saying, "Hey, the Meg girl is alright and I want to include her." I'm within the secret walls.

That morning at work, I was surprisingly focused on my job. I got more done in a few hours then in most entire weeks. I had to fill up my mind so as not to drift into fantasies of Regina. Both my boss and Pete were amazed that I kept running into their offices in search of the next tasks. But at lunchtime, I couldn't help myself. I took time out to call Regina. Her voice sounded as comforting as a teacher's voice should.

She mentioned that, unlike me, she was having a really difficult time concentrating in class. She was taking my call in the faculty kitchen. It must have been even harder when I remarked, "Can you believe how blue the sky is today?" And immediately, my adorable slave came under my control and whispered into the phone to avoid office ears, "Yes, Mistress?" Then, in a measured tone, I told her, "I own you." There was a slow response from Regina as she was trying to digest this before saying, "Yes, Mistress." I continued with, "You are my object. My property. You will never disobey me." "Yes, Mistress," she solemnly whispered. I continued, "As my property, I will take care of you and treat you with all the respect deserved of my most valued possession."

There was a long pause. Then, came something from her mouth that shocked me: "I love you, Mistress." This was completely jarring to me. I was flustered. I loved her too, but it all seemed so scary. Was she only in love with me in the game? Was she only in love with her mistress? I responded, "That was some kind of crazy day I had." Then I quickly hung up.

About a minute later, RING – RING! She called back. I answered as myself:

        ME
        Hello?

        REGINA
        (Clearly with a smile on her face)

Do you believe the nerve of some people?

ME
What do you mean?

REGINA
This really pushy person just called and rattled me!! So I gave her a piece of my mind and let her know exactly what I thought.

ME
(Not really sure who was in control of this call)
Glad you gave it back to her. People like her can really be annoying.

REGINA
Only if you let them.

ME
So are we still on at 4pm?

REGINA
Yep. I just wanted to vent a little.

ME
*Thanks for sharing. It means a lot to me.
See you at four.*

At 4pm, I pulled up to Regina's house on Potrero Hill. It was classic San Francisco architecture, tall and skinny. It looked cute, but simple. She hadn't done much to the outside other than keeping it clean and nice. It looked like any of the homes on the same block, except for one difference; there was a thick bougainvillea encircling her garage entrance with little fuchsia buds that would eventually explode with color. If things go well with Regina and I still know her in June, that plant will be absolutely stunning. I want to be able to see that!

When I knocked at the door, she immediately greeted me with a warm "friend" hug. There was a certain air of formality. Right behind Regina came Tucker. He was bright-eyed and seemed enthusiastic about my arrival. Little boys always seem to gravitate toward me. I gave him a big hug, which was a little bigger than Regina's. I wanted him to like me. I wanted to try to win him over. I figured if I could win him over, Regina would like me even more.

To some, it may have seemed like I was trying too hard with Tucker. But he is really likable and I was sincerely interested in him. Who wouldn't want to step off of the adult train to get in touch with their childlike sensibilities? I asked Tucker if I could see his room quickly before we went location scouting. Judging from her approving eye contact, Mom was having fun watching my interaction with Tucker. He was eager to show me his room and quickly lead the way.

As I stepped across the threshold into Regina's private world, I was taken by a feeling of warmth. Unlike the outside of the house, the inside was full of personality. It was charming. She clearly had fabulous taste in décor. It was cheery and homey, built on top of classic style. Stickley chairs graced the living room and there was a Ralph Lauren rustic feeling, accented by bold colored artwork and a sense of simple sophistication. Everything matched Regina: poised, charming, smart, graceful, and fun. That was her.

There was also a baby grand piano, which doubled as a coffee table book display. Her book collection was very visual: fine art, architecture, a whole book of orchids, a Rolling Stone magazine book of backstage shots of the greatest musicians, and… a big fat book of Helmut Newton photographs.

Wow! Her dark side! My whole life, I wanted to live inside a Helmut Newton photo. I wanted to be in there so badly. Helmut Newton, for the non-aware, is the mainstream kinky black & white photographer who shot for Vogue magazine and the like. His photos always show stunning people in very staged poses that usually involve themes of S&M and bondage. Even though the photos are in black and white, his trademark is giving the skin a "bronze" sheen that looks hyper real. Every photo pulsates with sex. But it's surprisingly mainstream. I can never get enough!

As I followed Tucker down the hall toward his bedroom, it was apparent that Regina worshipped him. Every square inch of the hallway was covered with Tucker's artwork from school and pre-school. It is a rainbow of finger paintings, watercolors, mosaics, and paper cut-outs. It was a happy hallway.

We arrived in Tucker's room. It looked pretty typical with Legos, toy cars, etc. There was a fishbowl on the dresser holding a single goldfish. "That's Barkley," Tucker said. "Hi Barkley," I said sticking out my hand to the fish bowl as if trying to shake its hand. "Nice to meet you." Tucker and Regina chuckled. When I asked about the origin of the name, Regina replied, "He just made it up one day."

Then I noticed something odd. "Where's your bed?," I wondered aloud. Tucker proudly responded, "I sleep with my mom." Regina quickly chimed in, "It has always been that way. But now that he is bigger, we are going to transition to having him sleep in here… with Barkley." Even though Tucker was nine, it didn't seem weird to me that he slept with his mom, especially when considering the effects of a divorce. They both seemed healthy and stable, so it really didn't matter where he slept. "Let's hope she doesn't snore like a hippo," I quipped. They laughed. Then Regina tried to somehow reassure me by saying, "We are bringing his bed up from the garage this week."

I really wanted to see Regina's bedroom, thinking I could glean more about her life. I wanted to know everything about her, to see her naked in her body and thought. But she didn't offer to show me her room, and I didn't feel comfortable asking to see it. I knew there would be more opportunities. She had already trusted me into her life so much my letting me be with her and Tucker while location scouting.

As we headed out to the car, Regina looked as adorable as ever! Some people can light up a room, she can light up a neighborhood. She was casual in her jeans and maroon puffy short sleeve top. It had a scoop neckline and faint little butterfly printed pattern. No boots, of course (I didn't expect to see boots on her). Instead, she wore these cute espadrilles that tied around the ankle with a navy cotton strap. The overall feeling, when coupled with her personality, was cheeriness. My kinky mind especially enjoyed the tie around the ankles. It was a wink of bondage.

And just so you know, I didn't dress like the Helmut Newton models. I just had on some salmon pants, a simple white blouse, a black cardigan, and some ballerina flats.

We drove around location scouting in San Francisco. It was more like driving around eye-flirting the whole damn time. I took any opportunity I could to make it fun for Tucker. I took a minor detour and went down the crookedest street in the world, Lombard Street, while pretending the car was out of control. He was laughing so hard!

Of course we had to make a stop by the Golden Gate Bridge to throw some paper airplanes off. It's didn't go so well, though, because they blew back onto the street. So then we decided to spit over the railing and track how far we could watch it. We'll have to try again one day with paper planes when there is no wind.

Even inside the various warehouse locations, we had so much fun. There was a giant utility cart in one of them and we got it rolling really fast and jumped on. We were zipping along pretty good and laughing our heads off when the security guard busted us. True, it wasn't very professional of me to represent our company like that, but I figured they would never know. I can't imagine an afternoon where Tucker could have had more fun. Regina was really enjoying herself, too. I could tell she liked the way I worked hard to make it fun for Tucker.

One time when Tucker went into the bathroom, we waited outside the door in this enormous space. The sun was low and huge shafts of light poured through the upper vent windows onto the floor next to us. I asked Regina to move over a bit to stand in the light so I could take her photo. She looked like she was in a Caravaggio painting. I snapped the photo. It was my first picture of her. I had captured an angel!!

Then we stood silently, arms folded, staring at each other. I could tell each of us wanted to talk about "the blue sky," but were not at liberty to do so because of Tucker's presence. So we just stood there, each of us daydreaming a kinky dream. If I had to guess, I would say that she was pretty turned on… I mean, physically turned on. It wasn't just her mind. I think she was physically aroused by staring at me, her mistress. I dominated her with a stern look.

When Tucker finally emerged from the bathroom, we were both slow to snap out of it. But we did. Tucker never had a clue that we had been undressing each other. He had no clue that I had his mom over my knee and was spanking her slowly with a hair brush while she masturbated herself the whole time.

After the scouting trip, we figured it was best to not have dinner together. It was a school night and Regina wanted to start the nighttime routine with Tucker. I completely understood. But still, I didn't want it to end. I dropped them off and went away very satisfied with life. I have never felt such a connection to a human as I had with Regina. This was bigger than a friendship like, "Hey, check out that hot guy!" This was about being on the same wavelength, meshing with another person.

--- THURSDAY MARCH 29 --- Sharing secrets

I'm writing this at the end of a very long day of developing my passion for Regina.

This morning I woke up to discover my ankles tied together with a belt. Then I got really aroused thinking about Regina. Here's what happened.

Last night, Regina called me after Tucker had gone to bed. She wanted to thank me for such a lovely time. She said they both had the best time. So did I. We talked for a while about our jobs, comparing notes.

We were both pretty happy at work. Regina has been teaching there a long time. To her, it was a job, not a career. That's not to say she doesn't adore her students and shower them with positive energy. But if she didn't have to work there, she would be happier. For me, I guess it's more than just a job. I see my work as a steppingstone to advance and ultimately become a commercial executive producer where the real money is.

Then the phone call turned deeper:

> **REGINA**
> *How are you doing with all this?*
>
> **ME**
> *It feels really good.*
>
> **REGINA**
> *I'm glad you feel that way.*
>
> **ME**
> *And what about for you?*
>
> **REGINA**
> *It's exciting. It feels like eating cotton candy.*
>
> **ME**
> *I know what you mean. Still, it makes me wonder if it is all fluff... not that I think it is... I'm just hoping that we will still feel this way next week.*
>
> **REGINA**
> *Me too. I still can't believe I'm romantically interested in a girl!*
>
> **ME**
> *You don't know the half of it. I was judging myself at first, but you're not just any girl. I*

could have never felt this way about any other woman.

REGINA
You're making me blush.
(Pause)
I think you should go look in the back seat of your car.

ME
What?

REGINA
You might want to check the back seat of your car for something.

ME
My car? Now?

REGINA
Sure. I'll wait.

So I dashed down to the garage to check the back seat. Under a throw blanket was a long shoebox. Any girl would know what is in a box that long: Boots! I opened it. It was Regina's new brick red boots! I was happily confused as I raced back to the phone:

ME
What are you doing?

REGINA
I thought we should share them... I mean... if you like them.

ME
Like them? They're hot.

REGINA

That way we can always feel close. You can know that your sweaty feet are standing in the very shoes where my sweaty feet were... and vice versa.

ME
Who says my feet sweat?

REGINA
Figure of speech. Do you like the idea of sharing them?

ME
I'm putting them on right this second.

REGINA
I want to please you.

ME
You mean in the game?

REGINA
In general. I want to make you happy.

ME
There's something strong going on with us. So how to we share the boots?

REGINA
I don't know. No rules.

ME
Ok. I'll get them back to you at some point.

REGINA
Tell me a secret about you... a secret that you have never uttered to anyone in the world... not even your therapist.

ME
(A little surprised)
You first.

REGINA
Me first?
(Pause)
Ok. This is real trust. I'll kill you if you ever tell anyone.

ME
Scouts' honor.

REGINA
Am I really doing this? Ok. Here goes. Ever since I was a freshman in college, I have been addicted to "The Young and The Restless."

I'm so embarrassed!!

ME
What? Millions of people watch that. So what?

REGINA
Yes, but I like to think of myself as wholesome, local and organic… a girl who shuns the nightly news and mainstream media. I watch a soap that is sponsored by the biggest, most detrimental companies of our society. And I'm supporting that by watching their stupid show. One time, one of characters died and I literally found myself mourning for 3 days. I was heartbroken. Nobody knows I watch it. It's oxymoronic with my lifestyle.

ME
Wow. That is shocking. You're right. Soap operas are the antithesis of the way I perceive you.

REGINA
I know. I know.

ME
The soap operas are misogynistic. All the characters are greed mongers... nobody is a millionaire, they are all friggin' billionaires! They are the polar opposite of local and organic.

REGINA
(Laughing)
I know! I feel stupid.

ME
But if you don't buy the products, then you're not supporting them at all. You are merely enjoying the story. I can't believe you are embarrassed about watching that.

REGINA
It feels funny telling you. So what's yours?

ME
I can't tell you. It's not balanced. Yours was so minor that it almost doesn't qualify.

REGINA
Yours will probably seem just as minor to me.

ME

I can't believe we're doing this!

REGINA
Go on.

ME
(Big sigh)
A couple years after I hit puberty, I discovered that…

REGINA
What? You can say it.

ME
I found out that if I tied my angles together with a belt, my orgasms would be stronger. I loved the way it felt because it was harder to get my fingers in there and felt more awkward to make it all happen.

REGINA
And that's your big secret?

ME
Part of it.

REGINA
What else?

ME
After I finished, I liked to stay like that… all night. I found it really sexy and comforting that my ankles were strapped together at night. I would sleep like that.

Sometimes I would wake in the middle of the night, having forgotten that my ankles were tied. At first I would be startled, then quickly I'd start getting turned on again. Sometimes that would happen three times in one night!

REGINA
Now I'm getting turned on.

ME
But that's not the whole secret either.

REGINA
I'm still listening.

ME
Sometimes I still like to do it... to sleep like that.

REGINA
(Joking)
You must be some kind of freak!

ME
Have you ever done that?

REGINA
No.

ME
Well, what do you think?

REGINA
Do it tonight. Sleep like that!

ME
You think I should?

REGINA
Yes! It sounds sexy. I'd join you but I'll

have Tucker in the bed.
(Pause)
Wait? Does that mean you are submissive? Maybe you should actually be my slave since you like to be tied up?

ME
Do you have a dominant side?

REGINA
I don't know. This is all so new to me. Articles about S&M in Cosmo and such have piqued my interest, but meeting you somehow brought all this stuff to the surface that I didn't really know was so strong in me.

I remember reading "The Story of O" when I was about 17. It's the story of -

ME
... a girl who consents to being sent away to a secret S&M society to serve as a slave. It's a very sexy book!

REGINA
Right. At 17, I thought the concept was ultra sexy! But I also thought regular romance novels were sexy too. I read all that stuff! But now, I feel what the "Story of O" was really about. It's about embracing your shadow self.

ME
Right. So... does your shadow self have a dominant side too?

REGINA

I don't know. No. I don't think I do. That may change; but right now, I just want to be your yours. I want you to degrade me.

What about you? If you like having your ankles tied up, maybe you have a slave side too?

ME
Sexuality is complex. In my fantasies, I'm both dominant and submissive. Whatever. Let's just say I'm kinky, however you want to define it. I've never been as turned on as when I think about being mean to you... in our game.

REGINA
We need to play again.

ME
Yes.

REGINA
But for now, I need to go to bed... and I need you to tie your ankles together tonight.

ME
Is that an order?

REGINA
No, it's a request from a loving friend.

ME
We have a fucked up relationship. Go watch your soap opera. Oh, and thanks for the boots!

REGINA
Goodnight.

We hung up. And I did it. I had her boots on. So when I awoke this morning and felt my ankles tied together in Regina's high boots, I took a few minutes for myself (wink, wink!) before starting the usual morning routine.

The sun was casting its warmth across my bedspread and I could feel it all the way under the covers. In my mind, I transformed the heat of the sun into the gaze of Regina watching me. I could feel her eyes generating warmth onto me as she stared. She watched me get my hands into position, despite the fact that I couldn't open my legs. As I began to caress myself, she crossed her legs and leaned back to take it all in. I rubbed deep. Then, as I was getting close, I saw her uncross her legs and put her hands between her own legs. She looked as turned on as I was. She put on some Ray-Ban's so I couldn't see her eyes anymore. My breath and heart were racing, as were hers. We were both completely enthralled with the moment. At the same instant, we both burst out in ecstasy. Passion was burning. Lava was coursing though my veins. I felt alive!

As I slowly came down, Regina in Ray-Ban's was gone. There was just an empty chair. But I had a warm smile on my face because I knew she had really been there with me. She was inside me… even though she was probably getting ready for work.

And now I had to get to work. That took a little longer than I wanted, but who cares? What a way to start a day! And things would even get better. Tonight would be yoga. Tucker would be back at his dad's after school and Regina could be my object again.

Once I was at my office, I couldn't help but text Regina several times to basically say nothing. It was just a matter of feeling a connection with her. She called me once on her lunch break. It was being in touch, feeling the energy of our new situation.

After work, I changed for yoga and grabbed a quick bite. I wanted to get to yoga early so I could meet Regina outside upon her arrival. Sure enough, she rolled up right on time on her electric Vespa. She looked really pleased to see me waiting there for her.

As much as I was delighted to see her and wanted to have fun together, I also found myself wanting to dominate her. I mean, we had been on the phone a good deal during the day and there wasn't much worthy of conversation since our last call a couple hours earlier. She clearly didn't feel that way, looking like she was game for a 4 hour talk-a-thon at a café. She was bubbling out of her own personality without having said a word.

She jumped off her bike and ran over to give me a hug. I hugged back. It was better than any hug with a boyfriend. Her small little boobs pushed up against my bigger ones and it felt amazing. If a picture is worth a thousand words, a hug like that is worth more. It was a whole story. It told me that she trusted me, that she adored me, that she was excited to see me, and that she valued me. I'm sure she could sense that I was feeling the same about her.

There was newness, not just to the romance, but to the very idea of being with a woman. It felt secret and special… secret because no guy could ever know what it felt like to be a woman falling for a woman. Even though Regina is technically older than me, I feel like I am the older one… by about 4 years. I liked feeling the power of being emotionally older. She looked up to me. I could exploit her and take advantage of her. She would do anything I say.

After that incredible hug at the curb, I gave her a quick kiss on the lips. It was natural and easy. She seemed not to have a care in the world. People on the street seeing that kiss would probably have assumed that we are dear friends. Do girlfriends sometimes kiss on the lips to greet each other? Anyway, it seemed innocent enough.

But after the kiss, I looked her deep in the eyes and said, "Can you believe how blue the sky was today?" She was jolted from the present and light mood. She was somebody else now. Really. Her whole face said, "I beg of you from the bottom of my soul, please fuck me as hard as you can on the cold concrete. I want to be your object of lust. I want you to punish me." Of course, I don't know what she was actually thinking. But she responded, "Yes, Mistress. The sky is blue."

To be honest with you, I had no intention of activating the game. It was not preplanned. But when I saw her arriving, it came over me in an instant.

Without saying a word, I grabbed her by the wrist and sternly led her up the stairs to the yoga class. There was a couple walking down against our path and I could tell they noticed the way I was holding Regina's wrist. People only hold a child by the wrist like that when he or she is going to get in trouble. I didn't care what the couple thought. I just wanted to keep Regina's slender wrist in my grasp. It felt good to be bossy. Regina's energy told me that she was totally on board, too.

When we got to the studio, everyone was laying out their mats. I privately told Regina to put her mat front center. "Yes, Mistress," she responded quietly. I placed my mat directly behind hers. Then I went right up to her ear and whispered, "Do not give me any eye contact. Do not say a word to me." She obediently nodded.

Regina's demeanor was different than usual at the yoga class. Instead of her usual sparky self, she was solemn and reserved as she played our game. Even, Carol, the yoga teacher, noticed the change. She asked, "Is everything okay, Regina? You seem like something's on your mind." Regina, looking to shake the conversation, responded, "I'm fine. Thanks for asking." Then she turned away for another stretch.

I loved that only she and I knew the secret, that she was being controlled by me. The funny thing is, because "Regina" wasn't in class, the whole energy of the group had changed. It took on a more serious tone than normal. It's funny how a catalyst like Regina can have a *butterfly effect* on a whole room. That shows you what a powerful force of light she is. It must be fun for her to turn it off for a while in our game and play someone so different!

The class itself was normal. I loved how earnest Regina looked in doing her poses. She was more stiff than usual. You could tell that being a slave was affecting her usual limber body. She was in a headspace that had her more reserved and self-conscious.

During the warm down, I quietly excused myself and sneaked out the side door without saying goodbye to Regina. She was face-forward in the front of the class and unaware that I had bailed.

But out on her motorcycle, I left a note on her seat, held down by a rock: "Come to my house immediately." And I signed it, "Your Owner."

Once at home, I was still hungry. I reheated some risotto, threw a quick salad together, and sautéed some tempeh to toss in the salad for my little vegetarian friend that I had hoped would obey and show up. I set the table and poured two glasses of Pinot. Music was my Pandora romance mix that I had been crafting for over a year during my days with Boyfriend X. (For some reason, I thought that if I found the perfect mix of lustful songs, it would make him get dark and nasty. Not.)

The table was set. Feeling a bit nervous, I took a couple gulps of wine, then quickly changed into a cotton LBD and put on our communal boots. The wooden heel was wonderfully high and felt feminine and powerful. The brick red clashed nicely against my pale skin. They were really sexy on me. I hoped Regina would think so too.

A moment later, there she was at the door. When I opened the door, it wasn't Regina. It was my object. She still wouldn't make eye contact with me, handing me fresh cut flowers. I gestured for her to come in and I closed the door.

Since she wasn't "Regina," it was easy for me to get what I wanted and toy with her. I told her to put the flowers in a vase. She immediately walked to the kitchen and opened cabinets in search of a vase. She found one, filled it with water and placed the beautiful flowers in it. She had not spoken to that point.

The second the flowers were on the table, I walked up to her and grabbed her face between both my hands and coldly addressed her… 1-inch from her face. The conversation went like this:

> **ME**
> *How dare you disobey me.*

She looked confused and didn't speak.

> **ME**
> *What did the note say on your scooter?*
>
> **REGINA**
> (Sheepishly)
> *To come here immediately.*
>
> **ME**
> *And what did you do instead?*
>
> **REGINA**
> *I swear, Mistress. I came here as fast as I could.*
>
> **ME**
> *Where did the flowers come from?*
>
> **REGINA**
> (Realizing her screw up)
> *From Betsy's Flowers, Mistress.*
>
> **ME**
> *So you disobeyed me, didn't you?*
>
> **REGINA**
> (Barely audible)
> *Yes, Mistress.*

ME
What?

REGINA
Yes, Mistress! I wanted to give you flowers.

I gave her a little slap in the face. Her eyes darted up to me with fear and remorse.

ME
Don't you look at me!
(She quickly cast her eyes downward)
Let's get something straight. You will never disobey me again. Is that clear?

REGINA
Yes, Mistress.

ME
I made this little dinner. I thought we could spend some time together enjoying ourselves with nice conversation. And then you come along and spoiled the whole evening by disobeying me.

REGINA
Yes, Mistress.

ME
Take off your sweatshirt.

Regina took off her yoga sweatshirt to reveal her coral-colored cotton workout tank. Her arms were so slender and toned. I pointed to a cardboard box on the counter.

ME
Go open it.

REGINA
Yes, Mistress.

She opened the box and was happily surprised to see a pair of shoulder-length, kid leather, opera gloves.

ME
Put them on... slowly... like you mean it.

REGINA
Yes, Mistress.

She took her cue. She played up donning the gloves in a slow and steamy reverse striptease. The leather looked sexy against her arms. I was getting turned on watching her work the gloves. While boots are my main fetish, the gamut is wide. Long leather gloves run a close second at getting me going.

ME
Here's a rule you really don't want to break. If, for any reason that may arise, you find yourself with an opportunity to touch my bare skin, you must always be wearing those gloves. It would disgust me to be touched by someone as lowly as you without gloves. Understood.

REGINA
Yes, Mistress. Thank you.

ME
I have one more gift for you. Turn around.

She turned away from me. I approached her from behind and gently placed my hand around her throat, giving her a firm feeling of being mildly choked as I pressed my breasts against her back. Her gloved hands were at her side.

ME
Rub me gently.

REGINA
Thank you, Mistress.

She put her hands behind her back as I kept a solid grip on her throat. Ever so gently, she placed her hands between my legs and started caressing me through my little black dress. I released her neck and allowed my hands to slide down her front side, my left hand landing around her waist and my right hand taking her breasts. I pulled her in snugly. She was rubbing me and I was gently playing with her boobs.

But then my left hand slid from her waist down to her covered clitoris. I held her close with my right hand as I stimulated her with my left. All the while, she was stimulating me with her arms behind her back. It was like spooning while standing up. We were both on the brink. I halted her with, "That's enough," and released her at once. She stood there catching her breath and waiting for the next command.

After a brief trip to the living room, I returned with the items I wanted. Grabbing her wrists, I locked them in steel handcuffs behind her back. The cuffs locked with that telltale ratcheting sound. She was my prisoner. The look of the steel handcuffs over her leather opera gloves was pleasing, to say the least. Then, I shoved a leather bit gag into her mouth and cinched it tightly behind her neck. The gag (one of my internet purchases along with the handcuffs and gloves) was made of a leather-covered dowel with a strap on each side. The dowel was a half-inch in diameter and about 4 inches long. It looked very sturdy and serious.

"Kneel down," I commanded her. She quickly complied. Then I went over to the dinner table, which by now held risotto that was a tad above lukewarm. In an unsympathetic voice, I scolded her, "No dinner for you. I will not tolerate being disobeyed. You ruined the whole evening with those flowers. Now you can sit there and watch me eat all by myself."

And there she was... on her knees, hands in full-length gloves bound behind her back in handcuffs, an uncomfortable gag across her bite. I was super aroused, but I played it cool by casually eating and sipping my wine while ignoring her. I walked over and picked up the Chronicle, then sat back down and crossed my legs right in front of her while I read and dined. She was studying my/our brick red boots. "They look so much better on me, don't you agree," I said. Regina, not being able to speak, nodded affirmatively with her gorgeous eyes.

After I indulged myself in her punishment for about a half hour, I decided to show some mercy. I took off her gag, which left indentations on her cheeks from where the leather straps had been. I gave her permission to answer me when spoken to. She stretched her jaw up and down a couple times as I think she had been quite uncomfortable in her bridle. I spoke, "You were such a good girl during dinner and sat so obediently, I think you deserve some dessert." Extending my right leg, I continued, "Lick my boot." "Yes, Mistress," she eagerly replied.

And she began to lick my boot as if it were the biggest cock in the world. She started at the tip of my toe and gradually covered more and more. Her tongue was driven by all the passion she had in her body. It was as sexual as anything anyone could imagine. She was in bliss. All the years of a crappy marriage and the heavy burden of being a single mom were finally shed away as she relished every bit of her feminine sexuality. She was alive. She was licking my cock.

On the Pandora mix came the sexiest song I have ever heard, an oldie but a goodie... David Bowie's "Putting out the fire with Gasoline" from the Cat People movie. It was the perfect soundtrack to watching her. She got to the top of my boot... and kept going. I didn't stop her. She caressed my leg with the same commitment as below, reaching my inner thigh and eventually, my sweet spot under my dress. I helped her a little by pulling my panties aside. There was some awkwardness as we worked to get the perfect angle. Her tongue was melting me. She was fire.

Nothing on the Earth has ever felt better to me. It was my slave. But it was Regina too. She had extremely detailed command of her tongue and carefully gauged my reactions so that she could better stimulate me at each moment. I grabbed her hair with one hand and pulled it tight to her approving moan. She brought me to an incredible crescendo... so much so that I leaned back, accidentally knocking a wine glass off the table.

I was floating. A breeze of love washed across my whole body. I had nothing left, as if having been in a sauna for 2 hours. Regina, hands still locked behind her back, rested her head on my thigh in order to feel close to me and have a connection. I gently played with her hair. With each pass of my fingers, she seemed to be purring, intoxicated by our passion and honesty.

I needed to be close to her too. "That was some kind of crazy day," I lovingly uttered. She quickly sat upright and shocked me by forcefully blurting out, "No, Mistress. It was NOT a crazy day. Please don't leave me!! I beg of you." And real tears came over her as she started to cry. I was rattled, not expecting this in the least. I had planned on getting her off, but not until later. By her reaction, I realized that she was still in the headspace of the game and wasn't complete. Even though it was a game, it was as real as real could be.

The mind is a powerful thing. I'm afraid of heights and if anybody recounts a story of their parachute jump, my hands get sweaty and my heart races. The parachute jump is as real to me as if I was doing it right then myself. That's how the game was to Regina. She wasn't a mom. She wasn't teacher. She wasn't happy and bright. She was Meg's object. She needed to be controlled and handled. Fine.

"Fine," I blasted. "You want more, you got it!" I shoved the gag back in her mouth and buckled it as tight as I could, causing a little yelp as she felt the force. Then I stood tall and pulled her upright with me. I took off her clogs, yanked off her yoga pants, removed my boots and put them on her feet instead. I zipped them up. This was all happening very fast and with a brusqueness that such an object deserves.

From the closet, I grabbed the heavy steel chain I had used on her before and locked one end tightly around her neck. I grabbed the other end and led her forcibly down the stairs to the garage. I loved dragging her by the neck with her hands locked behind her back. It felt like I was a Roman soldier dragging a slave to the coliseum. She struggled to navigate the stairs in her high heels without the help of handrails. Anybody seeing this would have immediately assumed that it was not consensual and that the poor girl was in danger. This was the game in full effect. I felt so tough in acting out with my aggression. I wasn't my own "Meg" self. And maybe I was a little over zealous because I was really in the mood to cuddle after my orgasm, but she screwed that up. Regina was completely in the zone.

Once at the garage, I took the loose end of the chain, wrapped it several times around the top of a workbench leg, so that she was secured with her cheek laying on the workbench surface. I snapped the padlock closed and she was stuck there, her head on the workbench, her hands in long opera gloves handcuffed behind her back… and a whole lot of aching need. "Is this what you are looking for? Is this doing it for you," I called out in a dickish intonation. Struggling to understand her through the gag, I heard a mushy version of "Yes, Mistress." But I wasn't going to leave it alone.

From the top of the washing machine, I snatched a couple of wooden clothespins. The real "Meg" had a hard time with it, but my dark side fought for me to clothespin each of her nipples that were suspended downward from her position (her head chained low and ass out). The clothespins easily overpowered the thin cotton barrier of her tank top and she gave a big wince when each clothespin was applied.

At the sight of her pain, "Meg" came forth with the most warm and sincerely loving tone, "Hey, baby… are you ok?" Regina, or rather, slave-object-girl defiantly uttered a mushy version of "Fuck you!"

"Really now?" I retorted, snapping right back to the game and away from Meg. I picked up a ping-pong paddle from the shelf and started paddling her bare ass. Her thong gave no protection to her derrière. I smacked her hard with three good swats to blow off my immediate steam. She shrieked with each blow.

Then, I calmed myself down enough to hit her with a softer, more measured cadence for about twenty times. Regina was euphoric and was helping meet the paddle each time by extending her ass for it. She wanted it. She wanted the paddle. And she was moaning softly as if she was in her own world without me. After the paddling, I put both of my hands on her bottom and rubbed gently with loving passion. She was still moaning in that same way. I removed the clothespins. With each one, she screamed as the blood rushed back into the area that had been clamped, causing a rush of sharp pain. But I wasn't done yet.

In an improvised stroke of genius, I saw the electric sander tool on the workbench and plugged it in. It vibrated like crazy. I wrapped it in a beach towel from the laundry basket and held the padded sander between her legs as her head was stills chained down to the workbench. Within about 10 seconds, she convulsed into an all out eruption of passion. She was shaking and writhing... burning rapture! She had an orgasm that seemed to go on an on. Slowly, it turned into a soft whimper with tears as she felt the discomfort from both the painful pose and the strict paddling she had endured. I could tell she was trying to hold back the tears, probably embarrassed to have her mistress see her so weak.

Fuck her. I decided to go back upstairs and leave her chained in the garage a for a bit. In fact, I went up to my room, grabbed my vibrator, and thought about how in command I was of her. I stayed about twenty minutes, playing with myself and getting so turned on thinking about her being chained in the garage while I was comfortably reclining with my vibrator. I exploded with lust in a very loud climax.

Finally, I thought the poor girl had had enough. I warmed a towel with hot water and took it to the garage. When I opened the door, she was still whimpering. I think the position was especially uncomfortable and causing her to ache. When I surprised her by putting the moist warm towel on her red and tender bottom, she recoiled at first touch... then slowly realized she was in tender care and relaxed herself. I removed her gag.

"That was some crazy day wasn't it?" I offered. Regina softly answered, "Yes, Meg, it was quite a day." I knew I had my Regina back. I quickly unchained her and gave her the biggest hug in the history of the world. Of course, she couldn't hug back since her arms were still handcuffed and the key was up in the house. But she hugged back with all her soul. And we kissed. They were sweet and warm kisses with nothing but joy and honesty for each other. She looked like she had been through the wringer. It had been quite a day, to say the least.

Back upstairs, I uncuffed her and we collapsed on the couch, arm in arm. We both felt like we had just been on a wild rollercoaster and needed to be still together. I took off her boots (or maybe they are mine) and rubbed her feet for a few moments while she laid back with her eyes closed. Touching her feet was like kissing her softly. We were connecting on a deep level. When I'm 38, I hope I look half as beautiful as her. She was very relaxed, content. In hopes of making up for the mean mistress's ways, I told her, "You must be starving. I'm going to make you a real dinner now! Poor girl never got a chance to eat."

But first, I poured her a glass wine and poured myself one too (since mine had been shattered in the commotion of violent passion). As she sipped the wine, a fun smile came over her… and then some giggles. "You're crazy. You're fucking crazy." I was laughing at the whole thing too. I gave her a full kiss on the lips and we looked into each other's eyes. "I just kissed a girl," I whispered softly with a smile. In each other's eyes, we saw an emerging friendship that had already been going on for a hundred years and was just now becoming visible.

"I'm going to draw you a bath," I said. She looked pleased. "After that, dinner will be ready and I promise I will not be mean to you, c'mon." I led her to the bathroom and started the water. There were some amazing Sonoma bath salts that would make her feel revitalized. I dimmed the lights, lit the candles and put my soft music mix on the Bose speakers. Haha. The first song was a delicate rendition of *It Takes Two To Tango* by Lester Young. "Oh my gosh, You're spoiling me," she remarked. "No, you're spoiling me," I responded.

As she settled into her bath, I went downstairs for a minute and returned with an ice-cold glass of cucumber/ginger water with slices of oranges in it. I also gave her the latest issues of my stupid gossip and celebrity magazines. I figured she might like to check in on actors of "The Young and The Restless."

In the kitchen, I started a stir-fry and listened to my own music, Philip Glass. The rolling minimalism felt just right for being in a place where I was floating with no boundaries.

I had a few thoughts like, "Am I gay now? Am I still capable of being turned on by a guy? Is this some kind of over-the-top rebound or revenge sex from Boyfriend X?" But as the Phillip Glass music started to penetrate and as I stared at the sizzling vegetables, I let all that go away. There was a beautiful woman in my bathtub with a beautiful soul. There was a woman who not only didn't judge my kinky sexuality, but also reveled in it. And before I knew it, the doubting self was washed away, leaving only the purity of Regina as a person.

Dinner was about ready. I wasn't going to eat (again) so I made Regina's plate extra fancy; the stir-fry was sitting atop a bright orange carrot puree and I clipped a little rosebud from the front of the house to complete the plate. During cooking, I had taken the thickest powder blue bathrobe you have ever seen and put it in the dryer on high for 10 minutes. I went to the bathroom to tell her dinner was ready and to present her with the warm bathrobe. She was nude and immediately slipped under the bubbles out of modesty. "Oh, sorry," I apologized, "I didn't mean to catch you like that." It was kind of sweet how we had this crazy sex and then she was worried about me seeing her body. But I completely understood. The body can take on a more utilitarian form when not viewed in the glow of a sexually charged moment. I excused myself back to the kitchen to give her privacy.

A moment later, Regina came downstairs in the bathrobe. "Best bath of my life. Better than a spa day. I loved the magazines. The robe is still warm!" In seeing her coming down the stairs, I was drawn to her and met her near the last few steps. I stood a step below her and she towered over me. On level ground she is almost a head taller than me. Now the height difference was exaggerated. I put my hands around her waist, craning my face upward to look in her eyes, and a conversation flowed:

> **ME**
> *The flowers you brought me are perfect. I'm really touched.*
>
> **REGINA**
> (Sarcastic)
> *Yeah, I could tell.*
>
> **ME**
> *Do you think the game is going to get us in trouble? You know, maybe someone's feelings will get hurt in the game and it would bleed into real life?*
>
> **REGINA**
> *I think we can keep it straight.*
>
> **ME**
> *I guess. But it could get tricky in some situations.*
>
> **REGINA**
> *We're two smart women. Let's make it work. I need to serve you. Let's just say that what ever we say in the game doesn't count in real life.*
>
> **ME**
> *So if I say something really cruel to you in the game, you will know that it doesn't mean anything in real life, right?*
>
> **REGINA**

Totally. When I told you "Fuck you" did you think there may be a kernel of real hostility toward you?

ME
No, but it did jolt me away from my real self quickly. I went instantly to the Mistress bitch.

REGINA
Bitch is right. You're a harsh one. Ok, the game is its own world. No crossover.

ME
Should we have separate names for the characters in the game?

REGINA
No. It's cooler to be called Slave Regina and Mistress Meg than some fake names we don't relate to.

ME
Maybe you're right.

REGINA
It feels real to me.

ME
What, the game?

REGINA
It feels like I'm literally a different person. It doesn't feel like an act. What about you?

ME
Oh, it's real alright.

REGINA
When I'm with Tucker, I'm mommy. When he's gone, I'm someone else. I listen to different music and have different thoughts. And when we play the game, I'm someone else entirely.

ME
I could never dream of hurting you or being mean to you in real life. But in the game, you bring that out in me.

REGINA
Do you want to be monogamous with me?

I must say, I was blindsided by this! First of all, it really put me on the spot. I didn't see this coming at all. Secondly, I was really afraid... afraid of being in some kind of gay relationship. It was so foreign to me. I have no idea why I was so scared of that concept. Mainly, it was because I never would have considered myself in such a category. Most of my adult life, I had practically been a sex-addict with guys. I needed some kind of sex at least once a day. Granted, it was usually by myself.

So there I was standing on the stairs looking up at this amazing creature who seems to fit me in every way I can imagine and the only drawback is that she happened to have been born with a vagina.

And that's another thing... what would it be like to never get dick again? Would I be cool with a monogamous relationship where no penises were involved... ever? Actually, I read that the average dick is only five inches long. That's not even as long as my hand! So why was I so hung up on the idea of guys?

And then does monogamy mean we are out in public as a couple? Does it mean we go to weddings, funerals, graduations, and Thanksgivings with each other? Would we be an "item" just like straight couples? Then does that all lead to the inevitable next step of co-habitation and ultimately marriage? Then would I be a step mom to Tucker? Agghh! It all just freaked me out!!!

On the other hand, I have never been as sexually turned on in my life as I have with Regina and our game. On a scale of hotness, it was fucking lava. During most of the time at work, I would be so turned on thinking of her that I had to swap out my panties for fresh ones a couple times. I'm serious. With thoughts like that, who needs a penis? Plus, it's even kinkier to play with strap-ons. That very word seems so naughty and hot… and they don't even shoot out gross stuff at the end. I'd love to wear a strap-on and watch Regina give me a blowjob on it!

But I guess the monogamous bomb made everything feel so serious. It would be crossing the ocean with no compass. My heart told me to go for it, but my head told me maybe I was just in "lust" with Regina and it would fade or fall apart once the novelty wore off.

Regina must have watched me process all of this in an instant or two. She looked really hurt and confused as I was standing there wondering how to respond. I think she was expecting an immediate "YES! Let's go steady" instead of my shocked expression. She looked like she was going to cry when the conversation continued:

> **REGINA**
> *No worries. It was a dumb question. I gotta get going.*

I grabbed her hand and tried in vein to pull her in for a closer conversation.

> **ME**
> *Wait, Regina! I didn't even say anything.*

> **REGINA**
> *Your face did. I gotta go.*

And she turned around and headed back up the stairs to change back into her clothes. I followed and begged:

ME
Regina, please! Let's talk about it. I was just surprised, that's all. I was just digesting the concept. That is something very serious and it needs serious consideration.

REGINA
It's not easy for me, either. But this is magic. It's beyond reasoning.

ME
I agree. It's amazing on every level.

REGINA
Then what's behind your hesitation? My age? You want to play the field more? It's moving too fast? Or… is it that I'm a woman?

She closed the door to the bathroom so she could change in private. I waited outside the door. A few moments later, she charged out and made a beeline for the front door.

ME
Regina, please give me a chance! I just want to process it a little bit. Everything is so new and crazy.

REGINA
Process all you want.

And she left without a hug or "goodbye." I had no idea what had just happened. There I was having the best day of my life with the most special person I have ever encountered and then it all blows up as soon as I don't immediately answer if I want to be monogamous with her or not.

For the past several hours, I have been crying off and on. In my heart of hearts, I can't envision a scenario where we won't end up together. I am so sleepy. I just drank a glass of wine and now I'm hoping I can go to sleep and wake up in the morning to learn that her departure was a little blip of a bad dream. C'mon, Regina. Let's be together. Today was the best of days and the worst of days. Goodnight.

--- FRIDAY MARCH 30 --- Exploring the game

Good morning, Diary. I hope you had better night's sleep than me. Mostly I tossed and turned and had dreams of Regina. All the dreams were good. I'm going to make a cup of coffee and take a bath where Regina did last night.

I just had a nice bubble bath. With a latte and a bubble bath, a girl can get a fresh perspective on things. I decided I wanted to reach out to Regina and have a mature talk about all this. I can be open with her. We agreed to never play games. She would surely be receptive. And right on cue, the phone rang. It was her. She said she was sorry about dashing off and wanted to speak with me about it. I told her I was about to call her to say the same thing. Her tone was warm and sweet and mine was the same. We clearly both wanted to work though the monogamy issue and get back on track. We decided to meet for early dinner at Capannina in Cow Hollow. (Vegetarians can always find comfort in Italian food)

At work, I was quiet. There was a meeting with the team about a new commercial. Part of me was in the meeting, my head. Everyone must have thought I was really together… like I was on my game, because they kept deferring to me for answers. But inside, I was wondering what Regina was doing. Meaning, I was wondering what she was doing in her mind with "us." Where did she see this going? How would it all play out? How could it play out? In five years, what would we be looking back on? Would it be a pivotal moment in a deep, lasting relationship, or merely a recreational activity between two people a long time ago? Even the very idea of looking 5 years out was nerve-racking to me.

Soon enough, it was time to head over to Capannina for dinner. I arrived 15 minutes early… and so did she. I guess we both took our future seriously enough to be ultra-punctual. In order to keep a straightforward tone to our meeting, I wore jeans, a basic black top, and flats.

But Regina apparently didn't get the memo. When I saw her walking up, my jaw dropped!! Along with an adorable butterscotch sleeveless, simple French floral print dress, she wore some classic mules. Oh, and she had on the shoulder-length, kid leather opera gloves I had just given her! Talk about making a statement with accessories! She looked like a hipper, more slender version of Jackie O. with a twist of Vogue Magazine Paris! The gloves had the effect of setting off both the outfit and me! She noticed me checking out her gloves and played coy. I could see the restaurant patrons checking her out and whispering strong approval for her outfit. She also sported a burgundy scarf around her neck. Friggin fashion plate.

We gave each other a gentle hug and looked into each other's eyes for a few beats. The hug clearly told us both that whatever obstacles were there about being together were only obstacles, not dead ends. We exchanged simple greetings that were loaded with more emotion than the few words we spoke. We were about to enter into a crossroads type of conversation that could literally change our lives forever.

Possible outcomes were agreeing to monogamy, casual sex from time to time, or worst case… breaking up. There was a lot at stake. It was best to manifest destiny now instead of later when we would be more entangled in each other's hearts. Que Sera, Sera.

But I was positive about one thing; I was determined to be honest and gentle with my new best friend. I was feeling optimistic that we could make it all work. But honestly, I had no idea how our relationship would look at the end of this dinner.

We sat at the side table and between ordering and dining, I remember the conversation unfolding like this:

ME
You wore the gloves.

REGINA
You noticed.

ME
How was your day?

REGINA
Confusing. I'm trying to make sense of all this.

ME
Same here.

And there was some awkward silence.

REGINA
I didn't mean to pout off last night.

ME
It's ok. I didn't mean to freeze up. There were just too many things racing in my head to process.

Question: were you ever submissive with your Ex?

REGINA
Never. He was abusive... but it wasn't consensual. It was ugly. And I have never kissed a girl before you. It never even crossed my mind.

ME
Do you still like Guys?

REGINA
Since we have been... ahem... seeing each other, I realized that maybe I was never fully attracted to guys. With you, it is fire. I have never felt fire in my life. What about you... liking guys?

ME
I was always attracted to their bodies. I still am. The idea of them always wanting to fuck is sexy too me... the idea of being overpowered by their sheer size and strength always appealed to me sexually. But I agree with you about the fire. With guys, it was never there in reality. But with you, it's there.

REGINA
Are you naturally submissive? Are we doing this wrong?

ME
No. I'm naturally dominant. My fantasies in the past have me hurting and dominating someone else. But then I like to think about what the "victim" would feel, and so I inverse the fantasy. I know, this sounds so complicated.

Here's an example: Right before I met you, I was fantasizing about this woman in my bedroom who would watch me masturbate. She was very powerful and had an air of superiority. In my mind, ***I was the woman*** *watching myself. I would tie up my ankles with a belt and pretend that I was the woman's slave. In other words, I was* *dominantly watching the slave masturbate, even though it was me. I'm sorry. Fantasies and dreams are weird.*

REGINA
I couldn't be anything other than your object. I want you to degrade me and use me. I want to be locked up and forgotten for hours until you eventually decide you need some pleasure. I want you to force your hand into my mouth while I'm tied up and choke me.

We fell into a flirty gaze.

REGINA
I've always felt like this, but I never knew you existed. There's no way in hell I would have acted on those feelings with anybody else I had ever been with.

ME
You really want me to go that dark?

REGINA
I want you to abuse me and neglect me with all your heart. I want to serve you, Meg.

ME
Regina, you are beautiful. You are amazing. I'm so turned on right now.

The waitress shows up to pour water and interrupts the flow with idle chit-chat. After she left, we both came down to Earth a bit and continued the talk:

ME
What would monogamy look like to you?

REGINA
It would just be whatever it is... without dating others.

ME
But what would it look like? Would we be gay to everyone?

REGINA
I haven't thought that far ahead. Excuse me while I go to the rest room.

She left the table. My head was really trying to grasp all this as I played with the breadsticks in the basket. But not even a second later, I was startled to feel Regina's gloves covering my eyes. She had faked going to the bathroom and sneaked up behind me to blindfold me by holding her gloved hands over my eyes. I could imagine a few restaurant customers must have been trying to guess what our deal was. Why was this woman in leather opera gloves blindfolding a girl in the restaurant? They must have thought some surprise was about to be revealed.

She whispered in my ear:

REGINA
You can't see love, can you?

ME
(Nervous about what she was up to)
No.

REGINA
(Whispering slowly)
Love doesn't look like a man or a woman, does it?

ME

No.

REGINA
But my loving hands are on you. You can feel it without having to define my gender.

I feel love coming from you, too. It doesn't come in a man's body. It just comes.

She had me. How can you argue with "Love has no gender"? Besides, this didn't have to be the final showdown I was expecting. Instead, maybe we could take baby steps in our relationship. The first baby step is accepting that we were fine the day before and we could be fine today. Nothing has changed in the way I see her. Nothing has changed to make me pull away.

ME
Let's be monogamous. Maybe I still need time to wrap my head around the how we act together in public. I don't want to be with anyone but you.

REGINA
Can you believe how blue the sky is today?

And just like Regina does it, I involuntarily switched on my game personality in an instant. It was real and visceral. Turning on the game is going into a place that isn't accessible to us otherwise. It is going into my parents' forbidden bedroom. It is opening the compartment of our compartmentalized personalities and climbing in. It's going down the stairs into the storm cellar as a child and playing naughty games with the neighbor boy. It's allowing darkness in and playing with it in the safety of its own world. Different rules apply. I can be a bitch. I can hurt someone and humiliate them, but outside the game they can know I am still a loving, trusted, sensitive person with a warm heart.

I quickly grabbed her wrists, clenching down with all the force I had, and pulled her hands down from my eyes. "Sit back in your seat!" I coldly demanded. She sat down. Regina was no longer with me. It was my object. Her demeanor had changed to submissive and unconfident. "Sit on your hands," I blurted. She obediently sat on both of her hands. I stared at her. "Don't move," I told her. Then I got up and went to the rest room. She was stuck there sitting on her hands, a pose which was delightfully accented by her long black gloves tight against either side of her dress. She dared not raise her eyes, continuing to stare at the middle of the table.

After I finished with the restroom, I paused at the back of the restaurant to spy on her… pretending to be answering text messages.

She was sitting there looking very awkward. A waitress, seeming to notice her withdrawn appearance, approached the table and asked if Regina would like anything else. Regina never moved a muscle or batted an eye. The waitress, not figuring her out, smirked and walked away.

I went back to the table and thanked the slave for respecting my wishes of not moving. Sitting on her hands was such a submissive look. To play with this idea a bit, I took a fork full of her lasagna and fed it to her, quietly calling for her to eat. She complied. A quick glance around the room showed three people had taken notice but were trying not to stare. For the duration of the meal, I fed her bite-by-bite. No words were spoken.

To "vanilla" people (the term for those without a kinky sexual orientation) the whole scene must have seemed bizarre and asexual. Here was a woman, sitting on her hands in a restaurant. Big deal. Ninety-nine out of one hundred people would probably not see any possible source of eroticism in that. But to us, it was hyper-sexual. I was literally aroused in Capaninna by merely watching her sit there. It wasn't the image of her sitting there that was the turn on; it was the idea of what was in our heads.

In her mind, she was seeing me as a (hopefully) beautiful woman who was literally controlling her every move. The sensation she felt in the "sitting-on-hands" scenario was a continuation of the dominion I had already imposed on her… Chaining her to a work bench while paddling her ass, teasing her at dinner by eating in front of her while she knelt before me in handcuffs, etc. The "sitting-on-hands" seems fully sexual when you consider all that had led up to it and all that was overflowing in years of repressed sexual fantasy. The vanillas were not privy to the whole story.

But there was more to Regina's state-of-mind as she sat there. She was submitting as an actual slave to me. She was allowing herself to be my toy.

She would tell me later that in surrendering herself to me that she felt more free than at any other time in her life. Imagine being able to step off the hectic rollercoaster of life and take a literal time out.

As a slave who is not allowed to make a single decision for herself, it is a break from stresses like fighting with her Ex about how to raise Tucker. As a servant to my wishes, Regina could forget all the worries about trying to date guys, about feeling lonely, about feeling pain, and about feeling pressure to make it all work and keep it all going. Stepping into my dungeon-world meant Regina could just *be* with no expectations from the real world. It's like going into a therapy session; an opportunity to explore aspects of one's self that are unacceptable to work through in the real world.

When handing off the check, the waitress was still trying to make sense of Regina's behavior. I loved watching the waitress awkwardly ask us how everything was. Regina didn't say a word, continuing to sit on her hands. I gestured to Regina and said, "She thought everything was perfect." The waitress, receiving zero eye contact from Regina, responded through her smile with "You sure wouldn't know it." We got up to head out and I clutched Regina by the wrist and lead her outside. I love holding her like that!

Outside, I told her to go home, pack an overnight bag and be at my house in an hour. And we each took off. I was looking forward to fucking with her.

I could have a set a stopwatch for the doorbell, exactly one hour and zero seconds! When I opened the door, there was my toy, eyes cast downward. She was in the same outfit and still wore those wicked gloves. I played bright and silly, "Oh, Regina! So nice to see you. That was some kind of crazy day I had."

But Regina doesn't always pop out of the game as quickly as she pops into it. I think it can take a few moments for her to downshift to regular old Regina. (Regular? She is anything but regular in real life!!). I hugged her softly as she was changing gears. I remember the conversation as follows:

> **ME**
> *It's okay, Sweetie. It's just me. It's ok.*
>
> **REGINA**
> *Hi Meg. Thank you so much for dinner. That was really generous of you.*
>
> **ME**
> *Thanks for coming right over. I don't know if you really want to spend the night or not, but I thought maybe you would in the game.*
>
> **REGINA**
> *I would like to spend the night in either case.*
>
> **ME**
> *Come in, please.*

Gently holding her hand (not her wrist) I led her to my living room and invited her to sit on the couch and get comfortable.

> **ME**
> *Can I get you a glass of wine?*
>
> **REGINA**

Sure. Thanks.

I smiled softly and headed off, then returned a few moments later with some wine and dark chocolate. I could tell Regina was still not fully Regina. I think the submissive has a harder time than the dom bouncing back to real life

> **ME**
> *Are you still in the game a bit?*

> **REGINA**
> *Yes. The restaurant was really sexy. As soon as you agreed to be monogamous with me, my heart soared. As your slave in the restaurant, I was feeling more loved than I could ever have imagined. It felt deeply satisfying to be yours. But that was in the game. Are we monogamous in real life too?*

I wanted to reassure her with everything I could offer and looked in her heart.

> **ME**
> *Regina, yesterday this would have been more difficult for me to say... but today something is different; I love you. I want to be monogamous with you!*

Her face warmed and tears started flowing. And mine started flowing too. We were just staring at each other processing all this. And finally she said, "I love you too."

After a beat of taking this in, we hugged a tender hug, which led to a wonderful kiss. Her leather gloves were magic on my face. If you've ever had a picture of a perfect kiss in your mind, this was it. It was soft and pure. We were in sync. There was no need to figure out the mechanics of the kiss or to have any self-consciousness. The kiss was guided by our souls... as natural as breathing.

Slowly, my domineering feelings started creeping in. Even though we were having an incredible connection, I could sense we were both getting turned on and I could feel her slave-self coming on. We probably could have easily progressed to our game without a word being said, but I think we both appreciated and needed the formal start and end of the game. We needed boundaries in order to keep each other's feelings safe from harm. And my lips uttered, *"Can you believe how blue the sky was today?"* The usual and expected "Yes, Mistress," didn't come. Instead, she just stared and me with eyes that burned, "Own me. Hurt me."

My hands drifted to her neck where I felt her burgundy scarf, which I removed very slowly and sensually… inch by inch. Making my hand into a pointed shape with my fingers and thumb all touching tips, I inserted my hand into her mouth and tenderly forced her mouth open by expanding my fingers and thumb outward. When her mouth was good and wide, I put her scarf across like a gag and wrapped it several times around her head, where I tied it super tightly behind her neck.

She wanted anything I was willing to give her. I hugged her and slowly began kissing her right over the gag. She kissed back. No matter that her tongue was blocked from reaching mine, it was still an ultra steamy kiss. Then I felt her arms around me, reciprocating the hug. I thought it was pretty presumptuous of her so I threw her arms off me with, "Did I say you could touch me?" Scared of my wrath, she quickly shook her head "No." You would have thought she was constantly abused in her life because she was so quick to completely surrender herself.

I pulled out the handcuffs and locked her wrists behind her back. Then I stood up and faced her as she was still sitting on the sofa. I pulled her head between my legs with a good deal of force and commanded her to "Please me." Even though I was wearing jeans and underwear, she immediately started "licking me" through her gag. It was like a dry humping version of giving head. She was doing a great job, too. The friction of her gag rubbing on me was an unexpectedly hot sensation that was driving me insane!

But I didn't want to go all the way yet. I pulled her head away from stimulating me and praised her for doing a nice job for her mistress. It seemed like a fun idea to punish her a little too. So I scolded her, "You didn't have to get me so turned on this early. I'm going to have to punish you for creating dirty thoughts in my head. Go upstairs and stand by the foot of the bed." And up she went.

I took a few moments to calm myself down by flipping through a magazine. I knew that no matter how long I took, even if it were three hours, she would still be standing their when I arrived. But I didn't take three hours; it was more like ten minutes.

When I got upstairs, there she was, obediently standing at the foot of my bed with her arms bound in the gloves behind her back. I loved the way the gag cut across the soft skin of her cheeks. She has perfect skin! It must be that vegetarian diet. I have to work at my skin a bit, but I bet Regina doesn't do a single thing except wash her face each night and drink water like people are supposed to. I should drink more water.

Upon seeing her, my creative mind starting thinking of fun, torturous things to do to her. My whole life, I have dreamed of having a willing person I could mess with and torture for fun. It's a dark streak. The sexual thoughts bubble up when I think of being in control of someone in a physical manner. The feeling seems to be magnified many times over with the idea of a woman I can torture. And it is magnified even more because the person is Regina who aches for my control over her.

I removed her gag, the burgundy scarf, and then planted a brief but luscious kiss on her lips. Because she had been standing there in full obedience with great anticipation of what would happen to her next, she received my kiss with hunger. But it was fleeting.

I silently left her to go to my top dresser drawer (my new armory of kinky toys from the internet). From behind, I covered her eyes with a heavy leather padded blindfold. It was like the kind they give you in first class on airlines, but this one was extremely sturdy and wouldn't let in the slightest ray of light. It was very secure and straps behind the neck. I removed her handcuffs.

As she stood there blindfolded, I secretly took off all my clothes and lied on the bed. I commanded her to give me a full massage... with special instructions to respect the privacy of my erogenous zones. A few other words were spoken:

> **ME**
> *Make sure the massage is worthy of my time.*
>
> **REGINA**
> *Yes, Mistress. May I move freely to fully provide this service for you?*
>
> **ME**
> *Yes, you may. Do not disappoint me.*
>
> **REGINA**
> *Yes, Mistress. Thank you for allowing me the privilege of serving you in this way.*

She was very solemn and dutifully took to her task as I turned over on my tummy. She straddled my middle back and put a little weight down as her hands went to work navigating their way up my body. I could feel her energy change when she realized I was completely nude. Her energy felt like she was unbelievably turned on.

Strangely, she first went for my hair and softly ran her gloved fingers through my hair over and over. At first, I felt a tendency to micromanage her with commands of what to do and not do. The hair stroking was not what I had in mind when I had ordered the massage.

But before I could fuck it all up by barking out some other instructions, I suddenly felt this vibrant tingling over my whole spine. My hair and had never been touched like that! My mother had never given me the long, sensual hair brushing that we have all seen in old movies. My hair was never sensual to me. But this was different. Regina was starting with her fingers on my cheeks and then slowly tracing the hair from my hairline, then tenderly pulling the hair all the way to the tip. The repetitive feeling of her fingers on my cheeks and then the long stroke was sublime. Her touch was light, but the sensation was grand. She must have sensed that I was particularly enjoying this because she kept at it for a good twenty minutes. I was beyond relaxed. It was putting me to sleep, a sexy sleep.

The weight of her body sitting on me was perfect. No guy could ever do that without either crushing me or making me quickly fatigue of it. She must have been turned on because her crotch on my back was exceedingly warm. The weight of her loveliness was pushing me into the bed, creating an extremely tight and intimate connection between us. Her dress fell softly on either side of my waist and her panties felt moist against me. I was wishing my back had a penis that was up inside her.

Finally, she moved from the hair stroking to my neck and upper back. She rubbed me with deep circular pressure, probably mimicking something she liked done to her by a professional masseur. My nude skin welcomed the cool leather of her gloves. I loved that she was blindfolded and just had to feel her way around me. But her fingers had vision. They could see me perfectly naked and found every cell. She sunk her thumbs into my armpits and hit some pressure points that must have been hidden in there. Her touch, for such a delicate creature, was surprisingly strong and forceful as she worked my shoulders.

Still in the game, my libido was warming up quickly and surprised me by calling her to stop. She did. I coldly told her to rise up a bit so I could turn over. Then she let herself back down onto my stomach. In a whisper, I quietly ordered, "Bring your pussy up here." And she shimmied up to my face and presented me with herself, sliding her panties to one side. And there I was… finding full passion in tasting another woman. It was my first time. As my tongue made contact, Regina twitched in reaction. Slowly, I sank into her… as she sank back into me in unison. It was a union of slave and mistress… of two loving beings.

She gyrated gently on my tongue and I moved it to caress her with careful attention. After a few moments, I discovered her secret spot… along with just the right timing and pressure she required. Her quiet whimpers and sighs were guiding me ever so precisely. Feeling her splendid thighs with my hands, I was inspired to follow them along the contour of her body. I took a grip on her waist and helped her gyration toward my mouth. Again, it was my first time ever holding a woman by her waist in such a manner. It was unlike anything I have ever felt with a man. Her waist was trim and so different from that of a man's. This is when I really noticed how different it was to be with a woman.

My hands continued upward to her breasts. I cupped each in my hands, stimulating them in the same rhythm she was using on my face. I played with the tips of her nipples at the same time. Sometimes I lowered my hands and loosened my hold to let gravity suspend each breast into my palms so I could better feel their curves. My own breasts are much larger and it was exciting to feel another woman's smaller breasts, a different form that seemed to be every bit as feminine as my own. In this case, size definitely doesn't matter. Body types are like personalities; each has its unique extraordinary charm. Regina's breasts felt delightful.

Her experience must have been heightened by the fact that she was prevented from accessing her sense of vision. She fell into some other state of consciousness that was neither of her nor of the game. She was in rapture by passion beyond what I was reflecting to her. Watching her in this state was also new to me. Never, ever have I been able to please a partner to this level. It was a culmination of both our history together, our newfound psycho-sexual exploration, and the extended trust that comes with a vow of monogamy. And of course, the hotness of being with a woman was surely heightened by the idea that it had always been forbidden in our pasts.

She blasted into a wail of orgasm that was so saturated with raw passion that it could have only originated in her deepest psyche, an erupting volcano of truth. That sound, that primeval exaltation, could not be anything but genuine. She was mine. In that moment, she was completely revealed to me in all her nakedness, even though she was fully clothed. Perhaps outside the game, she would be more grounded and practical with me, but no words she could say would ever be able to erase my secret glimpse into her very soul at that moment. I saw her. I owned her.

Envious, I wondered if I was capable of exposing myself so fully. If so, I knew it could only happen with Regina… nobody else.

Her explosive satisfaction was over, but the game was still on. My id was turned on by watching her, tasting her, and feeling her. I was craving to crush all that beauty and passion. It was time to take charge. "Did I say you could come?" I wondered aloud. "No, Mistress," she responded as she was coming down. "So why would you pleasure yourself so magnificently without my permission?" I pushed.

As she started to respond, I cut her off with, "You disgust me. Go in the shower and watch that filth off of yourself." She hopped to it with a concerned "Yes Mistress." Once she was behind the bathroom door, I told her to be sure to use the toilet because it may be a while until she gets another chance. I further instructed that after her shower, she needed to present herself to me blindfolded and naked. She understood.

During her shower, I dressed into my jeans and top, feeling relaxed and alive. I slipped into our brick red boots and pulled them over the bottom of my jeans. It's a strong look.

A while later, the shower water stopped and in a minute, Regina emerged from the steamy bathroom in classic angel lighting. As required, she was nude, with just the blindfold, her wet hair under the strap accented her loveliness. She took a couple timid steps into the room, fearing a bump or a trip from no vision. I told her to get on her knees… and lick my boots, which I presented to her. She didn't reply, but immediately did exactly what I had ordered.

I directed my foot to her hands; She held it, raising it to her mouth.

She was in a perfect downward dog position, her ass stretched high and her face low. I reached down to her ass and grabbed it forcefully, hanging on tight as I squeezed her flesh. It was a tad painful; she was moaning from the building ache, all while expertly licking my boot.

I released my grasp on her butt and caressed it tenderly for a few minutes to her satisfaction. Then I commanded her to stop licking my boot and aim her head upward to lick my hand. She was getting really turned on. We both were. She focused on connecting with me through her mouth on my hand. When she was working on sucking my thumb, I imagined it was a penis and I was getting the best blow job a guy could ever dream of. For her it was a penis, too.

I bet guys in her past, including her ex-husband, must have experienced the best blow jobs imaginable from her. She didn't give it out of mechanical technique, but out of full devotion of herself to the task. She was the same with my four fingers in her mouth at the same time. I loved looking down on her with my fingers in her mouth. It was such a submissive image. Then again, I'd like to think this level of passion was only possible with me. Maybe guys in her past got your basic mechanical blow job.

I told her to stop and lick my other boot. Again, she sloped into the perfect downward dog. I took my wet middle finger and ran it around her anus delicately. She was purring, a sound and sight so alluring that I had no choice but to slip my finger inside her ass. At first I went slowly… as she tried to comprehend the ecstasy of the feeling.

Then I stuck my finger in as far as possible and gently thrust in and out. When my finger was all the way in, I bent over to use my other hand on her clit and pussy. She was thrusting back at my hands to maximize her sensations. She was dripping wet and her mouth was delirious on my foot. I started fucking her hard in the ass with my middle finger and sometimes I would lift her ass a little with my finger, causing extra pressure in the top of her anus.

I sensed she was close to a giant sexual erruption and … instantly removed my hands with, "STOP!" It was hard for her, but she got a hold of herself. I continued, "You are never allowed to come without my permission first. Are we clear?" Straining for composure against her near orgasm, "Yes, Mistress. It's clear." "Get on all fours like a dog and wait for me." She obeyed and waited, completely frozen in that humiliating position while I went to the bathroom to wash off my hands that she had soiled.

When I returned, I let her know that she was about to receive her punishment for having previously come without my permission. She seemed willing to take her lumps. I had her lie on her back and put on her leather opera gloves again. I took off my boots and put them on her instead.

Then I commanded her to cross her legs (like Indian-style), pulled out a 4ft piece of heavy chain and chained her ankles together in that crisscross leg position so that she couldn't straighten them or stretch them out. I took the other end of the chain and wrapped it around her neck.

And to secure it at the front of her neck, I used a padlock, which I also used to lock the center of the handcuffs. I grabbed each of her gloved wrists and locked them in the cuffs at her neck. It was a beautiful sight. Her legs were locked in a crisscross position and that chain went around her neck, locking in the front. Her hands were locked in the cuffs on either side of her chin, which prevented her from touching herself anywhere. It looked like a very uncomfortable position. She could never escape. If I lost the key, she would be stuck there for hours until I could figure out how to cut the chain.

Because of her blindfold, I couldn't see her full expression, but I would venture to say that she looked extremely turned on. I lied down next to her and caressed her like a pet. I kissed her slowly. It felt so dominant to have a woman chained up like this; I could touch her all I wanted but she couldn't touch back. She was literally my object.

I decided I needed a little loving too, so I slid off my jeans and stuck my pussy right in her face. She immediately began licking me… licking me from that honest place in her. I could barely handle it for more than a few seconds and pulled away.

Then, blindsiding her, I firmly covered her mouth and pinched her nose closed to cut off her breathing. At first there was little reaction, but slowly, she began to squirm and moan as her breath was running out. In a calm and loving voice, I told her, "Listen to me. You can trust me. I will never harm you. I love you. Do you understand?" She desperately nodded "yes," clearly under duress.

Just as she was starting to flop and writhe to get air in a panic, I released her breath. She sprung to, desperately gasping for air, while bellowing, "I trust you, Mistress." "Good. I'm only punishing you for your own good," I assured her. And now that I had her trust, her mistreatment could begin.

I strapped the leather horse bit gag into her mouth and tightly cinched it behind her neck above the chain. She was blindfolded and gagged on the floor. Her arms were bent at the elbow and locked to handcuffs by her neck. That same chain locked her booted ankles in a crisscross position so that she couldn't stretch out at all. She was naked. But that still wasn't enough for me. Can you believe it! The kinky monster inside me was free to do what it wanted to this poor slave. And the monster wanted more.

I placed full earphones over her ears with a long cord that went to my Bose player where I put on a Pandora channel to send floating French and Italian arias to her ears. It had the effect of rendering her in a state of complete sensory deprivation: no vision, no hearing anything in the room, no mobility, no use of her mouth due to the gag.

I spoke to her as a test, and she couldn't hear my normal talking voice at all. She couldn't see. She couldn't walk. Basically, she was fucked. I took a few moments to play with her super wet and exposed pussy.

Lifting her earphones for a moment, I told her, "I'm going to get your keys out of your purse and sleep in your bed at your house tonight. You are going to have to sleep here like this. This is a very secure building and I will be checking on you from Skype on my iPhone from time to time. My laptop over there is broadcasting the video of you. I will be back in the morning. Do you trust me?" She looked terrified as she nodded "yes." Then I put the earphones back on her and walked out of the room, slamming the door for effect on the way out.

The power of having my own human object chained up in my bedroom for any use I desired is quite a feeling. She was an orifice or a plaything. She was fodder for masturbation whenever I wanted. She is willing to be degraded and uncomfortable in order to please me. And she is beautiful.

Being left overnight like that must be a rush… no mobility, no vision, no hearing, no way to check the clock. The only thing she has is trust. If she didn't have trust, surely full panic would quickly take over and it could be the most terrifying experience imaginable. She had to keep calm and keep faith that I would return to release her in the morning. But in her mind, I wondered if she had fears about me not returning at all. Perhaps I would get in a car crash. Perhaps I would get arrested for some strange reason. Who knows?

But God forbid, if anything like that happened, she would still be chained up and at the mercy of circumstance. It is extremely doubtful that she would ever be able to be rescued because nobody would know she was there. On the flip side, if something happened to her while I was away and I couldn't get to her in time, she might suffer grave consequences, even death. The whole scenario was really, really scary. That's what made it so sexy. The trust had to be deep. I had to use every precaution to make sure that she was safe… and that I was safe too.

I started wondering if, perhaps, her limbs might be too restricted for proper blood flow. It would be awful if I left her like that all night, only to discover in the morning there was no circulation to her hands or feet. To check on things, I reentered the room loudly so that she would both feel the door action and my footsteps in the floor's vibration.

I lifted off her headphones and said, "Before I leave, do you feel safe? Do you feel like anything is going to fall asleep?" "Thank you for checking, Mistress. I feel perfect," she struggled to utter against the gag. Of course she felt perfect. She was limber and fit from years of yoga and good eating. I replaced the headphones and stared up close at her for a moment. Then I slapped her face quite firmly. A sexual moan of approval escaped her mouth. I walked out the room and slammed the door again on my way out. At least, that's what she must have thought.

Instead, I only faked the door slam. I wanted to stay in the room for a while and spy on her. I stood quietly studying her perfection. I loved the contour of her bent elbows that lead to her wrists being locked in the handcuffs by her neck. And her legs, chained crisscrossed in the boots is an image I will certainly recall in the future when I need some good material for self-pleasuring.

I decided to test her hearing again. First I whispered her name. There was no response at all. I tried it louder and louder and she could never hear me at a loud room voice. I can't imagine what have been more torturous for her... to be chained up like that or to have to listen to opera all night! Either way, I was certain that she couldn't see or hear anything from me. I watched her another few minutes as she squirmed a little and tried in vain to adjust her position against her bindings.

Very quietly and slowly, I opened the door and exited. While leaving, I studied her to see if there was any reaction to the change in air due to the opening door. She didn't seem to have any awareness that the door had opened. I closed it and stealthily headed downstairs.

At the kitchen, I poured a glass of wine and then sat on the couch. With my first sip of wine came the thrill of thinking of all this craziness I could have never imaged just a few weeks ago. My libido was in charge and I felt sexually fulfilled for the first time in my life. It was a woman. It was bondage. I was in control. She craved it. The whole thing was feeding my lifelong yearning. I mean, I never yearned for a woman, but I yearned for this feeling.

In retrospect, I could have only been this satisfied with a woman; BDSM with a man could never feel this rich. A man could never look as submissive as Regina. A man could never surrender so fully from the inside like Regina had. I could never relate to a man's physical sensations like I am with Regina. I was she. I was chained up there in the bedroom and I could feel the chain around my neck and the blindfold cutting off my sight. I could feel my wet pussy and feel the freedom of surrendering to a beautiful mistress lover. I could feel the scariness of the situation and feel the sensual power of pure trust and honesty. I could feel that mistress loving me profoundly. As a woman, I was both slave and mistress. The control lies with me, but the sensation of being a slave is accessible to me.

I know Regina wants to surrender to me and that suits me fine. I want to own her sexuality. I own her by not being selfish, but by being strong and controlling. She must serve me. She is free with me and she relishes giving up the trappings and trials of daily life.

As I sat so comfortably in my living room sipping my wine, I enjoyed thinking that she was helpless and uncomfortable on the floor of my room. Her mind was filled with the idea that I was gone to her house. But in fact, I'm too chicken to leave her alone and completely helpless in such a dangerous situation. Too many things could go wrong.

I was bullshitting her about leaving her alone. But she probably thinks I really left for her house. Each minute to her must have felt like an eternity. Every heavy truck that rumbled by or vibration of the elevator must be a big event when all other senses are removed. She may be completely stressed about if I am ever going to return at all.

The contrast of being relaxed in my chair while she strained to get through each minute was particularly erotic to me. I started to play with myself as I thought of her stuck up there. Strangely, I wanted to feel a bit of what she was feeling. I grabbed a clothesline rope from the garage, lied down on the floor and crossed my legs like hers, and then tied them extremely tightly together.

I was pretending I was her. I was trying to be in her head as I massaged my vulva and clitoris. It was a vicarious torture. I rubbed and thrust into my hands. I was fully excited, dripping, and tingling with excitement over my whole body. My legs felt like Regina's. With one hand, I played with my breasts while escalating my pleasure to mind-shaking rapture. I exploded in ecstasy, trying to refrain from being too loud. It was Regina's orgasm I was feeling. I was her. She was mine. Ahhhhhhhhhhhhhhhh.

It seemed like a good idea to take a peek at my little slave. I went upstairs and quietly peered in. To my surprise, she seemed to be asleep; her breathing was different and she was completely still. I could tell she was not in peril. Can you imagine how shocking it would be when she awakens to rediscover that she is completely chained and immobile? Sometimes that happens when I sleep with my feet bound; I forget while I'm asleep. Then when I awaken to rediscover it, my heart races and I jump straight into being fully turned on in an instant.

One of these days I'm going to chain her up like that and wait as long as it takes for her to wake up. The second I sense she is realizing she is helplessly bound, I will shove a giant dildo in her mouth and ram it as far in as I can. Imagine waking up to that!! But that was for another time. I decided to go back down stairs, enjoy my wine and spend a good long while writing here to you, my dear Diary.

It's therapeutic to share with you, Diary. What started as a move to vent angrily about Boyfriend X has morphed into an unlikely love story. It has morphed into a wonderful exploration of my real self that was never able to have a truthful voice in the past. Thank you, Diary.

Never has my sexual orientation been so guilt-free. Until now, my kink was to be hidden and shamed. In our culture, BDSM people are stigmatized to a high level. It is usually expressed in media and television as goofy and clown-like. We've all seen the countless clichés of a black vinyl clad dominatrix comically whipping a male slave who usually has on a diaper or a dress and gaudy makeup. Or she whips the backside of an unattractive male slave who is strapped spread-eagled to a wall of a cheesy dungeon featuring garish red lighting. Why are the slaves always portrayed as unattractive buffoons? Why do all the dominatrices wield a bullwhip and smile crazily while pretending to whip a guy? A real bullwhip would immediately cause blood and irreparable damage in the hands of a novice. So the "clown" is one shaming version of S&M.

The other version is on the news: "Police discovered the kidnapped victim was held captive in a makeshift dungeon where there were implements of torture." People tend to associate the real S&M with violent and nonconsensual abuse. That's like thinking that making love is the same thing as rape; it is the same exact act. What difference does consent make? The shame of being kinky was always heavy for me.

Like being gay, many people think it is merely a choice. Sure, there may be cases of homosexuality arising out of circumstance or exposure, but ninety percent of sexuality is proven to be determined way before any choice is presented.

For example, it is not a choice to like chocolate. There is never a date when someone approaches with a Godiva bar and says, "You must now choose to like this or not to like it." Straight people never have to make a choice to be straight. Kinky people never make the choice to be kinky. But the shame is overpowering.

There is also inherent shame in hurting or degrading another human. In real life, I could never hurt a fly. I could never see myself abusing legitimate power over someone else. It would disgust me to the highest degree. The worst is when you hear about cops who cross the line and abuse their power of authority. It really repulses me to see cops hassling people for minor or nonexistent infractions. Police brutality or abuse is sickening.

All these feelings need to be understood and reconciled somehow with my sexuality. That's why it works best to have the role-playing game for a lot of kinky people. It is a way to set clear boundaries about real world versus play world experiences. Think of the actor analogy. In a movie or TV show, there is the time on the set and the time off the set. Each personality is a one hundred percent different mindset. As I have seen on the shoots for my production company, an actor can literally be irate or cry in the scene, feeling each emotion deeply. But when the shoot is wrapped, they are a different person entirely. Yet each mode carries its own set of emotions and rules.

During a scene, the make-believe emotions can be every bit as real as the stresses found in real life, even though they are manufactured for the sake of the film. And that's the same for the S&M game too. For once in my life I am able to get on the movie set and be a fucked up bitch without somebody being hurt in real life. I scream. I can look down my nose at someone. Once the director calls "cut," I'm back in a different world. Nobody will judge me for being aggressive on the movie set. No feelings are hurt in real life.

After having written quite a while, I wanted to check on Regina again. Plus, I was pooped and wanted to go to bed. It had been a fantastically full day. I thought maybe I would grab my pillow and sleep on the couch so that Regina would think I was still away for the night.

But when I got upstairs to check on her, Regina was squirming and violently thrashing about trying to get free. She looked in distress and I was immediately concerned on a high level. When I put my hand on her chest to let her know I was there to help her, she jumped with a major start!! I'm positive she thought I was nowhere in the house. So imagine if you think that and then all of the sudden a warm hand touches you out of the blue. I quickly removed her gag and pulled off the opera headphones. The second she was ungagged, she started blabbering in a frenetic desperation, "I love you. Thank you. I love you. Thank you. Thank you." I wanted to leave her blindfold on until I figured out what was going on with her. I needed to take her back to reality slowly. We had the following exchange:

ME
Hey. Hey, babe. You're ok now. I'm here. Everything's ok.

REGINA
Thank, you Mistress. I'm so sorry to make you come back.

ME
Huh?

REGINA
You saw me squirming on the webcam and got concerned.

ME
Tell me what's going on with you?

REGINA
I'm sorry, Mistress, but I can't take anymore punishment. This is a very uncomfortable position and I really need to stretch my legs out. I just can't take it anymore.

ME
I have to leave now. Your dear friend Meg is going to take good care of you. I love you, slave.

REGINA
Thank you, Mistress. Thank you for punishing me as I deserved. I will always love you. Will you please kiss me, Mistress?

I leaned over and softly kissed her a long and gentle kiss. She relaxed in the kiss and gave her whole body over to a sigh.

ME
That was some kind of crazy day I had.

After a moment of letting her digest the transition, I came back as Meg with:

ME
Wow. Looks like you are in quite a fix for

> *some reason. Let me figure out how to get these chains off you so you can stretch your legs out.*

I began unchaining her and taking off the handcuffs.

> **REGINA**
> *Meg! Thank God you're here! I was almost going to lose my freaking mind! That was impossibly uncomfortable after about two hours. I started getting really scared. I thought you wouldn't come back for several more hours and I went into panic mode.*

> **ME**
> *Baby, it's ok. I'm here.*

Once she was unrestrained, she stretched out with all her length. I lied down next to her and took off her blindfold. There she was staring at me with trust in her eyes. We kissed softly and hugged and caressed away the bondage stress. She started to cry quietly. The conversation continued:

> **ME**
> *Can you share with me what you're feeling? Did I cross the line by leaving you so long?*

> **REGINA**
> (Between crying)
> *No. No. It's was insane! I mean, "insane" amazing. I think this is just a reaction of relief. It was really hard to be left like that. I was afraid being alone.*

> **ME**
> *Yeah, I never should have done that.*

REGINA
No, I liked it. I'm serious. Being that helpless and under your complete control... being at your complete mercy... was the hottest thing in the world!! Even though I was scared, I wanted to be tortured by you.

ME
You mean, by your Mistress.

REGINA
Yes, by the Mistress.

ME
I kind of freaked out when I saw you in such distress. Do you feel ok about me?

REGINA
Meg, this is the most exciting time in my life.

ME
Me too. I lose myself in the game with you. I literally want to hurt you and piss on you.

Regina broke into a laugh

REGINA
*We are so kinky! It feels amazing!
But if you ever make me listen to that opera music again for hours on end, I will fucking kill you!! Oh my God, I thought my head was going to explode!*

We laughed for a moment and then she continued:

REGINA
Did you really go to my house?

ME
Maybe you should ask your Mistress friend.

REGINA
No, it would probably piss her off and I would get in trouble.

ME
Judging from the way I found you just now, I don't think it would be too wise to piss off your Mistress.

REGINA
Can we sleep in your bed together?

ME
Under two conditions: One, you don't try to take advantage of me... and two, take off those damn boots. You'll get dirt all over my sheets for Chistsake. Why are you always in boots anyway? It's almost like you have some kind of fetish.

REGINA
(Laughing)
Fuck you! You need a spanking now!!

And she lunged for me and tried her best to give me a playful spanking. We were both laughing so hard as she was chasing me around. Finally, I threw myself over her lap and stuck my ass up for fun. She started swatting it in a crazy, silly way. I was pretend screaming. She started seriously getting into it and her laughing subsided. The spanking was actually starting to feel good.

REGINA
Now who's your daddy, bitch?

She started laughing again as she was delighted to be spanking me. But from inside me came:

> **ME**
> *Can you believe how blue the sky is today?*
>
> **REGINA**
> (Still laughing)
> *What the fuck? You can't take a little spanking and have to call for backup?*

Jumping with both feet into the Mistress character, I turned the tables on her, jumping on top of her, and starting to choke her with both hands with:

> **ME**
> *Don't you ever disrespect me again by not recognizing my arrival with a proper greeting. Understand????!!*

Her smile shut off and she became slave Regina, fear in her eyes.

> **REGINA**
> *Please, Mistress. I beg your forgiveness. It won't happen again.*
>
> **ME**
> *Close your eyes.*

She closed them and waited for something, a command or a slap. After a hefty pause, I told her:

> **ME**
> *That was some kind of crazy day I had.*

I could see her let out a sigh of relief. I think she had already been through too much during the evening to endure another session from the mean mistress lady.

I asked her to open her eyes. When she did, I was lovingly gazing at her. We kissed and hugged tenderly. Then we brushed our teeth, washed our faces, and settled into bed next to each other. We were completely nude. She spooned me. I will never forget the feeling of her bare breasts on my back. They were warm and soft and they felt like love itself. If love could be physically present, it would be in the form of her breasts pressed against my back in the sheets. I reached over to her bum and softly stroked it over and over. We were together in a way I have never felt before. We were sexual, dangerous, friendly, trusting, and loving. It was like all my life of dating and experiencing others was designed to clarify that Regina and I were made for each other. Kinky little troublemaker.

--- SATURDAY MARCH 31 --- Balance of worlds

Last night, after Regina spooned me in bed, we were both asleep within 2 minutes and never woke up until morning. It had been a stellar day together and sleeping never felt so natural. The sleep really did its job. I woke up first and quietly started writing here about yesterday while it was still fresh in my head. After a while, Regina awoke and ambled downstairs to see me. We both stared at each other in a warm buzz. It turned in to a giggle, drawn from all the crazy feelings we had both been having. When she laughed, her nose crinkled in the cutest way possible. We both felt entirely refreshed and anew.

We decided to go out for a morning-after-fuck coffee. That's when lovers and one-night standers hit the café to relish the night before and get reacquainted in the daylight (usually in the same clothes as the night before). You know, two people with bedheads radiating afterglow towards each other.

I asked her as myself (not as the mistress) if she would wear my thigh high boots and a casual solid olive dress from my closet. She loved the idea and immediately got changed into it, looking like a Seattle vibe, kind of grungy and cool, but feminine. The thigh boots were a great accent, sexual but not sexy or clubby. They had a rounded toe and a heavier heel. (I generally hate stilettos because they always seem like trying too hard). The dress just barely covered the top of her boots, such that if she sat down and crossed her legs, the dress hemline would rise up just enough to reveal a slash of her buttery skin between the boots and the dress. The outfit gave her the look of a Paris model on her day off.

As for me, I wore the same jeans and black top as last night, but instead of the flats, I tucked my jeans into our brick boots. And to tie both our outfits together, I came up with the ultimate accessory: Her Vespa! Imagine two cool girls zipping around San Francisco in high boots on an electric Vespa! It's the photograph in Vanity Fair or Interview Magazine that we all want to be in. And now it was happening. When we got to her bike, she looked every bit as cool in real life as the picture was in my mind's eye. I got on the back of her bike and held her tight around the waist to complete the image.

We were going to hit Rose's café on Union St. But once we started zipping around the city, by the time we got there, we didn't want to stop riding so soon. We were having a blast and being all goofy together. We decided to cruise the city for a while.

For kicks, we asked a few tourists where the Golden Gate Bridge was. We made faces to kids in car seats to crack them up, switching to a normal face when the parents would turn toward us. We got a few odd looks from people too. Maybe they thought we were best friends zipping to an acting class. I wondered if anyone thought we were, in fact, a couple.

When people see two women riding a motorcycle together, or holding hands for that matter, they generally think that the two women are best friends out having a fun time together. I doubt "lesbian" comes to mind right away. Even for me… whenever I would see two women out having a happy time together with a little physical contact, I would never think that there is more to the story. But that was before I met Regina!

Now, when I look around at paired girls in the city, I run scenarios in my head; Does that little one lick the bigger one's pussy while she is handcuffed and gagged? Are they straight like me and got hit with the love bug that suddenly turned them gay? Do they like it rough and nasty? Do their parents know about them?

As of today, it has been exactly one month to the day that Boyfriend X stood me up on my birthday. Fucker. It has been one month since I learned that I meant nothing to that self-absorbed douche who never got turned on by me. It was strange because wherever I went, guys would always flirt with me and light up when I walked into a room. Then once they started talking to me, understood that I have a career, understood that I make money, understood that I have a brain, my appearance suddenly seemed to dip on their rating scale. Sexy and feminine is hot… unless the woman is independent, enthusiastic, and thriving. Then she's just a plain threat to the penis.

With BX, I never felt beautiful or desired. In a relationship, that sort of apathy toward a woman makes her play all kinds of mind games with herself. Am I ugly? Does he want someone younger? Do I have some lines or cellulite that turns him off? Do I deserve a guy less handsome that is more of a match for my appearance? Am I dating out of my range?

Cut to Regina! She adores me and worships me. Well, maybe she adores me and *worships* her bitchy mistress. It is the exact opposite of BX's apathy. It is full-pathy! Suddenly I feel beautiful again. I feel sexy and self-assured. One month ago my self-esteem was in the toilet. I doubted myself in a terrible way. The only partial remedy was to throw myself at my work and fill up every dark place with compliments from my co-workers and bonus paychecks from my inspired account handling.

Now I'm a different person. My whole life is glowing! When I look in the mirror, I still see my flaws, but I see a face that somebody loves and wants. My imperfections become part of the rich experience of Meg, instead of shameful reminders of her inadequacies. Regina makes me love myself.

I couldn't help but wonder… what if a guy had treated me the way Regina does, adoring me and longing to spend another second together? Would I ever have met someone who inspires me to be my true self? Would I ever be able to throw myself sexually into a relationship without feeling ashamed about being kinky? Would I ever have considered crossing the stigmatized gender line to be with a woman?

Whatever the case, a single month has brought the surprise of my life. I have discovered that being in love transcends gender and old models about how life is supposed to work. I know that sounds dopey and cliché, but I feel like a different person since meeting Regina.

I have never felt freer or more in tune with my sexuality. She has no dick, but she has so much more. To share my kink with someone who doesn't judge me is the most amazing thing. She probably feels the same way. Ninety-five percent of people would be repulsed by real BDSM, the kind that is not based on gimmicky notions of vinyl corsets and black dominatrix wigs with the Bettie Page bangs.

So there I was, holding tight on to Regina as we bopped around the city on her electric scooter having the time of our lives. It felt like the most beautiful city on Earth, vibrant and thrilling. We zipped over to the Marina district, which immediately reconfirmed my love of the city. The fog was smothering the Golden Gate Bridge but the sun was everywhere else. Alcatraz was winking at me in the sunbeams. Windsurfers and sailboats were zigzagging around the bay.

I had a micro fantasy of renting a sailboat and restraining Regina below deck in the cabin while sharing drinks with a few friends on deck as we sail the bay. Of course, the guests would have no idea my slave was on board. Every so often, I would disappear to the ladies room where I would take a detour by the slave's quarters to fondle, kiss, and torture Regina.

Then I had another micro fantasy about Alcatraz. See, when people are kinky like me, almost anything in daily life can kick you to a feverish lust. So about Alcatraz, I'd love to be mega-rich and rent the island for a full week. I would drag Regina into that compound in manacles and shackles. I could lock her up in the darkest cell and be her fucked up prison guard. She would have to sleep on the cold concrete floor with no blankets with her neck chained to the floor.

Occasionally, I would enter through the giant iron door and give her a meal of plain rice… after she polished my boot with her tongue and begged for a bite to eat. Sometimes, I would take her to my warden quarters and lavish her with a two-hour vacation of a hot shower, toasty flannel jammies, a cheese plate, and a bottle of merlot. And I would rub her delicately and show her the softest side of my warden personality. Then it would be off to her cell again where she would have no light and would not know whether it was day or night. She would not know if she would ever escape. I would be her lifeline to human touch. I would own her.

Poof! Fantasy over as she commented, "Shit. We're running out of the charge on my scooter. We better stop for breakfast and charge up." So we crossed our fingers and hoped to make it to Rose's Café. Too bad! The bike pooped out two blocks away at Greenwich and Fillmore. "We'll push it," she resolved. We both got off the bike, two cute girls in high boots and bedhead hair, and she began to push the bike. I immediately jumped in to take over. She had no business looking that beautiful and pushing a motorcycle.

But I wasn't pushing for three seconds when a fine gentleman from the street, briefcase in hand, jumped to our rescue. He said if we wouldn't mind holding his briefcase, he would push the bike. And so it went. It seemed like the sight of two girls, a dead bike, and a businessman was an interesting sight; We got quite a few looks.

After a few minutes, we made it to Union St. We would be able to coast downhill the last block to the café. We rubbed the guy's ego a bit with our feminine wiles, and he was on his way with a smile. Oh, and he turned around for one parting shot directed toward Regina: "Your boots are magnificent! Absolutely great!" Regina responded through a coy smile, "Thank you. I borrowed them from her (pointing to me). She has a boot fetish and wanted to see me in them." The guy delighted in trying to process this, then gave a wave and was off. The kindness of strangers!

We hopped on the bike and rolled a little above walking speed down the slight grade to the café. I asked Regina what we were supposed to do with the bike after breakfast. She said, "No worries. Watch." She lifted the seat to reveal a little compartment which held a seventy-five foot extension cord. She grabbed the plug and sauntered into the café. A moment later, she came out without the plug in hand and a telling smile. The bike could charge while we dined and then we would have enough juice to make it to my house for a proper charge.

Once we were seated and ordered, Regina had a request:

> **REGINA**
> *Meg, Let's not talk about the weather here, ok?*
>
> **ME**
> *Why, is something wrong?*
>
> **REGINA**
> *That whole scene last night wiped me out... emotionally.*
>
> **ME**
> *Is there anything you want to talk about? Are we cool?*
>
> **REGINA**
> (Sharing a warm and sincere smile)
> *Everything's great!! I'm in heaven with you. I love being your object!! I love the game!! It's like yoga, I love it so much... but you can't do yoga all day... or dessert for that matter.*
>
> **ME**

123

I getcha.

REGINA
And maybe I'm a little afraid of losing you to the mistress. I need both of you, not just one or the other.

ME
And I need both of you! But I'm extra horny these days because you have come to my sexual rescue and allowed me to experience a fullness that I have never known in my life! Thanks, Regina.

I leaned over and kissed her briefly on the lips. That one little kiss sent the electricity of hope and caring through my whole body. I was in love with this woman. She must have felt the same thing because she took my hand from the table and held it close to her cheek as if she was hugging me dearly.

"Hello, Girls." interrupted an unknown male voice from the side of the table. We turned to see a couple of lads looking at us with pickup lines ready to roll off their tongues. They were a couple of dot-commers, you know, in their 20's and loaded with stock options about to go public in a major way. I was able to size them up so quickly because they were very confident, but very nerdy, and accessorized on the high-end. One's shoes were one-of-a-kind leather booties that felt like Nieman Marcus. The other had designer prescription glasses and a Tag Heuer watch.

Dot-commers like these have just enough moxi to come out with this: "Say, would you two like to have some lunch guests?" Nieman Shoes chimed in: " By 'guests', he means we'll pick up the tab." Regina and I shot each other a look and approved the deal in our glance. We simultaneously gestured for them to pull up chairs. Nieman Shoes continued:

MR. NIEMAN SHOES

I'm Josh; this is Dave.

The conversation continued:

REGINA
(Extending her hand)
Pleasure.

JOSH
How about a bottle of wine for the table?

ME
It's lunchtime. I think we'll pass.

DAVE
We saw you on the scooter and thought we should stop by and say "hi."

ME
We're glad you did.

DAVE
(To Regina)
Is your name Wi-fi? Because I'm feeling a connection.

REGINA
Yeah, I'm feeling it... as strong as a dialup modem.
(The guy's face turns dejected)
Just kidding.
(Gesturing to the empty seats)
Sure. Pull up a chair.

ME
Actually, I didn't give her permission for that.

DAVE
Whoa. What are you, her owner?

REGINA
As a matter of fact, she is.

JOSH
(Thinking it's all a joke)
She owns you?

REGINA
Yes. She certainly does.

JOSH
You mean, you're her boss?

ME
In a manner of speaking, yes.

REGINA
She even told me what to wear today. She has a boot fetish.

DAVE
Wow. Ok. Well how about you ask your "boss" if you can give me your phone number?

Regina and I both start laughing. Then:

ME
Awesome!!! You can come over and give us both backrubs.
(Changing to an unsmiling tone)
We're a couple.

You should have seen both guys' eyes widen! They were a little embarrassed too. But Josh was quick on his feet to save face:

JOSH
And an amazing-looking couple you are! Too bad people like us will never get to shower you with the man's love you deserve.

> **ME**
> *Thanks. We'll enjoy showering together instead.*
>
> **REGINA**
> *She's not really my boss. You can't own a person.*
>
> **DAVE**
> *Either way, you two are gorgeous. Your beauty rivals the graphics in "Call of Duty"*
>
> **ME**
> *I have an idea. Let's get the waiter to take our pictures together. You two can Instagram it and tell everyone you had a great lunch date.*

Both guys were overjoyed at the proposition.

We all got up and stood by the table. Josh flagged down a waiter and handed him a phone to take the picture.

We used all our feminine allure to make this a photo that any guy, especially dot-commers, would be thrilled to show their friends. They could put it on their office cork board. "Cheese!" and the picture was snapped. The boys thanked us profusely and then headed out. We sat back down to continue our meal and conversation:

> **ME**
> *I bet those fuckers are rich!*
>
> **REGINA**
> *Did it give you pause? Would you want to be with a guy like that?*
>
> **ME**
> *I would be a whore. There would be no reason in the world to be with a person like that. I would never fit. I could never be emotionally or sexually satisfied.*

REGINA
Me neither.

After the meal, we thought we should split up for the rest of the day. She had laundry to do and I had to take care of some errands. We could have done everything together, but I think we were both feeling like a little air between us would be good. It's super important for everyone to have their own space. Besides, we had had a pretty incredible and intense few days and there is no way we could keep that pace up without flaming out in our lives outside the relationship.

She unplugged the extension cord and we headed out on her bike with a nice new charge!

When she dropped me off, we both got a little melancholy and decided to have dinner out together, making a promise not to play the game or end up at either of our homes together. Dinner would just be Regina and I catching up. The mistress would have to stay home and pout.

I finished doing my errands and paying a few bills, still buzzing with thoughts of Regina. It was a pretty warm day (which is funny because Regina had been wearing thigh boots), so I thought I'd hit the beach and crash on a blanket.

I went to Ocean Beach. First, I took a walk along the water, then put out a blanket and crashed out. I was asleep in just a couple minutes. Everything felt cheery and magical. I must have slept a really long time because I woke up, freezing from a foggy breeze coming in.

I checked the time and found out it was almost 6pm! I was supposed to meet Regina at 7. Shit. I raced home as fast as I could and jumped in the shower at 6:28 to wash the sand off. At 6:50, I called Regina to let her know I was running a tad late. She was already at the restaurant! Well, it wasn't really a restaurant. We were meeting at Steep Brew, a basic burger/Americana pub at 17th and Rhode Island St. We thought a mundane place would be less sexually charged than a fancy romantic joint.

I zipped over there as fast as possible and made it just about 12 minutes late. "Hey, Stranger," she welcomed. We hugged and I sat down. It was funny, we had been so intimate and exposed to each other in private that now it almost felt like we were college roomies meeting after 5 years apart. It was like war buddies getting together later. We had to reacquaint ourselves with each other in the light of the everyday world.

Clearly, we still had a giant chemistry toward each other, but we both wondered if there was more to explore with each other than kink. We bounced back and forth with some meaningless small talk, while trying to size each other's personalities up. Would we be best friends if we had never explored kink together?

My question would be answered within the first 5 minutes of ordering. We were at a table where my side was the booth and Regina's side was a chair. Regina left her chair and came over to park on my side in the booth, scooting in as tight as she could to me. That quasi-awkward start across the table only turned out to be the result of two people with entirely different lives suddenly trying to merge with someone new.

Surprisingly to me, being close to her physically in that moment was a much stronger feeling than my fear about being seen in public "with" a girl. It was that same excitement I remember feeling in junior high when I went on a date with a guy I really liked and he put his arm around me.

It was shocking that someone could actually like me enough to hold me in public and not be ashamed or nervous that it would damage their reputation. Maybe it is my self-esteem, but I have often felt like an imposter in cases like that. You know, they must think I'm someone else from my façade. Or… maybe they wouldn't be so affectionate in public if they knew the real me inside.

I was always fine in public as the life of the party… the "hot" girl in the black dress who would do daring things. But when things got up close and personal, I tended to be less confident. For me, it has always been easier to fuck like a whore than to have someone hold my hand.

In retrospect, I think I also felt like my kink was shameful and could never be revealed. So in a sense, I was somewhat shallow with people who were interested in me. I didn't want them to know that there was something wrong with me.

But there I was with Regina. She had primed the pump by sitting so close to me and suddenly I felt safe to reciprocate the touching. I was rubbing her neck and ear as we chatted about the vanilla parts of our lives.

She told me how Tucker is really complex. He has an amazing sensitive side, super empathetic. He writes poems like this one Regina pulled out of her purse to read me:

"Love is a triangle between a healthy body, a healthy soul, and a friendly smile. Love is mommy when she reads to me and looks at me."
Remember, this kid is only 9!

Regina said it is really common for him to write and say things like this. And he doesn't always focus them on her. He tends to exude this sensitivity that seems out of place for a kid his age.

But Regina went on to describe how he is complex. While he does have this extremely sensitive side, he also has a bit of a self-righteous streak. It is common for him to put others down and judge others. For example, Regina says Tucker often says stuff like, "That guy has a big fat gut! He shouldn't be drinking that soda."

So Tucker has this yin yang thing that seems a little extreme on either side. Regina tries to never talk about people pejoratively or in a judgmental way and she didn't remember her ex doing it either. She thinks it is the way Tucker is coping with the divorce somehow. But he does well in school and seems to have balance, so she isn't worried about him.

After explaining all this about Tucker, she hit me with a zinger: "Can you believe how blue the sky was today?"

Shit! I was coming to terms with trying to be close to this woman and she has to haul off and start game playing. I really wanted to be with Regina, not that fucking slave. I wasn't in the mood. We never came up with rules about what to do when one person wants to play the game and the other doesn't. Great. Frustrated, and being yanked out of my warm and fuzzy bubble, I scoffed as the Mistress, "What do you want? This had better be good."

Regina, I mean the slave, apologized for bothering me, but said she wanted to give me a present. She handed over a box with a bow on it. I opened it to discover a very expensive-looking black leather corset. This was the kind of corset that was functional, not just lingerie. It was boned and had a very stiff feel that could easily be laced up tightly to constrict breathing and also substantially suck in one's waist.

I always thought corsets were sexy and feminine, especially when they were the real thing like this one. A flimsy little lace one wouldn't do it for me.

Regina looked at me for approval of the gift she had given me. I wasn't quite sure how to react so I just decided to be honest. "Come with me," I commanded, leading her to the bathroom. She followed me across the restaurant and into the single toilet bathroom where I locked the door behind us. I took off my top and bra and held the corset in place against my bare skin. "Lace it up," I told her. The corset was foreign to both of us and she struggled for a moment to figure out the lacing in the back.

But it wasn't long before I felt the leather tightening up to my tummy. Corsets are designed to be laced from the center first, then tightened outward from the middle. She was really cinching my stomach and I was literally feeling constricted.

She heard my groans growing as the tightness increased toward discomfort. She had the awareness of my discomfort and finally started moving outward on the lacing. The corset was pulling in around my chest and also around my lower back and I was getting turned on. It was a half-cup corset and gently lifted my breasts up as it got tighter. My nipples were exposed just above the top of the leather.

When Regina got everything about as tight as I could stand it, she tied off the balance of the string firmly around my waist. The thing about a corset is that the more you tighten, the more left over string there is when you are done. I would say there was at least 5 feet of extra string when I was all cinched in. I could actually feel my pussy getting wet from the mere act of being constricted by Regina.

It felt like no kind of bondage I could imagine. I felt solid and powerful, even though every single bit of my torso was compressed beyond comfort. It is kind of like heels, they make me feel strong, even though, technically they make a woman more vulnerable.

I looked in the mirror as Regina watched on. It was clear that this was definitely a great look on me (although maybe not the greatest look with my yoga pants). I wanted to enjoy the appearance a bit. She was standing behind me and I told her to put her hands around my corseted waist and show me that she adores me.

Her arms went around and she hugged me close from behind. She began kissing my neck as I watched in in the mirror. It was unbelievably sexy to see her delicate hands on the dark leather as she licked and kissed my neck. Either she got bolder or lost herself in the sensuality of the moment, but she started playing with my nipples just above the corset. It was super hot to watch.

She was really in touch with me and quickly read my mind that I wanted her to finger me. With one hand on my nipple, she used the other hand to stimulate me where I was aching for touch. Simultaneously, she had moved from kissing my neck to alternately focusing on my ear and mouth. As for me, I was just taking it all in, spying from the mirror. It felt like I was someone else watching. It was a sexy movie in the mirror. But things escalated quickly as she played with my clitoris and gently fingered me under my yoga pants.

For real… the corset made it hard to breathe. I was short of breath and it got worse the more I got turned on. Just then, Regina shocked me by slipping her left hand over my mouth and pulling in tight, while pinching my nose to cut off my breathing. I was suffocating and writhing under her touch and started to come violently. The whole time I was coming, she kept her hand over my mouth and nose. It was a burning orgasm that took me to places I have never been before. I was weak, suffocating, and could hardly stand.

She sensed when I was finished and removed her hand from my mouth. I gasped with all my might for air and kept panting desperately. She softly hugged me as I gradually came down. Keep in mind, the entire time we were in the bathroom, the only words spoken were "Lace it up." The silence stood to heighten the sensuality of everything that was going on.

Finally calming down, I turned around and hugged her with incredibly warm feelings. She smiled softly, realizing that her gift was a success with her mistress. We kissed for a long time; there was such a connection to the moment… to each other.

I broke the silence by softly speaking, " You are very thoughtful slave. You will be rewarded." Then we kissed again before separating. It was a strange scene because she had dominated me, but the mistress didn't seem to mind. It all happened organically. The slave had been suffocating and fondling the mistress. I guess sometimes you have to turn the other cheek when a slave is presumptuous or disrespectful. It's a matter of picking one's battles.

I put my top on over the corset because I really wanted to keep it on. With no bra, my erect nipples were super visible through the fabric. Also, that fact that my boobs were pushed upward was adding to the effect. Oh well, people would have to deal with my nipples. The corset felt amazing and I was certainly not going to do anything to stop that feeling.

We walked out of the bathroom and there was a line of 3 girls that were waiting. Oops. They looked at us… and clearly knew that we were up to something in there. When we were walking back to our table, I felt the swagger of a real dominatrix. That corset is like a cape to superman. It gives powers. Regina was beaming as we sat back down. I decided to fuck with her. "Did you give me that corset because you think I'm fat?" A look of horror came over her as she quickly defended, "Mistress, not at all. I merely wanted to give you a gift that I thought you would like." I gave her a disapproving look with, "Fine. Then I accept your gift. But you are never going to bribe me into being soft with you (and I grabbed her face firmly), do you understand?" She answered sheepishly, "Yes, Mistress." And then I put a stop to the madness with "That was some kind of crazy day I had."

We both shifted emotional gears. It took a few moments because we were so in the zone. And there we were, together again as ourselves. I was as emotionally naked and unguarded as possible when the following words flowed from my mouth unconsciously: "I'm in love with you."

Regina blushed. The girl who had just been suffocating me and rubbing my pussy was now blushing. It was really cute. Then I remarked how the corset was really uncomfortable still being so tight. We both laughed. So much for a casual meeting without kink.

After more sharing about our regular lives outside, she surprised me by blurting out, "Your breasts are beautiful!!" And now I was the one blushing. Guys always said that to me, but it felt so different hearing those words from a girl. It felt sweet and sexy, rather than lusty. From anybody else, I tend to brush off compliments like that, but with Regina, I felt like it was real enough to take in and enjoy.

We finished up with some airy conversation about plans for next week, Tucker's schedule, and which grocery store we each liked, all while holding hands on the table.

After bussing our table like good girls, we and said our goodbyes, each with an inside glow that was moving us happily on our separate ways toward home.

But before we actually left each other, I pulled her in close and honestly said, "Regina, I love my corset! Thank you so much!" Regina, realizing we were not in the game, flashed a heartfelt smile with "You're welcome."

Even though the mistress's slave had given the gift, I was the one thanking Regina outside of the game. This was peculiar because it clearly showed how complex emotions and sexuality can be; I was thanking her… as a person… for doing something nice for me. It wasn't a sexual thing. In fact, I couldn't wait to get the corset off of me. It's super uncomfortable outside the game.

The kink helps to compartmentalize the sex from the rest so that we can share on a deeper level in both worlds. The sex is supercharged and insane, while the rest is so completely human. That's why it was odd that I felt like thanking Regina for the corset in real life. The corset was from the other world. But the gift was from Regina and I had to reconcile all this within my feelings. One thing was clear though, the real gift was Regina. We said goodnight and headed out.

--- SUNDAY APRIL 1 --- April Fool's Day / Hating Surprises

This morning I awoke to discover the entire city was buried in snow 3 feet high and none of the roads were open! San Francisco has never seen anything like this!

Ahhh, bullshit. You are so gullible, Ms. Diary. That's my attempt at an April Fool's prank. Stupid. For whatever reason, I have never been fond of pranks. I hate when people are punked. I hate April Fool's day, and I hate surprises. Please NEVER throw me a surprise party. I mean it! Who likes that stuff anyway?

Pranks and being punked always equate to someone has to be the butt of a joke. Someone has to be made foolish. Why is that fun? There must be a million Youtube videos of pranks that have millions of views. Why? I don't find it funny to see someone come into their office only to find that it has been filled from floor to ceiling with popcorn.

Frankly, I see that crap and I think… "What a disgusting waste of food and resources." Think of all the water it took to grow that corn. Think of all the diesel fuel it required to tend and deliver the crops just so some asshole can fill up his buddy's office with it for a 10 second laugh. Hilarious. Think of all the people who go to bed hungry and would do anything for that corn.

I know what you're thinking: "Jeeze, Meg. Lighten up, it's just a silly thing we all do to each other." Ok, perhaps I am a little overboard. And of course, I frequently get a chuckle from watching a prank. But it is more of a human reaction, rather than true amusement. Then after a moment of laugher, I put myself in the prankee's head and feel embarrassed for them.

That embarrassment and shame is what is at the heart of my problem with the practice of pranks. As a child, I always felt like I was an outsider and that groups would single me out for humiliation. It wasn't until I was much older that I learned that the humiliation wasn't directed at me specifically. It was merely directed at the nearest or easiest target. But the pranks always made me feel even less adequate and even more like an outsider.

One time on St. Patrick's day in 6th grade, I was eating hot lunch by myself in the cafeteria. I had on a cute green leprechaun hat and was minding my own business. All of a sudden, I felt someone lift my hat off from behind. Then a hand came down to my lunch tray, grabbed my bowl of peaches, dumped them on my head, and then pulled my hat back over my ears, squishing the peaches all over my hair.

The entire cafeteria burst into humiliating laughter and waited for my reaction. However, to their disappointment, I didn't react at all. After wiping off my head, I simply continued eating my lunch as if the event hadn't even occurred. I took a surreptitious look behind me to see who the culprit was. And there was Marsha Spencer, getting hi-fives and pats on the back by her laughing cronies. Mental note: "Marsha Spencer will die." It's true what they say about revenge being best served cold.

Even though I appeared to the rest of the cafeteria to be completely unphased by the peaches, what they couldn't see on the inside was that I was thinking of what type of revenge would be ten times more humiliating to Marsha. Fucking bitch.

After stewing on it a few days, I finally came up with the perfect revenge. About a week after the great peach incident buzz had petered out, I circulated little notes around that school that said, *"Marsha Spencer is going to eat shit on Tuesday on first break on the soccer field – Meg"*. Of course, I expected this to circulate back to Marsha as well.

When Tuesday arrived, I was prepared. When the bell rang for first break, everyone headed to the soccer field, a place without yard duties because kids didn't usually hang out there.

Everyone gathered around me and waited for the show. Out of her little clique, came Marsha. Everyone knew she could kick my ass because she had been known to fight dirty. But I didn't care. I just wanted revenge more than I feared getting my hair pulled or whatever.

Marsha, cocky as ever, came out with "So I hear you are going to kick my ass." I responded calmly, "No. You must have heard wrong. I said you are going to eat shit… and I meant it." Everyone started laughing. Marsha was laughing too. While she was mugging to her crew and not paying attention to me, I reached into my coat pocket, pulled out a baggie that had one of my actual shits in it, grabbed it out of the baggie with my bare hand and I shoved it forcefully straight into her open mouth!! Then I wiped my hand on her face and hair! The look on her face was priceless. I will remember it forever. She was frozen in shock. I turned and walked away without expression.

The crowd, rather than standing there laughing, was absolutely appalled and disgusted and reacted in deafening silence! It was like the famous diner scene in Pulp Fiction where the lowly petty thieves come up against Samuel L. Jackson, a bad ass murderer who makes them look like babies. I was Samuel L. Jackson. She was the baby. Later in school, I heard that Marsha had barfed right after I left. Imagine having to barf in the dead silence of all your cronies as they look on in disgust. Yeah, it was a satisfying day. Neither she, nor any of her friends ever messed with me again. The point is, I don't like pranks.

Sorry for going off topic. I guess seeing April 1 on the calendar really hits a nerve with me. To be honest, I realize that I have an overly sensitive view on the topic. Maybe some other prank trauma happened to me in the past. I can't remember any major ones. But I clearly have issues around this. That's probably what made me turn kinky (Just kidding).

The strange thing is, humiliation plays such a big part in my kinky fantasies, Regina's too. Shame is a giant component of S&M in general. It's sexy to feel the shame and play with it in a safe context. Not being a shrink, I really have no idea how humiliation fits into someone's psyche or how the satisfaction is manifested. When Regina and I are walking in public, and I'm holding her wrist instead of her hand, it's a form of humiliating her. It is saying she is not equal and that she is lesser than. It's a shameful posture. It's also fun to do verbal humiliation (or to receive it) in a sexual context.

Within the bounds of a BDSM scene, humiliation feels amazing. It's surprising that it is so awful to feel in real life. But it comes down to consent. The faces of power I despise and loathe in real life such as humiliation, dominance, cruelty, sexual exploitation, police brutality, and even rape, are all elements that can be used erotically when consent is mutual. In fact, that's the entire basis of my sexual identity. I want to feel the dark side of sex and power. Just like a horror movie, it's a safe form of exploration and satisfaction. Consent is everything.

That's why I hate pranks. They are built on the idea of emotionally harming someone who hasn't given consent. That's why Marsha had to eat shit.

So back to the only important subject at hand: Regina. Last night, we decided we would meet tonight to barbecue at my house. She asked if the mistress was going to be here. I replied, "Well, she does live there." Regina seemed pleased. We agreed that it couldn't be a late night because it was a school/work night. We also decided that during the daytime today, we would each do our own thing. Cool.

So when I got home last night I emailed Victoria and asked her if she wanted to come over for lunch. She sounded really excited to see me and catch up, saying she had a lot of news to share. I said the same thing! We set it up for her to come over at 12:30.

At 11:30, I get a call from Regina. When I answered, there was no greeting, no "hello," no small talk, just these words "Can you believe how blue the sky is today?" Obviously, I'm always thrilled to hear from Regina on the phone, but when I'm surprised by Regina the slave calling me, it messes with my groove; I instantly shift into another personality. Sometimes I'm not ready for that.

Again, it's not really a deliberate choice to switch personalities, it has become an automatic, Pavlovian changeover. Think of it like hypnosis… you know… "when I snap my fingers you will become a dog and bark." It feels like that. I don't control it or consciously switch it. Here's another analogy: If someone flips you off while you are driving, you don't simply decide to be mad at the person, you just see red and it turns to road rage. It's automatic.

Anyway, so there I am on the phone with the slave who says: "Forgive me Mistress, I know we are seeing each other tonight and you may have your own plans during the day, but I am craving to be in your presence. Even if I could be under the same roof as you, I would be most grateful to be able to serve you."

My wheels started turning, "Fine. Get here right away. Wear your leather opera gloves and our brick red boots." "Yes, Mistress. Thank you Mistress," she groveled.

When I hung up the phone, I was about to call Victoria to let her know that "something came up and I would have to cancel." But then I thought, "Forget it. I'm not going to change my plans to accommodate a lowly slave's whim."

Sure enough, Regina arrived in a New York minute. When I opened the door, I saw a walking dream! There she stood in our boots. She had on an avocado-colored mini-skirt, an adorable sleeveless grey top with a subtle black pattern, the long leather gloves that went up to her shoulders, and… a three inch wide heavy brown slave collar around her neck! But it wasn't really a slave collar from an S&M store. It was more like she had found a high-end brown belt from Macy's and had it altered to be just long enough to fit her neck.

It was a really striking accessory! I never really thought about a collar in all my kinky fantasies, but suddenly, I had a new fetish. You can't imagine how hot she looked!!! Her slender white neck was contrasted by a heavy leather belt that said, "I'm your object." It was the perfect combination of classy and sassy at the same time. The look was sophisticated and could easily be worn in public as a fashion statement. Come to think of it, you never see that done. Other than a necklace or scarf, you never see any other type of neckwear. This slave collar was completely original and very striking. It was a smart look. It looked kinky and sexual, but could easily pass for being ahead of the vogue curve. Sure, I've seen cheap bondage collars on tattooed goth girls before, but this was something entirely different. This was Barney's of New York style.

I swear, Regina, is the answer to any shame or guilt I ever felt about being kinky. She makes it feel so natural and acceptable. She makes kink feel as ordinary and emotionally fulfilling as putting on a favorite song. It's just a great feeling. God, even her hair is beautiful!

Even though a slave owner is probably not supposed to tip their emotional hand, I started with, "Wow. Your mistress is very impressed with your outfit. For a slave, you look stunning."
Without raising her eyes to me, she responded, "Thank you, kind Mistress."

In my customary manner, I grabbed her by the wrist and led her into my house, closing the door behind me. I dragged her straight over to the living room and commanded her, "Assume a downward dog position." And her perfect yoga body struck the familiar pose that I had seen so many times in class. But in her outfit, in her slave collar and gloves, it was beyond sensual for me. It was an aesthetic mind bomb.

I sat on the couch in front of her and commanded her to raise her head and look at me. As her eyes met me, I felt her burning lust... and started masturbating before her. Her face was warm and focused, but I could read little else of her. It was clear she was trying not to reveal her thoughts to me.

Then I commanded her, "come over here and pretend my feet are a cock that you crave." And with a "Yes, Mistress," she crawled over and began licking and sucking on my toes as if there was no bigger turn on to her in the world. She was moaning and completely overtaken by the task. She was in another world and she licked the arches of my feet and sucked each toe. What's funny is that this sort of contact with my feet would usually have me busting out in ticklish laughter. But the treatment from Regina was so direct and sexually charged that laughter was far from the moment.

It was really hot to watch her take her sweet time in massaging my feet with her mouth. All the while I was playing with myself. Finally, I was getting really close. I ordered her to stop with the feet treatment, and to go across the room and watch me. I wanted to come in front of her as she watched, just like the dreams I had had. As I carried on, it was obvious by her urging expression that she was really enjoying being the voyeur.

As for me, I took in every square inch of her as eye candy. I loved looking at her figure and posture. She stood a little awkwardly in a pose that was completely unpretentious, feet slightly pigeon-toed and her hands clasped gently and submissively behind her back as if she were in handcuffs. The collar on her neck struck a formidable contrast to her feminine gracefulness, as her eyes gazed on me intrusively. I stroked myself ever more rapidly toward climax.

Throwing all modesty aside, I let my orgasm gush at full force, rolling with it, writhing, working it as deeply as I could. Regina was softly biting her lower lip in solidarity with my experience. I closed my eyes for the final rush of passion and exploded with a primal moan that would have indicated harsh pain in any other context. It lasted and lasted until I finally collapsed like a spent dish rag, slipping off the sofa and right onto the floor.

After a few moments of gaining back my senses, Regina took it upon herself to slowly walk over to me, coming to a rest with her feet just inches from my head. It was unusual for my slave to take any action whatsoever without being ordered to do so. But there she stood, towering over my head as I lay on the floor. Then, shockingly, she looked me straight in the eye and deliberately put her right boot to my lips. My first thought, was, "How dare her!"

But before I even processed that notion, my hands grabbed her boot and pulled it tight to my mouth… where I started licking her sole with the same passion and commitment that she herself had used on my toes. I was imagining her licking my feet and replicating that same action on her boot. It was other-worldly. It was a drug. I was not in my house or my mind, I was in a mysterious roman orgy where dreamlike lust cascaded around every inch of my body.

It didn't matter that I was in a submissive position, serving my own slave. It was pure sexual fire that was more an expression of our desire for each other than of which body part was receiving which stimulation. That was all irrelevant in light of the power of our passion. This stunning woman was sticking a boot in my face and I was attacking it as if my hunger for her could never be satisfied. If she had only offered her pinky instead of a boot, I would have been just as fervent. But the boot had the added sexuality of allowing my fetish to access my lifetime of self-shame.

Only with enraptured lovers can boundaries be so blurred, if not invisible between physical versus non-physical, dominant versus submissive, respect versus disrespect, shame versus confidence, and leather versus skin.

Regina's expression looked equal parts pained and turned-on. She had this darkly curious gaze and was completely captivated by watching me work on her foot like this. But she also showed twinges of fear... like when a child deliberately acts naughty as they test the boundaries of authority. Oh, she was naughty alright.

Gradually, I started coming to my senses and realized that I was practically making love to the shoe of my own slave. My intellect finally put the brakes on my libido and interrupted the scene. I frustratingly shoved her boot aside with, "Keep your disgusting feet off of me!" Regina, instantly falling into full submission, realized she had crossed a line. She pleaded desperately, "I'm sorry, Mistress. I'm so sorry. Please forgive me! Please, let me make it up to you!"

I sprung to my feet, then immediately slipped my fingers under her collar and pulled her head in close to my face. "You need to be punished." With a firm grip on her collar, I dragged her forcefully to my small laundry room where I pulled her head toward the ground until she ended up on all fours like an animal.

Dread was in her eyes and it was starting to look like she would cry. I told her to wait there and not to move a muscle. She was still as a rock as I left the laundry room to fetch some implements.

A few moments later, I returned with of a box of bondage gear, the use of which would leave no doubt about who was boss of whom.

First order of business was to let this slave understand her position in life. I took off my pants and panties, yanked her head back by pulling her hair and then I shoved the soiled panties deep into her mouth, causing her to react with a slight gag sound. I grabbed her hair and spoke to her coldly, "Do you taste me? Do you see what you did? You spoiled my fresh panties by making me come." Then I pulled away her skirt and swatted her ass with a solid spanking. She was yearning deeply for it. I smacked her 20 times in a row in a steady rhythm about a second apart. With each contact, she moaned into my panties, growing ever more aroused as I continued.

Once her ass had a rosy burn, I stopped, kneeling down to offset some of the pain with some soft licking to the area. My tongue on her buttocks almost created the same level of moaning as the spanking. In a sense, Regina only wanted contact from me and didn't seem to make a distinction between the kinds of contact, be it harsh or gentle.

After a few moments of licking her perfect bottom, I wanted to play things a little more strictly.

The leather bit gag was next out of my magic box of playthings. I crammed it in her mouth right over the panties, then cinched the strap firmly around the back of her head. The gag, combined with her newly fashioned "belt" collar made for a striking aesthetic. I had always wanted to live inside a Helmut Newton photograph and this was definitely getting close to that feeling! Here was a gorgeous woman on all fours with a bit gag in her mouth and a thick leather collar around her tender, alabaster neck.

Next, I commanded her to lie down on the floor, after which I pulled her slender arms behind her back and locked them there with handcuffs. From the box, I pulled out a length of heavy steel chain and chained her ankles in a cross-legged position. The chain looked imposing against the leather of our brick red boots. Taking the end of the excess chain, I locked her crossed legs to the middle of her handcuffs with a heavy padlock.

Even though this is not everyone's idea of comfort, for a yoga girl who likes punishment from her lover, she seemed quite content. It was time to leave her for a good long time to ponder the disrespect she had shown for me.

Just in time too. I needed to hop in the shower and get ready for Victoria who was supposed to arrive only about fifteen minutes later. That's right. I planned on leaving Regina while I met with Victoria in the living room. It's a win-win. Regina gets her punishment, I get to visit with Victoria, and then I have a horny slave to play with after Victoria leaves. Perfect.

After finishing my shower, I checked on Regina in the laundry room. She was squirming a bit, but seemed okay and aroused. I spoke sweetly to her, telling her she was a good girl and that I loved her very much. I kissed her softly on the check and told her she was impressing me by taking the punishment so gracefully. I also asked her if anything was cutting off circulation or if there were any other physical problems with her position. She shook her head a definitive "no."

Seeing her all tied up and helpless like that and feeling relaxed after my nice shower, I wanted to break from the game to be with Regina and tell her I'm crazy about her. But I knew that exiting the game would be a buzz kill for slave Regina who was in the SLOW process of foreplay. The mean Mistress took a few moments to give a gentle and loving back massage in the space between her handcuffed arms. She purred at the connection. Next thing you know, I was slipping my hand into her pussy and rubbing her. She was making sounds of sublime pleasure… just as… DING DONG!

It was the doorbell. I quickly rinsed my hand in the sink and left Regina in the laundry room, closing the door behind me.

At the front door, there was Victoria. My first impression, having just seen Regina's perfect body, was that Victoria was so much heavier than I remembered. I don't know if my perception was skewed by having Regina as a reference point or if Victoria had been putting on weight. Either way, I was really glad to see her familiar face. We have a long history together and have been each other's sounding board for so many relationships and dramas.

She charged right in with, "You gotta any red wine in this joint?" She was like one of those neighbors on the sit-coms who pop over and help themselves to the fridge while spouting on about some goofy topic or another. Before I could answer, she had already found a bottle and cork screw and was helping herself to it.

She poured us each a glass and immediately took off her shoes and plopped on a kitchen chair. We toasted each other and hugged. During the warm-up small talk about jobs and landlords, etc, I started prepping our enchiladas and salad for lunch. She was babbling like crazy, cramming to make up for lost time together. After taking a breath, the conversation shifted to a more balanced discourse that went like this.

> **VICTORIA**
> *So tell me about the new beau.*
>
> **ME**
> *There is no beau.*
>
> **VICTORIA**
> *It's already over? That was fast. When I dropped by a while back, it seemed like love with you... or at least something more than the usual dating nonsense.*
>
> **ME**
> *Well...*
>
> **VICTORIA**
> *C'mon. What's going on?*
>
> **ME**
> *It wasn't a beau. It was...*
>
> **VICTORIA**
> *Was what? Spit it out already.*
>
> **ME**
> *It was a belle.*

Victoria was confused. Her brain was working double speed to try to compute this concept.

> **VICTORIA**
> *A "belle." Meaning... A girl?*
>
> **ME**

Yes. This is insane but I have fallen wildly in love, Victoria. I'm in love with a girl!

VICTORIA
Holy shit!

She gulps some wine and struggles with it all.

VICTORIA
You? In love with a girl? Are you sure you aren't just searching for something new and crazy? It's probably going to pass.

ME
Victoria! I'm really in love. It's real.

VICTORIA
Fuuuuucking un-be-lieve-able! What's her name?

ME
Regina

VICTORIA
Are you suddenly a lesbian?

ME
I don't know.

VICTORIA
What do you mean you don't know?

ME
I don't think I could be in love with just any other woman. In fact, I know I couldn't. But this woman is beyond special. She accepts me. She accepts that I'm kinky and is okay with it all.

VICTORIA

Plenty of guys could easily accept it too. That's no reason to all of a sudden turn into a carpet muncher. Wait... do you actually do that with her?? I can't picture it!

ME
That's private information. But think about it... two people are in love. There is deep physical sharing. It doesn't matter whether tab "A" goes to slot "B" or not.

VICTORIA
What about the "kinky" part? You mean she likes it rough too?

My need to share was really bubbling up and I couldn't hide my enthusiasm any longer. I really wanted to express all the goodness that I had been experiencing in this truly amazing relationship.

ME
She is kinky just like me! We play bondage games. I'm happier than I have ever been in my whole life!!

VICTORIA
Bondage lesbian. Nice. Is she butch? Tattoos everywhere?

ME
She has the body of an Audrey Hepburn, fashion plate! She's beautiful and elegant!

VICTORIA
Wow! I can see in your eyes that you are for real about this.

ME
And guess what else?

VICTORIA
What?

ME
I have her tied up, actually chained up and gagged, in the laundry room right now!

Victoria's eyes bugged out! She immediately jumped up with a big gasp of surprise.

VICTORIA
Show me. I want to meet her!

I literally had to block Victoria's path.

ME
Stop! It's private. You can't see her. Just relax.

VICTORIA
Why not? Are you making this all up?

ME
Hey! I'm sharing with you because you are my dear friend. This is not a joke; it's serious. This is not some kind of put-on or sorority prank! She let me put her in a very vulnerable, compromising position. She has trusted me with taking care of her. She is depending on me to respect her privacy and guard her safety.

VICTORIA
Sorry, I didn't mean to make light of it. It's just a pretty surprising bit of information. I mean, who keeps a girl tied up for no reason?

ME
It's not for "no reason." This is what I have been trying to explain to you for years. I'm not like you. Neither is Regina. We don't live our lives looking for the next big stud to screw. My sexuality is dark and complicated. I finally met someone who has the exact same sexual desires as me. We have the same sexual orientation. Believe it or

not, she is hogtied and gagged and left alone for an indefinite period of time, and she is probably 100 times more turned on right now than during the best vanilla guy sex she has ever had.

VICTORIA
Don't you have to be kissing her or something?

ME
Not at all. She gets aroused by being a worthless slave to me. She licks my boots while she is handcuffed. She washes my dishes while I spank her. It is much deeper than mere intercourse. It's a type of sex that transcends mere physical contact. The arousal comes from completely submitting to someone and being their doormat. Because the mind and body are both deeply involved in the scenario, it carries far more sexual power.

VICTORIA
So I take it you are the dominatrix and she is the slave?

ME
It's not as black and white as that. But basically, yes.

VICTORIA
Do you whip her?

ME
It's not like in the movies where I have a bullwhip and studded bustier.

VICTORIA
But you hurt her, right?

ME
That's kind of like the same question as do I carpet munch. You are focusing on the mere physical act instead of the psychological aspect. The real turn-on comes with

mindfucking.

For instance, right now, she has no idea if I am going to leave her there for a few minutes or until tomorrow. For all she knows, I may show up in five minutes and cram a coke bottle up her ass. Or maybe I will give her a loving massage while she is completely restrained.

She has no idea what I am doing right now. I could be masturbating or watching a movie on Netflix. I could be completely disinterested in her. She just has to wait there until the moment I decide to come back. She has no control over it. For once in her life, she has no decisions to make. She has no obligations to others. She has no deadlines. She just has to stay there and be at my mercy.

VICTORIA
You're explaining it. I'm hearing it. But, I'm sorry... that just doesn't sound sexy to me. It feels a little like trying to explain modern art to me.
(Thinking a moment)
Maybe I can understand what she gets out of it, letting go of all responsibility and all that. But what's in it for you? The Master?

ME
That would be "Mistress," the female form. Well, can you imagine what it would be like if your whole life, you wanted to have someone you could physically dominate and humiliate in a socially acceptable way. Then one day, you actually meet a person who gives you permission to act out your life-long fantasy of being cruel and heartless. Imagine having your own slave... not just a slave, but a sex slave too... someone who will wear any clothes you want them to and worship your feet and touch you anyway you want them touch to you. Can you imagine the power rush of having someone tied up in the laundry room that you could either hurt, ignore, or play with? It's intoxicating to

not filter or hide my true sexual desires anymore.

VICTORIA
Again, I'm hearing it. But frankly, I don't think it would turn me on very much to have a slave I could spank or make wash the dishes. Well, I take that back about washing the dishes. I actually need a slave like that. But still, I wouldn't find it very sexy.

ME
Obviously, we're different. And that's why there are so many flavors of ice cream. Everyone needs something different and they can't explain a desire.

VICTORIA
I really want to meet her. Can we meet at another time soon?

ME
Sure. I bet she would love to meet you.

VICTORIA
If we all go out to dinner sometime, am I supposed to do anything different?

ME
Like what?

VICTORIA
I dunno. Am I supposed to be condescending and bitchy to her?

ME
Victoria! She's just a regular person. She's a schoolteacher. You would treat her with the same respect as anyone!

VICTORIA

So how do you decide when to whip her? And when are you supposed to be dominant with her?

ME
Think of it like regular sex. You don't just go into a restaurant and start fucking. Same thing with S&M. You only do it when each person is in the mood.

VICTORIA
What do you plan on doing to her after I leave?

ME
I don't know. It will unfold on its own.

VICTORIA
Are you two going to move in together?

ME
We can't. She has a little boy. She's a single mom. And I must say... she's the hottest single mom I have ever encountered!

VICTORIA
Listen to you lusting over your MILF!! You must have been gay your whole life and were just hiding it from me.

ME
I told you. I'm not attracted to girls. Just Regina. We were made for each other! When I see other women walking down the street I may think they are pretty, but I would NEVER fantasize about having sex with them. Regina threw a monkey wrench into everything I knew and believed about my sexual identity.

VICTORIA
What if Mr. Perfect S&M showed up all of a sudden? I mean, if you had to choose between the perfect kinky guy or this perfect kinky schoolteacher girl, which would you

choose?

ME
C'mon, Victoria. That's stupid. Soulmates are not swappable.

VICTORIA
Now she's a "soulmate"?

ME
She's my soulmate.

VICTORIA
(She shook her head in a doubting expression)
I'm sorry. It's just hard for me to believe that anyone would want to keep their soulmate tied up and gagged in a freaking laundry room. I'm just not feeling the romance.

ME
Trust me, it's there.

VICTORIA
Then again, I did think it was strange how you never fit with relationships up until this point. I've never seen you this passionate and enthusiastic before. This girl must be really amazing…. that or you really, really needed to release the dominant bitch in you.

ME
I'm telling you. I found my person.

VICTORIA
Just imagine… this whole time we have been casually talking, she has been tied up and uncomfortable. You know, I better get going. I feel bad for her.

But then again, she's probably in need of a big ole spanking for being such a bad girl (wink!)

ME
I apologize for being so distant from you. Now you can see that it was nothing personal. I promise, we can all go out sometime so you can meet each other. She's so fun.

VICTORIA
You're a weird fucking chick. I wish I could be a fly on the wall and watch you punish her.

ME
You'll have to use your imagination. Thanks so much for stopping by!

VICTORIA
I love you. Thanks for sharing.

ME
Love you too. Have a good rest of the day.

And off she went. That was the main thrust of the conversation. Throughout eating the enchiladas, I also learned about her new diet and the usual problems with her dysfunctional family. She may be a crazy mess, but I think she will find a great guy one day. She would be a constant source of fun in a relationship.

After she left, I really felt like racing back to Regina and connecting with her. But the dom in me decided to pour a lemonade and write in my diary. Which I am doing now, "Hi Diary." But now I think it is way past the time that I should untie her. She probably has to pee sooooooo badly! Shit . I better go get her. Type to you later.

Ok. It's three hours later and Regina hates my guts! I'm so scared! I've spent the last couple hours bawling and trying to make sense of what when down with her.

Here's what happened. After Victoria left, I took more time to give slave Regina more time in her bondage scene. She has always told me that she loves being retrained and left in the corner like a worthless piece of shit while I go about having the freedom to do as I may, drinking a glass of wine, watching TV, taking a shower, whatever.

But when I finally got back to her in the laundry room, she was laying there hogtied with a completely blank expression. I was expecting her to be insanely turned-on and ready for a spanking and a big fat kiss. But she was just lying there. Clearly, something was up.

My first thought was that something was going on with her physically. Maybe she had been chained up too long and was completely numb or something. I ran several scenarios through my head but none of them added up to the way she was looking. "Oh, Baby. Are you ok?" I inquired. But she didn't answer. Clearly, there wasn't a single hint of sexual energy coming from her, no charge of any kind. The one thing that was clearly present in her was a foreboding sense of indifference. It was completely unlike her to ever be anything but beaming with full emotional expression. So to see her like this gave me a pit in my stomach. Something was definitely up... and it wasn't good. God, I just wanted to hug her and kiss her and tell her I loved her. I couldn't wait to get her out of those chains. I wanted to cuddle with her and warm her with a solid connection.

I asked another time, "What's wrong?" But it was like I was invisible... persona non grata. Realizing she was obviously still in the game, I changed tack with, "That was some kind of a crazy day I had." Instantly, she jolted back to reality and demanded in a icy, sterile tone, "Unchain me and get these handcuffs off me." Absolutely destroyed by her tone, I began babbling sheepishly as I started to unlock her, "Baby, I'm so sorry. I'm getting you out right now. What's wrong? Are you hurt? Can you share with me?"

Once she was free, she stood up, stretched out her aching muscles and then bolted past me without a sound. Ok. Now I understood. She was enraged at me. I scrambled to keep up with her as she headed toward the front door; "Can you share with me what's wrong? Let's talk about this, Regina." But she wasn't going to let me in at all and marched right out the door without uttering a word or giving me the slightest inkling of what had ticked her off. She took off without ever even looking back at me. Like I said, persona non grata. FUCK ME.

The pit in my stomach swelled over my whole body and grew until I exploded in tears. What had happened? She loved to be treated badly. Why was she suddenly livid with me? What could I have possibly done that was that bad to elicit such a dramatic reaction?

Then if flashed on me. It must have been something with Victoria! All these possible causes raced through my head. Had I said something to Victoria that Regina somehow overheard and was offended by? Had I broken some unspoken promise by sharing about my new relationship? Maybe I had outted Regina as a lesbian when she wasn't ready for that yet.

My mind kept racing to figure it out. Maybe I had outted her kink and wasn't supposed to. What the fuck had I said? Or maybe I had forgotten that she had to leave at a certain time and left her too long. No. That wasn't it. Was she jealous that I had Victoria over? Did Regina think that I was too chummy with Victoria? As that thought crossed my mind, I started remembering back to her mood and tone. In retrospect, it completely felt like jealousy… a slighted lover. Crap. This was bad!

After waiting several agonizing minutes to allow time for Regina to travel home, I started calling to try to reach her. Nothing. I tried texting and emailing saying, "I really need to speak with you. I love you." Nothing. Her lack of response felt like I was buried alive and suffocating in a coffin.

Feeling more desperate, I texted her, "We have too much invested in each other to cut it off in a single instant. We owe it to ourselves to talk this through. We owe it to our hearts."

Again, it was an excruciating black hole! Shit. I decided to take a shower. Feeling the hot water pour over my head, along with the repetitive water sound, tends to clear my head and pull me off a ledge. But when I got in the water and exposed myself to those healing negative ions, I still felt buried alive. I left the shower to text her one more thought I had: *"One of our rules we set up was not to play emotional games in with our relationship."*

The more I thought about it, the more I couldn't stand that she was playing this non-communication game. My suffocation feeling turned toward anger. I thought, "Ok, maybe I screwed up somehow, but that doesn't make the silent treatment okay. We had a freaking rule."

I hopped back in the shower to try again. But my mind was still a swirling mess of sorrow, confusion, anger, and deep yearning. All of the sudden, my phone started ringing!! Holy shit! I jumped out of the shower and sprung for the phone. Sure enough, it was Regina calling. I stood there sopping wet for the conversation that went like this:

>**ME**
>*Regina!*
>
>**REGINA**
>(Clearly under emotional strain)
>*We had another rule, didn't we?*
>
>**ME**
>*Regina. Thanks so much for calling! What other rule?*
>
>**REGINA**
>*Think about it.*
>
>**ME**
>*No playing games. That's all I remember.*
>
>**REGINA**
>*And no third parties in our slave game... EVER!*
>
>**ME**
>*Oh. Of course. But...*
>
>**REGINA**

Victoria was a third party.

ME
What? She just stopped by to catch up.

REGINA
While we were in the middle of a sexy scene with each other!

ME
Regina? Really? Are you really thinking I violated the rule by having Victoria over?

REGINA
I was chained up as your sexual slave. There was a third party involved.

ME
But she wasn't involved. In fact, I ended up telling her that you were my life-long soulmate and sexual fantasy come true and that you were chained up in the laundry room. She really wanted to see you to check if I was lying or not. But I told her I would never in a million years break that trust I have with you. I would never involve a third person like that.

REGINA
She was involved.

ME
I feel terrible. I didn't think you would feel that way.

REGINA
Feel that way? It's like you don't accept the fact that a third person was involved. Fuck.

ME
Regina. I swear to God I had no idea having Victoria over

> *would bother you or be breaking the third party rule. I was just so excited to finally share with someone about our relationship. It felt good to admit that I am in love with you. I think I needed to get it out into the open. I'm really in love with you.*

There was a big, long pause from Regina's side. I was starting to get really cold from standing naked and dripping. The conversation continued:

> **ME**
> *I must say, I was actually getting really turned on that you were chained up as my slave while I was casually having lunch with a friend. Isn't that what you want in your sexual fantasies? Don't you love the idea that you could be tied up and helpless while I am having a relaxing lunch as I completely "ignore" you? I thought it would be hot for you. You know, my slave isn't worthy of being at my lunch and has to wait to suffer alone until I'm good and ready to stop her punishment. I swear, I was getting turned on by that idea and I thought you would too.*
>
> **REGINA**
> *Maybe that could be hot if I had agreed to it in advance.*
>
> **ME**
> *So it was the surprise that bothered you?*
>
> **REGINA**
> *Fuck if I know. I just felt stupid.*
>
> **ME**
> *I'm really sorry, Regina. Do you think you would have felt differently if you had previously met Victoria?*
>
> **REGINA**
> *I dunno.*

ME

Is it because she's a girl? How would you have felt if I had my office buddy Pete over for lunch instead?

REGINA

(Thinking pause)
Maybe that wouldn't bother me as much.
But I would still want to know in advance.

ME

I'm really sorry, Regina. I guess I didn't think it through very well. I swear I never meant to make you feel bad or violate your trust by bringing in a third person.

REGINA

When we play the game, emotions are heightened. As your slave, I feel a hundred times more vulnerable. I started playing all these head trips on myself that you were flirting with Victoria the whole time and that I was the butt of a joke.

ME

Oh no. I'm so sorry. You have to believe me that I don't feel anything like that for her!! Nothing at all!! We have been buddies forever. That's all it could ever be. Do you believe me?

REGINA

Yes. I believe you. I realize you didn't know it would upset me.
(Thinking a moment)
I want to meet her.

ME

Ok. I'll arrange something. You'll see that we merely have camaraderie and a history. Nothing else. I swear.

REGINA

It's ok. I'm ok now, Meg. Well, except that my face is all puffy and red from crying so much.

ME
Mine too. I love you, Regina.

REGINA
I love you too.
(Long pause)
Can I whip you?

ME
Whip me? You mean in the game?

REGINA
No. I want to whip Meg, not the Mistress.

ME
You want to whip me?

REGINA
Yes.

ME
Ok. You can.

REGINA
Leave a key under the mat and handcuff yourself to the bed with your bottom up.

ME
Jesus. You mean right now.

REGINA
I need some catharsis.

ME
Ok. So, you're going to come over to whip Meg?

But the call went dead. She had hung up on me. Never have I been so happy to have someone hang up on me. We were going to be ok. We worked it all out. I felt like I could fly!

I dried myself off as fast as I could and put a key under the mat. I raced to my bedroom, found my new corset and put it on, and laced it as best as I could by myself. It was pretty tight, but nothing like the feeling when Regina had done it. I handcuffed my wrists together to the lower headboard railing. My ass was exposed as she had requested.

Can you say rollercoaster of emotions? That was the big fight and it looked like make-up sex was up next. Then there was this whole confusion about our slave game. Clearly, she was going to dominate me. Did that mean she was no longer going to be my slave? Did that mean the roles had completely reversed in a single instant? Even though I was excited to see what was going to happen, I really wasn't ready to give up my slave. I wasn't ready to stop topping her. Like I said, rollercoaster city.

I heard the front door open and I felt myself literally dripping with anticipation. I was super turned on to have myself exposed like that. I was so curious.

Regina came into the room, not saying a word. No bright smiles or forgiving expression. She just looked at me coldly. But it wasn't the same sterile expression she had when she was chained up and emotionally wounded. This cold stare was full of emotion that read, "Hey you, Girl – The one in the corset; now you are going to pay."

I really couldn't believe this was all happening. She went to my closet and pulled out a plain leather belt, then stood over me menacingly. Even though my face was down, I could feel her staring at me. Still, she didn't say a word.

Smack!! I felt a soft blow from the belt. It felt like magic. Then there was dead silence for what must have been two minutes. What was she doing? What was she thinking? Whatever was going on, the giant lapse had me dripping even more than I thought was possible. I was hoping she was going to shove a giant dildo up me and fuck me blue. It was such an unbearable anticipation.

Smack!! She hit me again, this time a bit harder. Smack!! Another blow came after only a second. Smack!! A hard one came a second later. Smack!! Now with the steady pace of a metronome, she whipped me with the belt at a consistent medium painful level. Smack!! Smack!! It must have been thirty blows at a second apart. Now it was starting to hurt. I was moaning with equal parts pain and ecstasy. Instead of craving more spankings, I was ready for our bonding. I really wanted her to kiss me and fondle my clitoris.

But that didn't happen. Smack!! She kept up the pace of a whipping every second. The blows were getting more severe. She still never said anything. I moaned and whined under the pain. Smack!! She kept the pace. My ass was on fire. I was starting to really struggle to get away and felt the handcuffs cutting into my wrists. Smack!! She kept going.

Pretty soon, I was really in pain. It was beyond sexual. It was raw pain. I begged her to stop. Really. I was begging her as in, "Please! Please stop!! I can't take any more! Please!! PLEASE STOP!! I BEG YOU!! PLEASE" But she wouldn't stop. I started to thrash around involuntarily against the pain. Then I started to cry. Smack!! She kept going. I turned into a bundle of nerves, bawling at full force and begging her with all my might under my tears, "PLEAAAAAAASSEE STOPPPPP!"

And she did. It was quiet. Again, I could feel her staring at me as I lied there sobbing, handcuffed. I was literally weeping uncontrollably. There was nothing left in me.

Finally, she put her hand on my shoulder with a soft and loving touch. It was just a hand, but it conveyed everything. It conveyed that the revenge was over. It conveyed that I was safe. It conveyed that she loved me.

She got the handcuff key from the nightstand and unlocked me. I immediately turned over on the bed and extended my arms to beckon her. She came to me and we hugged souls. We hugged and gave gentle kisses to the neck and cheek. My ass still burned like a blowtorch wound. But the hugging and connecting did a great job of masking the discomfort of a non-consensual whipping.

Pulling back the sheets, she gestured for me to crawl in; which I did. She joined me in bed and we hugged some more. The contact was heavenly. During the hug, she untied my corset and gradually unlaced it, then tossed it to the floor. She broke the embrace long enough to remove all her clothes and our sexy brick boots. We were two nude lovers in bed, two girls together… staring in each other's trusting eyes.

After a long, but silent communication, she started to softly cry and finally spoke:

> **REGINA**
> *I really wanted to hurt you. I'm so sorry. That was infantile of me. I don't like surprises like that. I don't want to be the butt of a joke.*
>
> **ME**
> *Regina, I know more than anyone exactly what you mean. That's why I despise April Fool's day. I promise I will always protect our boundaries.*
>
> **REGINA**
> *And I promise I will never harm you again outside of the game. I love you, Meg.*

Needless to say, I melted and offered a warm smile that forgave her for her revenge. She didn't need to hear the verbal words. Our connection said it all. And then came a sweet chuckle from her. "I don't want to dominate you. I want to be your slave," she confessed. Chuckling myself and taking note of the pain on my ass, I responded with "Thank, God!"

We French kissed. It was easy. It was natural. We fell asleep together, totally nude. We slept straight through until …

--- MONDAY APRIL 2 --- Making sense of surprises

"Oh Crap!", Regina blared out, alarming me from a dead sleep! She sprung from bed and started throwing her clothes on. "Oh no! It's 7:20! I gotta get to school. I can't believe I slept so long."

I offered to make her a quick cup of coffee, but she had to race home for her papers and a change of clothes. She told me to stay in bed and we would catch up later. It was the start of a Tucker week, so it would be a while until we saw each other in person again. As she was about to take off, she stopped by the bed for a brief connection of looking in my eyes and a sweet little kiss. She kissed each of my boobies too. "Can I see your ass?" she requested. I pulled down the covers so she could get a look. GASP! She was visibly affected by the sight of my bruised up and cut up ass. It had welts all over the entire surface of both cheeks and thin horizontal cuts where the belt had occasionally broken the skin.

She instantly recoiled in remorse. Clearly, she felt awful about doing this to me. Very sincerely, she said, "Oh My! I feel so bad. I'm really sorry, Meg. I didn't mean for it to go that far." Even though I was really feeling the pain of her whipping, I wanted to assure her that everything was cool, "Don't worry. Everything is ok. We are clear. There is no problem. It might be very hard to sit at work today, but I will be reminded of you any time I move in my chair. I like that."

Regina made a funny little "painful" face as if she could directly feel my wounds. "Ok. I can't wait to be your slave again," she commented. "You mean the mistress's slave," I corrected her. "Yes," she assured me, "That's what I meant." Worried about any more delays, I told her to take off. What a naughty little teacher! We shared a solid hug and a light kiss, and then she dashed out.

Aching along, I dragged my pathetic submissive ass to the kitchen to make some much-needed Black Cat coffee (a San Francisco brand that blasts out flavor). I put the teapot on and prepped the French press. At that point, I noticed both my wrists had perfect circular lines around them from where the handcuffs had been cutting in during my whipping. In fact, I had never had outwardly visible residual marks from kinky play. They were so prominent on my wrists that it would be awkward to explain away.

Instead of having flashbacks to the torturous struggle I had endured, the sight of the cuts took me to the sexiest part of the evening. It brought me right to that moment when Regina was standing over me with the belt… just staring down at me as I was in that vulnerable position. I was remembering the how unbelievably turned on I was with anticipation. The handcuff cuts gave me that same sexy feeling teenagers get when they get hickies and are proud they have them. It's a mark of having had an exceedingly passionate sexual encounter. (Later when I was making the bed, I discovered lots of little bloodstains from my wrists and ass).

I kicked on the heater and settled into the sofa with my coffee to wake up. Sitting there, I meandered through a bunch of thoughts as I reflected on the night before. First off all, I was really glad April Fool's day was over. I don't like surprises and luckily nobody punked me.

Speaking of surprises, I was coming to understand how Regina was so hurt by me surprising her with Victoria's visit. Reading between the lines with Regina, it was easy to see that she was, in fact, jealous. There I was, dominating her and sexually controlling her in a very private and intimate experience. Then suddenly, that privacy is pierced by a new person who could be seen as a threat to the moment or even the relationship. And not knowing Victoria, Regina could easily think that Victoria may unfavorably judge Regina as one of those S&M clowns from the movies like "The Gimp" in *Pulp Fiction.*

Without the right setup of context or mindset, most people who would hear of someone being chained up alone in the laundry room, would think it is some kind of joke or fucked up mental disorder. So in that sense, I can understand how Regina felt violated. It was pretty uncool of me to play the game knowing Victoria was coming and not tell Regina in advance.

However from my perspective, I thought it was fantastically hot to think that I had a beautiful woman chained and waiting for me while I took my sweet time to visit with a friend. Thinking of the power... the sexual power, is super arousing to me. It seemed like Regina would have been totally cool with it if she had known Victoria first and if I had told her about the visit first.

I'm positive that when the two of them finally meet, Regina will clearly see that my rapport with Victoria is anything but romantic. I think it could be a really hot element to include from time to time in our games. For example, I think it would be amazingly sexy to bind and gag Regina in the trunk of my car, then pick up Victoria for a trip to the movies. Of course, Regina would be left in the trunk while I enjoyed popcorn with Victoria.

After the movie, I would drop Victoria at her house and then ravish Regina with loving passion afterward. I would prove to her that being tied up in the trunk would have rewards far greater than the discomfort of being restrained during a movie. I would be the most loving mistress in the world, rubbing her feet, giving her a bubble bath, and reinforcing that she was loved and had served me brilliantly. But of course, it would all depend on Regina's consent to redefining the *no third party* rule, which I will never violate again.

See what a little dark coffee can do to me after a ride on an emotional rollercoaster! In further analyzing last night, I reflected about that whole submissive element that reared its head for me.

It was interesting how dominant and callous Regina became. I had never seen anything like that with her. She was a completely different person. Our sexual roles were one hundred percent reversed. For me, it was easy and comfortable to be submissive to her. And she seemed ultra-comfortable as my dominant. Like I've said, I always craved kink in the worst way. It really doesn't matter who is wielding the whip as long as it's sincere and both people are on the same page.

Given the choice, I would prefer to be dominant over Regina. I love that feeling of controlling her and bossing her. It feels hyper-sexual for me to see her perfect yoga body in restraints.

What was particularly interesting about her domination last night was that she was using it outside of our game. She was dominating me from her real-world personality as an outlet for having been emotionally hurt by me. At first, I didn't mind that she was harming me outside of the game. But when she wouldn't stop, I was starting to get really scared. I was in so much pain and my trust was starting to fade in her. It almost seemed like she had snapped into a true sadist who wanted to torture me for real. It wasn't fun any more.

But when the beating stopped, my trust came rushing back. I knew that she had slipped and lost touch a bit. I didn't blame her. She was just working out some emotions from feeling really violated by me just a little while before. This whole relationship (and all its peculiar sexual trappings) is new to both of us and we are trying to sort it out and make sense of everything as we speed along getting closer to each other. I really don't blame her for crossing the line into sadism. And upon reflection, I'm sure she doesn't blame me for bringing Victoria into our private scene. When you are doing something this extreme and emotional for the first time, it seems natural to have a bit of a bumpy road while working out the kinks ;-)

--- MONDAY APRIL 2 --- Just before lunch

Dear Diary, My butt is killing me!! It is so freaking sore! For the past hour, I've been writing in you and need to take an immediate break to get off my seat. Oh, and I ended up wearing a top with overly long sleeves to hide my wrist hickies. Back later.

--- MONDAY APRIL 2 --- Back at home

The rest of my workday was great. I swear I rock that job! It seems so easy for me to excel. Everyone loves me there and I never disappoint. Out of college, I always thought jobs would suck. But this gig really suits me and I'm so efficient at it that I can easily get my work done in thirty percent of the time that they think it requires!

When I make calls, I don't beat around the bush. I always tell the person on the other end that I only have a couple minutes until I need to be somewhere else. Invariably, they accommodate and we get the call done in three or four minutes, but anybody else could have taken a half hour messing around with un-related conversation. Anyway, I get paid for doing a good job and keeping our production company moving. So it really doesn't matter if I do it fast. They are still getting quality work out of me.

But man… my butt was killing me so much I had to take an Advil. I never take stuff like that. I pulled down my skirt in the restroom to check it out. The welts had turned to bruises. I took a selfie of my ass and texted it to Regina with a note saying, "Thinking of you!" But rather than laughing about it, she still seemed sensitive and responded with. "Ouch! I'm so sorry!" And of course, that led to a big sexting session on her lunch break that went like this:

>**REGINA**
>*I promise I'll make it up to you.*
>
>**ME**
>*Oh, you'll make it up to me alright. Actually, you'll be making it up to your mistress.*
>
>**REGINA**
>*I would love to please her in anyway I could.*
>
>**ME**
>*Can you believe how blue the sky is today?*
>
>**REGINA**
>*Yes, Mistress. How may I please you?*
>
>**ME**
>*You can tell me that you love me.*

REGINA
I adore you, Mistress. I love you with all my heart. I want you more than anything.

ME
Tonight, I'm going to sleep in the corset you gave me.

REGINA
If it pleases you, Mistress. Forgive me for not being present tonight. I have obligations.

ME
Yes. I'm perfectly aware of that. I'm going to have to punish you severely for neglecting me with your other "obligations".

REGINA
Yes, Mistress.

ME
You will need to be tied and gagged in the garage for a long time. You will need to feel some pain on your nipples.

REGINA
Yes, Mistress.

ME
You will need to have a dildo shoved up your ass that you will have to keep in place the whole time you are being punished. Do you understand?

But there was no reply from Regina.

ME
You must answer me. Do you understand?

Minutes ticked by. Pretty soon it was ten whole minutes! Finally, a new text popped in.

> **REGINA**
> *Forgive me, Mistress. I was unable to control myself. Went to restroom to pleasure myself. Thought about serving you.*
>
> **ME**
> *That is unacceptable. You can never do that without my permission.*
>
> **REGINA**
> *Yes, Mistress. I am weak to your allure.*
>
> **ME**
> *Weak and pitiful.*
>
> **REGINA**
> Yes, Mistress.
>
> **ME**
> *That was some kind of crazy day I had.*
>
> **REGINA**
> *Me too, Meg. I gotta get back to class. I love you.*
>
> **ME**
> *I love you too.*

And that was our little sexting tryst for the afternoon. I can't believe Regina's audacity. Not only did she do herself at work, but she did it without her Mistress's approval. Oh well. She'll reap what she sows.

As I wound down with a glass of wine at home after work, I was thinking more about how she turned crazy sadist on me and how I had betrayed her by bringing in a third party. We had both done something that had tested each other's trust. We had both acted without consent of the other.

But we came through it. Something else came through it too. From the minute we awoke this morning, I was feeling like there was a fundamental shift in our relationship. We were different now. I'm sure she feels it too. I'd like to talk with her about it. But things are very different. You cannot un-ring a bell. You cannot unbake a cake.

We both went through something very emotional together, something very traumatic. Even though it was of our own fault, we went through something hard. In the wake of it all, I noticed that there is much more solidity to us, more gravity. Our relationship changed from honeymoon love to solid, sober, unyielding love. The momentary trouble was a rehearsal for how we would be in the event of even heavier circumstances or obstacles that we are bound to encounter.

It was an emotional breakthrough. We are ready to be with each other through thick and thin, corny as that may sound. We are wiser. Strangely, having violated each other's trust ended up making that trust stronger. I never want to hurt her again. I never want to make her distrust me.

When I was in 8th grade, I thought it would be fun to try alcohol for the fist time on New Year's Eve with my girlfriends. The parents were out of the house and we were raiding the liquor cabinet. Before you knew it, we were plastered and started calling every boy in school to flirt and reveal secrets. I liked the feeling so much and wanted to keep it going. So I started chugging scotch and rum. Disgusting. But having no prior experience with alcohol, I quickly found myself in over my head. I completely blacked out, waking up the next morning completely naked in a fetal position in my friend's bedroom. I asked my girlfriend's what had happened.

They said that I was puking all over myself and they had to take off my clothes because they were so gross. Apparently I had completely ruined my friend's carpet. So in the morning, I was freezing and freaked out when I discovered myself like that. I stood up to try to find something to put on, but immediately started puking all over again.

Lucky I didn't die from alcohol poisoning. But after that, I vowed to never ever do that again. I never wanted to be so helpless and scared again. I vowed to never pass out drunk again as long as I lived. And you know what? That's how it's been. Sure, I get a little drunk now and then, but I never let myself lose control. I will never drink to that point again. I changed that night.

It is the same way with Regina. I never want to lose her trust again. I want to be good for her. I want her to believe in me. So last night was a healthy step towards solidifying everything we are to each other. We aren't going to wake up naked in a fetal position.

I just called over there to say hi and see how Tucker is. She seemed so happy to be with him. She said he was really clingy after being gone so long. He's got some new video game he was excited about and he was trying to teach her to play it. She made him soy hot dogs, mac & cheese, and broccoli. After dinner, she told him that she is really excited about having me as a friend. He asked who is better at yoga. Of course, Regina joked that she kicks my butt. Too bad it's true ;-)

After dinner, she read to him for a half hour in bed from a Shel Silverstein book. Even though Tucker knows how to read perfectly, there's nothing like being next to your mom as she reads Shel Silverstein. That's because Silverstein is a book of crazy short rhymes that are geared toward older kids. The themes are a little dark. Regina read me a chapter on the phone. I'm not even her son, but I loved hearing the crazy, lyrical rhyming. I can only imagine being Tucker and having her next to me and seeing her form those words with her darling mouth!

When I said goodnight to Regina, I suddenly felt lonely, kind of like an outsider. She had the full life and I had half the life. Even so, I was warm inside about my feelings for her and where we were going together. The funny thing was, my bruised ass was still hurting a lot. It was a souvenir of our time together, something to remember her by. But just like a souvenir, it never really can bring back the full joy of being in Paris and serves more to show how mundane life is after the holiday is over. It's kind of like the Monday blues after the weekend.

--- TUESDAY APRIL 3 --- Daily Life Connection

Regina woke me up this morning with a call to say "Hi" while Tucker was in the shower. Because she was in Mommy mode, I was embarrassed to tell her that I slept in my corset with my ankles tied together. It was a quick, but nice little call. After we hung up, I started thinking of how Regina had been chained in the laundry room while I was with Victoria. The corset helped to bring me closer to Regina. I was recalling how good if felt when she first cinched it on me in the restaurant bathroom. I thought about kissing her and licking her. It didn't take long before I was starting my day with a bang. Hi ho, Hi ho, off to work I went.

The rest of the day was pretty standard. But having Regina in my life really gave an extra bounce to my step, as they say. Everything seemed to have a sunshiny feeling. I usually don't get too wrapped up in my troubles, but the feeling all day was bright and cheery. It was love, alright.

There's a little shop by my work where I came across a perfect postcard to send to Regina. It was a vintage-looking black and white card of Bettie Page with her hands hoisted above her head in bondage and a ball-gag jammed in her mouth. The little thought bubble coming out of Bettie's head said, "Every girl needs a little time out now and then." Of course, I bought the card and jotted down on it, "Worship me. – *Your Owner.*) I popped it in an envelope, stuck a stamp on it and sent it off to my little plaything.

We texted each other quite a bit, sending photos of our daily lives. It all started when I asked for a shot of her classroom. And she asked for a shot of my desk. It was great to see a concrete visual to help picture each other's worlds. She also shot me a picture of Jonathan Martin, III, the class guinea pig. I guess kids take turns taking him home for the weekends (God only knows how they came up with that for a name). Then a few minutes later when the class was on break, she shot me a little 10-second movie of Jonathan Martin, III cruising around on the carpet. He just "happened" to be crawling around our brick red boots she was wearing to school. Ding! Nice job getting me turned on, you little tease!

When I got back home, I shot her a fifteen second movie of a pile of dirty dishes in my sink. My off-camera commentary was, "I hope you want to still be my friend knowing what a slob I am. Guess the maid took the day off."

After her school day, she texted that she was really happy having Tucker back. They were having a nice time together. She was grading papers and baking with him. They made brownies with marshmallows and chocolate chips inside. Yum!

After Tucker had gone to bed, she cozied in to watch her soap opera. That is still so funny to me! We texted about once an hour until she finally pooped out at about 10pm. School teachers need a lot of rest on school nights, especially when they two-time as a sex slave.

--- WEDNESDAY APRIL 4 --- Regina's X

More Tucker. Normally, Tucker returns to his dad's (Alex) on Wednesday evenings and every other weekend. But this week, Regina is helping out Alex by taking Tucker all the way until the next Wednesday to help cover some kind of trip Alex is taking. Luckily, he reciprocates when she needs the extra coverage. Regina still can't believe Alex got 50/50 custody, considering all his past drug use, drinking, and erratic behavior. But few people see that side of him. He's good at hiding it. Tucker never describes any bad episodes and Alex treats him like a prince.

Apparently, Alex went after Regina with top-tier lawyers. The custody was not as much about having Tucker, but about punishing Regina. But she thinks that Tucker does a great job of ignoring all the bad stuff Alex does. She also said that Alex isn't a total dick all the way through… or she wouldn't have married him in the first place. He is more like manic-depressive. He's great when he's great. He's terrible when he's terrible. He's like a petulant child with a big bank account and a lot of power because of it. His grandparents were in Texas oil and it still keeps pumping!

It's pretty hard to imagine Regina or Tucker with a Jekyll and Hyde who has the ability to be so awful to people. She also feels that Alex won't harm Tucker when she is not there. She has spied on them a few times and Alex is very loving with Tucker. Regina says Alex's hatred was always triggered by Regina being in the mix and calling him on his bullshit. Without Regina there to push his buttons, the temper is more or less diffused in the home. It's hard to be angry and fight against someone who is not there. It would be like if Alex went hiking alone somewhere. There is nothing to trigger a fight with himself. Perhaps from fear of witnessing past aggression, Tucker tends to mind Alex and lay low so that nothing can suddenly aggravate things. Kids are smart that way. They do what they have to in order to stay out of the fray. Tucker has made a few comments about how his dad often blows up at people on the phone.

Alex takes Tucker to the park for Frisbee and baseball time. Regina says if you took a picture of them, they would look like a living Hallmark Father's day card. But Alex has real demons. I can't even imagine how someone could ever find enough anger to harm Regina, the embodiment of grace and warmth. So glad she got out of there!

Anyway, looks like it will be a while until I can share one-on-one time with Regina. It's cool, though. I can use the time to catch up with things. It would be great to visit with Victoria again, but I don't dare do that until she meets Regina. I don't want to fuel any jealousy Regina may have. But I would like to go out with Pete (the gay guy from my office) some time. He's so funny! I can never be with him without getting a good belly laugh. He also has a sincere and philosophical side that I love. He's a solid guy with no baggage or drama. You gotta love that.

--- THURSAY APRIL 5 --- Calendar days

It was a typical day of missing Regina. We had a few texts back and forth, but not as many as yesterday. I figure she was just getting momentum in her mommy/teacher groove. I didn't want to bug her.

But every once in a while, just when I was clearing my head with some distractions, she would surprise me with a text about how she missed me. It was really nice hearing from her. I didn't always want to be the one to initiate things. Noticeably missing were any texts from the slave Regina. I wondered if she was deliberately refraining from contacting the mistress or if slave Regina was no longer present while in mommy mode. Hmmm.

But then a text came in: "This is slave Regina. I'm most grateful for the correspondence I received from you today. Very thoughtful! Thank you, Mistress." Obviously, she had received my Bettie Page postcard. I didn't give her the dignity of a reply.

--- FRIDAY APRIL 6 --- Apart but connected, right?

I went to yoga last night. Regina wasn't there. It felt really strange to me. I knew that she loves me, but not seeing her at yoga felt like she was not into me anymore. I know that is stupid and unrealistic. But I was kind of taking it personally. Call me a baby, but I want her to be everywhere I expect her to be.

I'll hit yoga again tonight. I bet she won't be there so I will try to use my big girl brain to tell myself that out-of-sight is not necessarily out-of-mind. For all I know she probably let Tucker play his Minecraft video game and was masturbating about me as I was in yoga class. Either way, I'm not real fond of being away from her.

As for the rest of my day, it was pretty good. Pete and I went out to lunch together. We took a hefty two hours. Of course, when he asked me what was going on, I had to tell him the whole story about Regina. Surprisingly, he was more shocked by the fact that I was in love with a woman than the fact that she was kinky. I mean, here's a gay guy surprised by someone else being gay (Am I gay? I guess that's what I am now?).

To me, the really shocking thing would be that I have a sex slave. He told me that the shock came from him completely misreading me as the straightest person imaginable. But to him, the kink was more of an activity than a sexual orientation. No matter how hard I tried to explain it to him, he couldn't grasp the fact that being kinky is a true sexual identity. Whatever. It's like I said before, sexuality is really complex and doesn't fit into a neat box.

Even in the kink world, nothing is standardized. There are for-real masochists who REALLY love pain by itself, as opposed to masochists like Regina who only love discomfort when it is at the hands of her lover. There are fetishists like me who can get turned on by wearing thigh high boots. But then there are other barefoot fetishists who think thigh high boots are a disgusting, obscuring of the legs and feet. There are transvestites who aren't gay and there are gays who are transvestites. It's all over the freaking map.

Pete was really supportive. He said that he had known something was up with me because I have been daydreaming and less talkative than usual and showing all the other signs of a person with new love.

After work, I went to the movies alone. I like doing that. It was a French flick about a teenage boy who fell in love with his best friend's mom.

I wore my corset under a loose sweater and felt sexy. I had a secret. "Regina" was hugging me around my waste very tightly for the whole evening. Sometimes when I thought about the feel of the snug corset mildly restricting my breathing, I found myself getting moist. I wore my thigh boots and black leggings, resting my legs on the chair in front of me in a mostly empty theater. None of the people in the movie had any idea that I had my own private property, a beautiful woman who would love to polish my boots with her tongue as I enjoyed the movie. Too bad she wasn't with me to prove it!

--- SATURDAY APRIL 7 --- Blurred Boundaries!

Dear Diary, Waking up on a Saturday without any Regina plans on my calendar is a bit depressing. Obviously, she has her life and I have mine, but when you're in love, it's hard to be apart.

I started the morning with a nice bath and a latte. A great bath usually helps my spirits. For me, a great bath always includes a mellow and soulful playlist. It's amazing how much music can turn and shape a person's mood.

Sure enough, just as I settled into the suds and took my first sip of the latte, one of my favorite songs came up: Nina Simone's classic "Real, Real". The lyrics go like this:

> *I say, real, real*
> *Our love is real to me*
> *It thrills me*
> *With perfect liberty*
>
> *When you tell me you love me*
> *And you hold me and kiss me*
> *Then I know it's real, real*
> *It's so real to me*
>
> *I say, real, real*
> *Our love is real to me*
> *Please thrill me*
> *With your kisses sweet*
>
> *Tell your papa and your mama*
> *One day soon we're gonna*
> *Have a great weddin' day*
> *It's so real to me*

So there I was in my blissful bath, listening to this blissful song about love when the lyrics suddenly jar me. "One day we're gonna have a great wedding day." Crap. That's a lot of pressure. It's one thing to be in love, but it's another thing to consider where the relationship is headed. It's one thing to think about going on a date, having some fun, and kinking it up a bit. But where is it headed? Where is it supposed to lead?

The way I see it, there are pretty much only three paths. Path number one: Breakup. Path number two: Long term monogamy. Path number three: Commitment forever (aka marriage). And number two (long term monogamy) seems just like marriage except that it preserves the angst of being perpetually unsure of when the relationship may take a turn to option number one, the breakup. And then there are all those nebulous legalities of legal marriage between the same sex. Fuck.

After a healthy dating period, for me, the real choices are either breakup or marriage. I mean, what's the point of staying together without a solid commitment as a couple? It would only be a means of postponing the inevitable breakup when either party tires of the other's ways or seeks greener pastures.

It could be argued that marriage could and often does just as easily end from the same fate. But the thing about marriage is that both parties state a solid intention to be together forever. That means you can plan. You can stop with the dating scene. You can buy a house together. You can invest in the relationship... nurture it. Sure it can blow up, but the intention is there to build on.

To me, long-term monogamous dating for years is like renting a home versus buying a home. When you rent, you are not as likely to invest in the property with improvements because you know it is only temporary. You are less likely to get involved in the community for the same reason. By contrast, owing a home gives one the confidence of knowing that any improvements or personal investments in the home or community can be foundations for a more solid and positive future. You can always lose your home from circumstance, but at least you can bloom until then.

In a marriage, there could always be a fire or a divorce or any other number of unfortunate circumstances that remove all the gain of any personal or financial investment. But if those things don't occur, the relationship will be better off in many ways. It will have a foundation, a base, onto which improvements can have a cumulative and multiplying effect.

Baths are usually really relaxing to me, but I spent the whole time running scenarios about my future with Regina.

Yeah, yeah. I know it all sounds really premature. We have only been together a few weeks. But I don't really see much point in barking up the wrong tree, emotionally investing in someone and heading down a path that will lead to heartache. I need to ask myself if Regina is someone I could potentially be married to.

It sounds so stupid when I put it in such black and white terms. Then there is the whole problem that we are both women! Two women marrying each other is even harder to digest for me and everyone else than two women having a little dating exploration. When two women are married, it is called "gay." It is not called, "I'm actually straight, but I just happened to meet the right person who happened to be a woman."

So the question regarding the future of our relationship is now expanded into two big questions: One: Is Regina marriage material? And, two: Could I be married to a woman and accept the "gay" label? Could she? Okay, that was actually three heavy questions. But really, Regina would have to be okay with the gay thing too.

What a fucked up bath! After I got out of the water with my head spinning, I got a *good morning* call from Regina. Hearing her voice (and feeling the buzz between us) grounded me again. Talking with her made me feel like that big decision about our future doesn't have to be made for a long time. We are great together in the present. We care for each other and lust for each other. I just need to keep my head in the present and go with the good feelings that Regina brings.

It was a brief phone call, but it was really necessary to assure me that we are on the perfect course, wherever that may lead us. It is just a matter of focusing on the present and enjoying all aspects of the relationship as it unfolds.

Regina said she missed me a lot. She's been having a nice time with Tucker. She made French toast today and discovered he only likes pancakes. He wasn't being a brat about it, but he didn't care for the egg flavor of the French toast. Never mind the fact that she has made it for him multiple times for the past 9 years. She chocked it up to him coming into his own personality with his own tastes.

I must say I still feel a little jealous that Regina has this whole life outside of my relationship with her. It's like I only get to share half of her.

To shake off my obsessive desire to be with Regina for the day, I called up Pete, who was fresh on my mind and asked if he would like to go rollerblading with me in the Marina today. He's not much of an outdoor guy, but he welcomed the opportunity. We decided to meet over there, skate a while, then have a late lunch. Perfect.

I showed up at the Marina and Pete showed up too… with his boyfriend! He commented, "I hope you don't mind if Ed joins us too. His other plans got canceled."

Dammit. Ed is a cool guy and he is a good fit with Pete, but I was looking forward to hanging with Pete by himself. Oh well, it was a nice enough time. But as they say, three's a crowd. Plus, it was hard to see them with their PDA's and inside flirting jokes and not have Regina with me to do the same thing. When it came time to have lunch, I wasn't into it anymore and told them I was going to bail to take a nap.

I went home and poured a glass of wine and watched the Discovery channel about how Hawaii was formed. Lava is sexy the way is oozes and undulates. As the wine kicked in, I found myself daydreaming about Regina. During one of the commercials, I decided to get a little kinky with myself. I went to my new kink stash and pulled out some handcuffs and small vibrator. Stopping by my closet, I grabbed my thigh high boots and put them on. The second that leather hits my legs, I feel ten times sexier. Sitting back down with the lava show, I handcuffed my ankles together over the boots. The lava was a pleasant and neutral visual that let my mind drift.

I pretended I had handcuffed Regina's ankles in the boots and that I was she. Slowly, I rubbed myself with my fingers very softly. The more I studied Regina's ankles in the handcuffs, the more turned on I got. I imagined that my mistress had given me full permission to go all the way and I turned on the vibrator.

It was really hot being Regina. It was hot to be owned by my mistress. The vibrator, the lava, and the bound ankles had their effect on me and I was soon exploding in delight. I let out a passionate scream, something I don't normally do when masturbating, but it erupted from the moment and I was fully embracing the turn-on and the freedom of an empty house.

Completely relaxed, I lied on the sofa with the comfort of my hands between my bound legs and drifted to a warm and gentle sleep.

Next thing I knew, my phone blasted me awake. It was in the kitchen and my ankles were still cuffed. So I let it go to voicemail instead of making a heroic effort to make it to the phone in time.

After uncuffing myself, I walked to the kitchen, still in my thigh highs. Even though I am so accustomed to the sound, it always sounds sexy to me when my boots walk on a hard surface. Heels are hot. They have always been hot!

Sure enough, it was Regina who had tried in vain to reach me. She left no message. Rather than immediately jumping to return her call, I took time to pour myself a sparkling water and make a plate of cheese and assorted green olives.

Once my brain had joined the real world after having been in such a deep sleep, I called her back. As she answered, I felt a rush of warmth in hearing her lovely and familiar voice. It was like connecting with an old friend I had known and loved forever. The conversation proceeded:

> **REGINA**
> *Hey. Whatcha doin'?*
>
> **ME**
> *Nothing. Just woke up from a nap after masturbating about you.*
>
> **REGINA**
> (Laughs)
>
> **ME**
> *It's not funny.*
> (Pause)
> *What are you doing?*
>
> **REGINA**
> *I want to wash your dishes. Can I come over with Tucker and his friend, Jason? There is a new Blaze*

Man movie they want to see. They can watch the movie while I do your dishes.

ME
Regina!

REGINA
Sorry. That was pretty presumptuous of me to invite myself over.

ME
It's not that. We can't be playing the game when Tucker is around. Duh!

REGINA
No. I didn't mean within the game. I would never do that!!

ME
Seriously. We can never do that.

REGINA
I just want to feel close to you and would love to clean your kitchen.

ME
Are you saying I'm a slob? What if it's already spotless?

REGINA
Then I'll vacuum for you.

ME
Too loud if the kids are watching a movie. Besides, what's wrong with just hanging out and talking over popcorn.

REGINA

You don't want me to clean your kitchen?

ME
I'm not saying that. But you don't need to.

REGINA
Yes. I need to. I want to be of service to you.

ME
Regina, We're not in the game. You don't have to serve me.

REGINA
Whatever. Can we come over? I'll order pizza for the boys so there is no hassle for you.

ME
Sure. C'mon over.

REGINA
The boys are going to be so psyched to watch Blaze Man 3 on your huge TV!

ME
And I will be excited to have clean dishes! Just kidding. I just want to hang out with you both and get to know Tucker more.

REGINA
See you soon.

ME
Do me a favor, Regina.

REGINA
Anything.

ME

> *Can you please wear something simple that won't trigger my crazy lust for you?*

REGINA
Don't worry. See you soon.

ME
See you soon.

I did a once-over on my place to make sure it was kid friendly and kink-free. A little while later, they all showed up. Regina, ever the lovely and fashionable one, had followed my request and wore a basic A-line dress in a muted plum. And for shoes, she wore some Keds; only a teacher would own those.

Tucker came right in and gave me a full-blown hug… like he meant it. Either he had attached to me somehow or Regina had been singing my praises… or a combination of both. At first I was a little surprised and didn't know how firmly to reciprocate the hug. But I quickly yielded and startled myself by giving him a kiss right on his mouth! I surely didn't plan that. It just kind of came out of me… as if I was his dear aunt.

Right after that, bouncing Jason (Tucker's acrobatic friend) comes in with full boy energy. He said "hi" and then immediately went into, "Watch this!" Then he dove into a handstand, which morphed into a roll. My banister heading upstairs caught his eye, "Cool!" He proceeded to climb the stairs from the outside of the banister to the alarm of Regina. "Jason," she quickly intervened in her teacher voice, "that's not the best idea. C'mon down please." He quickly obeyed. As he was coming down, he picked something off the floor and exclaimed, "Hey look! The world's tiniest key!"

Taking a look in his hand, I was mortified and instantly blushed as I realized he was holding my handcuff key!! Shit. I grabbed it from his hand with, "Great. Thanks for finding that key to my jewelry box! It's pretty small alright."

They had only been in my place a few seconds and I was already feeling both stupefied and eager to please. Two full-on boys and my beautiful lesbian lover. Nice combo. I didn't know whom to give my attention. So I started with some introductory small talk with the boys about school and their interests.

I asked Jason about his family and was confused when he told me he has no idea how many brothers and sisters he has because some move out to go to college or their own place and others move in. Regina, sensing my confusion, chimed in with "Jason's parents run a foster home. He has a lot of brothers and sisters." If that was the case, Jason sure seemed well-adjusted and outgoing. He and Tucker seemed really close and would finish each other's sentences.

I started the popcorn and set the boys up with their movie in the living room. They were delighted by the size of my screen and the sound of the stereo quality as the trailers played. I turned to Regina:

> **ME**
> *Can I pour you a drink?*
>
> **REGINA**
> *No thanks. I'm fine. Do you want to watch Blaze Man?*
>
> **ME**
> *No. I'd rather sit on the veranda and chat with you?*
>
> **REGINA**
> *I'll clean your dishes. You can sit and talk to me.*
>
> **ME**
> (After a chuckle)
> *Boy, you really want to do the dishes don't you?*
>
> **REGINA**
> *Yes, Mistress.*
>
> **ME**

What!!!!!! Shhhhhhh!!
(Whispering)
We're not playing that!

REGINA
Sorry. It kind of slipped out.

ME
(Pointing to the pile of dishes)
Help yourself.

Regina flashed a warm smile and hopped to washing the dishes.

REGINA
Have you ever seen Blaze Man?

ME
(Taking seat on the counter)
Of course. Who hasn't.
Last year we did a commercial tie-in for Blaze Man 2.

REGINA
How cool. Did you get to meet the actors?

ME
No. They just gave us movie footage to work with.
(Pause)
What did you do today?

REGINA
Mostly just graded papers while Jason and Tucker played Legos and made parachutes out of plastic baggies.

ME
You missed washing off some of the soap on that plate. See the bubbles?

> **REGINA**
> *You're right. Sorry.*

She appeared to have instantly and unexpectedly shifted into her slave personality and seemed ashamed and embarrassed by her mistake. We hadn't enacted the game, but somehow… we seemed to have slipped into it.

> **ME**
> *I don't want to be embarrassed if a guest comes over and discovers that my dishes haven't been rinsed properly.*

> **REGINA**
> *Please forgive me.*

Realizing that things could quickly get out of hand with us, I hopped off the counter and approached her from behind, firmly pulling her by the throat so that her ear was close to my mouth as I whispered: "That was some kind of crazy day I had." It worked. Her eyes changed personalities and I could see Regina again. I continued, "I'm going to go watch Blaze Man with the boys. Come join me." Continuing with the dishes, she responded, "I'll be right out." Just then, the popcorn was done. I took it with me to join the boys on the sofa as Regina kept at the dishes.

The boys seemed happy to see me joining them. I think there is no easier fit than young boys with cute women in their mid-20's. (Of course, that is assuming they would find me cute.)

We watched the movie for quite a while, maybe twenty minutes, before I started to wonder what happened to Regina. Wasn't she coming? I excused myself to go check on her.

When I arrived at the kitchen, I spied on her quietly for a moment. She was scrubbing a dish in her rubber gloves. But her head was clearly somewhere else, some kind of daydream. She had that look that I had only seen on her when she was completely aroused. Was washing the dishes that hot for her? Was she really digging it that much? There was a deeper thought going on.

Stealthily, I crept up on her, then softly surprised her with a gentle hug from the back. She recoiled as if caught red-handed doing something naughty. "Hey," I said, " why don't you come join me on the couch?" She looked at me, mildly ashamed and responded, "Sorry, I'm about done." But when I looked in her eyes, I could see she was still in some kind of fantasy. I gently slid my hand down her hips and slowly went under her skirt where I pushed up against her vulva. Her panties were dripping wet! She was on fire.

Completely surprised by how turned on she was (by merely washing the dishes), I figured I needed to take charge right away. "Can you believe how blue the sky is today?" I wondered out loud. She snapped into slave mode, "Yes, Mistress."

I continued to spell out my demands by whispering coldly in her ear," Listen, I'm very disappointed in you. I'm going to give you one order. Then I am going to go away. Do you understand?" "Yes, Mistress," she answered in near ecstasy. I continued my dark whisper, "You need to go upstairs to my room, put on my boots, and get yourself off. Then I need you to put yourself together and go away. I'm expecting my friend Regina to join me in the living room to watch a movie. Are we clear?" "Yes, Mistress," she whispered back. "Fine," I said, "Good bye." I kissed her ear and whispered, "That was some kind of crazy day I had."

Regina, still the slave, understood that the game was over for me but not for her. She took off her gloves and headed upstairs, completely ignoring me as Meg.

There we were, trying to have a platonic afternoon together and she has to go get herself all worked up washing the dishes. It had the effect of getting my head in the same space, especially since I knew she would be upstairs wearing boots and masturbating. Suddenly, I wanted to go upstairs and join her, instead of going back to the boys.

But acting as the big girl I am, I took a deep breath and let out a sigh to expel my sexual energy. I poured a couple glasses of sparkling water to take to the movie for Regina and I to enjoy once she would finally show up.

The thought crossed my mind that the boundaries of the game were getting blurred and misused. This could lead to trouble. It was the first time that I had given orders within the game and then exited the game while one of us was still playing. I wondered if that was okay or if we would start getting messed up. It could certainly lead to big complications, especially when we are out in public or with friends and family. I think it would be best to keep the game completely separate and go back to the rigid border rules.

The thing is, Regina seemed to have drifted into slave mode while washing my dishes without having a formal start to the game. Fuck. Just imagine if she does that at work or some inappropriate setting. She could get fired, embarrassed, or in some kind of trouble. Or I could. Yeah, we certainly need rules!

After I had been back with the boys… right at the part where Blaze Man and his girlfriend had been captured by the Russians at gunpoint, Regina shows up. And yes, it was the real Regina. She looked like she had just come from a day at the spa. Her cheeks were rosy and her eyes were bright and happy. She was bouncy and light. No trace of the slave anywhere to be found as I handed her mineral water. The boys were happy to see her too. It was a better energy when we were all there and present.

A few moments later, Blaze Man's female sidekick was literally chained at the neck to a dungeon floor as a giant drill was coming down from the ceiling to skewer her. She and Blaze were breathing through a scuba tank setup because the bad guys had removed all the air from the dungeon. Blaze Man, forced to watch her demise by being handcuffed to a machine, was helpless to rescue her. The bad guys had rendered his powers useless by keeping oxygen out of the room. (In case you didn't know, Diary, Blaze Man can only use his powers of fire when there is air in the room).

Regina and I exchanged flirty glances as the bondage of the girl was featured in a prolonged shot. "Don't worry, Mom," reassured Tucker, "they are going to be okay. Watch." Regina responded with an obvious bluff, "How awful to be tied up like that! It would be so scary!!" I shot her a condemning look.

At first, Regina had been sitting in the armchair at the side of the sofa. But to be closer to the popcorn, she squeezed in between me and the sofa arm. The order was, Jason, Tucker, me, and Regina, all sitting in a line. It felt nice to me. It felt like we were all connected and that I was included in Regina's life. Even though it was just the experience of watching a movie, it was a form of connecting us all.

Luckily, for the tied up girl in the movie, Blaze Man kicked the valve off the top of her scuba tank, causing oxygen to escape all over the room. His fire super powers had enough air to be activated. He shot bolts of flames like spears through the bad guys and freed his girl by burning off her chain with laser-focused fire. Too bad, I think Regina and I could have use a little more time of her squirming.

At one point, Regina grabbed my hand as she eagerly watched the plot unfold. That contact melted me. I wanted to hug her and snuggle with her. Too bad. It was a little premature in our relationship to be having PDA's in front of Tucker.

When the movie was over, Regina made comments about having to leave to get back home with the boys. But the boys protested and nagged and wanted to hang out more. I assumed they were both enjoying being in a new space with new energy. I think the chemistry between Regina and I also created a good feeling for them. That type of chemistry is appealing to anybody. It feels safe and fun. It feels joyful. Who doesn't love to be around the feelings of joy?

To help things along, I offered up, "Sure, we can hang out and I'll order Mexican food for dinner. Maybe we can play a board game afterwards. Of course, after that, we'd have to hit *Mr. and Mrs. Miscellaneous Ice Cream Store* on the way back to your house."

There was an chorus of "Please! Please! Please!" from the kids. It was a quadruple win and Regina could stop pretending she had to leave.

So that's what we did. It was really fun. We ordered Mexican and played several rounds of a game called *Telestrations,* which proved to be quite a hit with the boys, even though they may have been a tad young for it. I suck at drawing but it didn't matter in this game. It's a variation of the classic telephone game that uses crude drawing to communicate ideas. There was laughter all around. In fact, we all seemed so free and light playing together. I think Regina was delighted by the idea that I could fit with Tucker and Jason so easily. In other words, the kids seemed to have not only approved of me, but really enjoyed my company too.

The evening perfectly illustrated the contrast of Regina's sexual and vanilla personalities. Here was this quintessential mommy playing board games and watching movies with her boy when, just a few minutes earlier she was pleasuring herself with the kinky thoughts of being sexually controlled by another woman.

It's funny how she can be such an adored and respected schoolteacher and then have this wildly kinky streak. Then again, I guess I'm the same way. I have my work life that is so different from my sexual life. But for me, the contrast between the two worlds seems less sharp because I am a single and have no child depending on me. If Regina weren't a mommy or didn't have a teaching job, I wonder if she would be wild across her whole life.

That's stupid. Of course, she wouldn't. She would just be Regina with the same kinky needs. She would still be a vegetarian with a great fashion sense. She would probably balance it all just like I do. Sex may bleed into my real world, but there is still an overall sense of compartmentalization.

That's where it gets tricky with our game. It should be perfectly compartmentalized. But as I saw in the dishwashing episode, Regina is really longing to serve me... so much so that she may drop her compartmentalizing walls down when it's not appropriate. I think we should have a sit-down talk about it all and make the rules explicitly clear. We don't need problems. Most importantly, we don't want to do anything to cause confusion or unease for Tucker or the others in our lives.

After the evening at my house, we all went to ice cream on the way to Regina's. I drove my own car so that I could get back once Regina and the boys were home. The boys wanted to ride with me, leaving Regina in her own car! I was flattered and so was Regina. To the boys, I figure they were excited about the chance to change it up a bit with something/someone new. Of course, I had to blast the radio, roll down the windows, and hit the crazy San Francisco hill crests with enough speed to make the kids laugh their heads off.

After the ice cream date, we went straight to their house. It was late. Regina told the boys to immediately go brush their teeth and put on their jammies. They each gave me a hug before heading off. It was so sweet!

Regina ended up walking me to my car. We were both smiling at the nice time we had all evening. When I was getting in my car, there was a moment where we ended up staring at each other as enchanted lovers. We kissed. It was a sweet and lovely kiss, without kink. The kissing made me feel really in love. We were in lust too, but this kiss was about honesty and appreciation of each other. I love Regina!

--- SUNDAY APRIL 8 --- Out and About

I woke up this morning feeling great about life. There were no plans to see Regina. Of course, that's what I said yesterday before the whole dishwashing and Blaze Man business.

But I think Regina and I felt comfortable in letting the day pass without being too clingy. That kiss last night will keep me going for quite a while.

Instead of drinking my coffee at home, I decided to cruise over to Pacific Heights to have breakfast at The Grove, a hip coffee joint I've always liked. It's fun to go there because I can window shop in some of the most exclusive shops in San Francisco. Once I saw some Donna Karan boots there that were $1,920! Really, I'm not shitting! The funny thing was, they looked like they were worth every penny. It's hard for many people to understand what separates a two thousand dollar pair of boots from a pair that costs two hundred. Some people think the difference is merely in having a designer label slapped on. But that's completely false.

When I go shopping in Barney's or Nordstrom, I always gravitate toward the most amazing boots on the floor. Many have no clear designer markings at all. But when I turn the boot over to see the price on the bottom; BAM! There it is, a shoe with a price tag over $1,000 dollars. I have good taste! The difference is in how finely the boot is made, stitching quality, nuance in the shape, type of materials, workmanship, etc. The high-end designer shoes and boots have a certain gravitas, a feel of importance that the $100 dollar shoe lacks.

For that matter, it's the same with couture clothing and bags versus the cheaper ones. Maybe they would look similar in a photograph, but in real life the difference stands out like a tulip in the snow.

Needless to say, I'm not going around dropping 2K on shoes. However, I have always heard that male shoe and boot fetishists, guys with really serious fetishes, will buy you shoes and clothes and send them to you free. The only catch is you have to pose in them and post the pictures online. I've heard they want you to thank them online and do particular poses to prove they had the control over you in the photo. Bragging rights, I guess. This whole idea really intrigues me.

But I could never do it. Exposing anything too specific or personal on the net really freaks me out. No way! Instead, I will just have to settle for walking along Fillmore Street for some window-shopping on my way to The Grove.

Anyway, excuse the sidebar. I had a nice breakfast and some great coffee while I took my time reading the paper and answering emails on my laptop. After a while, Regina called. Since I was in the restaurant, I spoke quietly in my phone's mic. She said I sounded sexy.

I told her that I really wanted to dial in the rules for our game and PDA's so that nobody (especially Tucker and our co-workers) gets surprised with something uncomfortable or confusing. She was totally onboard and we decided on the following:

RULE #1: The game needs a complete start and stop. No sliding in or out of it.

RULE #2: If we are in the game and the real world intervenes or calls for our immediate attention, it is perfectly okay to step out of the game without using the code or getting the other person's approval.

RULE #3: Rule #2 is only valid when not exiting the game could result in bad consequences. Mild awkwardness or embarrassments are not grounds for stopping the game. For example, when I hold Regina firmly by her wrist while walking along may be embarrassing to her but will not result in real-world bad consequences. Therefore, I can always hold her by the wrist in public when we are in the game.

RULE #4: Neither slave nor master can commit acts that would be physically, legally, or financially harmful to either party. Of course, by "physically" we mean permanent or potentially permanent harm. Bruises and other temporary physical harm is okay, so long as it doesn't cause problems in our real-world environments.

RULE #5: We are never allowed to play the game in anger or as a real-world tool to work out issues in our relationship. For example, it's not okay to for me to physically torture Regina to get her to reveal real-world private thoughts (i.e. how she feels about a certain subject, whether she flirts with anybody else, etc.)

RULE #6: Verbal abuse or anything said in the game is never allowed to be tied to our real-world feelings. In the game I may call her "a pathetic piece of trash" and she may shout out, "Stop whipping me, you heartless bitch!" but that is only related to the characters in the game. Period.

RULE #7: Absolutely no photographs within the game… ever!

RULE #8: We never tell anybody else when we are playing the game or not. We never disclose what we are doing. It is a hundred percent personal. Nobody needs to know what we are doing because, even though we may be in public, it is very intimate and sexual.

We both felt strongly that these rules, a sort of constitution of kink, would really help us keep things clear. We both get so fully transformed into our game characters that these rules are necessary.

Now we have parameters to help keep the flow from overrunning its banks. There is a time to let the kink run wildly and a time to be present in the real world.

After sorting all that out, we had a little more chit chat before she had to go. She was taking Tucker and Jason to the roller rink. That would be so fun to skate with her!

I got through a few emails and finished up my coffee at The Grove. Just when I was about to close down my computer, an email popped in from my mom. She invited me over for dinner next Saturday. Jenna and Mark would be there.

It was just a simple invitation. But the implications were huge! My sister and her husband and my parents each will have their significant others there. Was I supposed to go there as usual and pretend I'm single? Am I supposed to be a 5th wheel? Am I supposed to pretend I am still incomplete and incapable of finding a quality relationship partner? Shit. Do I bring Regina as my new "friend?" It's not like I used to bring Victoria over there. Do I announce that I have a girlfriend? Do I say I'm gay? Maybe I respectfully decline the dinner and say I'm booked. But that only prolongs the inevitable. At one point, I'm going to have to deal with this... unless, of course, Regina and I break up and I turn full straight. Then it would be a non-issue if I postponed.

But honestly, what are the chances of Regina and I breaking up anytime soon... if ever? The way it's going, I'm already deeply in love and feel like I want to go the long haul with her. I'm positive she feels the same way.

I can't believe I'm faced with all these questions from a simple invitation to dinner! Could I really come right out and say "I'm gay?" I don't feel gay. I just feel in love. Fuck. But I suppose if I'm in love with a woman and have sex with her, I'm gay. I could just hear myself now, "Hi Mom and Dad. A few weeks ago I met this amazing woman and now I'm gay." Great.

But you know what? That's pretty much the way it happened. I'm a lesbian. I'm not "bi" because I haven't thought about dick a single time since meeting Regina. If I were "bi" I would probably be having straight fantasies. But I don't at all. I can't imagine ever missing straightness, especially since there are plenty of toys available to accomplish the same thing without all the headaches of being with a dude.

You know what would be super hot? I'd love to force slave Regina to fuck me in the ass with a dildo. Guys always love to put it in the ass. But with Regina handling the tool, I think the experience could be amazing because she would be sensitive to me as a woman. It wouldn't be merely wham, ram, thank you ma'am.

Sidebar: I think I should start having slave Regina service me more as a top. I could order her to be dominant and mean to me as part of the game, like my minion. She would still be submissive, but playing the role of dominatrix by means of satisfying my orders to her. Make sense?

Anyway, back to this dinner thing. I talked myself through it. I need to come out and introduce Regina as my lovely girlfriend. Life's too short to pretend otherwise. I will bring our relationship into the sunshine! If you think there's a boogeyman, turn the light on! Too premature you say? Have you ever heard of love at first sight? It's a real thing. When you have it, you know. I've never had it before Regina. But now I know for sure. She's my angel. We were meant to cross each other's paths at this time in our lives.

Next question: Do I tell my parents and sister in advance or spring it on them at the dinner? In the mere act of asking that question I discovered my own answer. I need to tell them in advance. There is no need for drama and surprise.

Dear Diary, I just did it!!!!!!! I'm out!!!

I texted Regina to see if she could make the date. She said she could.

Then, I just did it!!!!!!! I'm out!!! I responded to my mom's email and cc'd my sister with the following:

"Dinner sounds great. I'd love to make it. Also, I have some news, I met someone and I'm in love. Would it be ok to bring her to the dinner too? Yes, you read that right. It's a "her." I'm in love with a woman. She's amazing!

Love, Meg"

My mom wrote back about five minutes later, *"Wow! Congratulations. We're a bit surprised, but happy for you. We are only surprised because we never saw any indications that you had those leanings."* She also had a few questions about how we met, where she lives, etc. I responded honestly.

Jenna wrote back too: *"Glad you can make it. We'll see you both there."* For me, Jenna's omission of any questions about details led me to read between the lines that she either didn't approve of me being a lesbian or was terrified of it. Either way, it felt a little cold. But I don't blame her. It's like my mom said, *"we never saw any indications that you had those leanings."* It was clearly out of left field for Jenna. It's okay if it takes her some time to digest it all, especially since she thinks it's against the bible. Ha ha. Can you imagine what she would think if I told her I want to put Regina in a corset, handcuff her to a post and French kiss her while pinching her nipples!

After these emails, I called Regina to tell her how it all went down. She seemed really tickled and bubbly that I would be so bold as to officially call her "my girlfriend" and that I had the conviction to tell my family I was in love. I'm pretty sure Regina thought we would continue in the dark for a while, so she seemed delighted that we could come out as ourselves. And actually, it wasn't really as hard as I had made it up to be in my mind. Maybe Jenna is judging me behind my back, but I'm true to myself and my relationship seems less shameful now that it is in the open. It should be an interesting dinner.

Later in the day, Regina and I talked on the phone for about an hour about nothing in particular. It's so nice to fit with someone so well that conversation flows so comfortably. I went to bed happy.

--- MONDAY APRIL 9 --- Paper Doll

Damn!! I had the worst headache when I woke up this morning!! I think I had too much dark chocolate before going to bed. I was channel surfing and popping chocolate squares like they were grapes. Stupid. I've had this headache before for the same reason. Late night chocolate gives me headaches and salty food makes me puffy in the mornings.

It's only a couple more days until Regina is mine again. Don't get me wrong, Tucker is wonderful and I respect their time together, but... I need my girlfriend back.

We texted back and forth a bit in the morning, but at lunch (our usual time for connecting during the work week) she was booked in some faculty crap. So I took my laptop to a restaurant and surfed the net for new boots I could send Regina for fun.

I found these extremely hot Ugg boots called "Georgette." I know it sounds impossible for Uggs to be sexy, but these shoes are killer! They are actually booties, which isn't usually my thing. They kind of look like a high clog with fur lining around the top. The stacked wooden heel is super high. They look really natural and casual and would be fantastic with jeans.

I ordered a pair for Regina and had them mailed directly to her house. I can't wait for the day when she wears them out with me on a casual date for a beer. I love the idea of her dressing down (maybe with a tee under a flannel shirt) and having these suede heels as a show of nonchalant sexiness. It's fun to think that I own her and can dress her anyway I want, just like a paper doll.

In the evening, Regina was busy with Tucker and grading papers. At one point, we were Skyping and Tucker commandeered the camera and started mugging and using an app to make crazy funhouse mirror faces to me. We were all cracking up. After he got bored and went away, Regina gave me a sweet goodnight kiss right on the lens. I felt it on my lips.

--- TUESDAY APRIL 10 --- Apart but together

Nothing much happened today. Regina and I exchanged a few emails and greetings about missing each other, but there was nothing else interesting outside of that.

Oh, there was one thing... In a phone conversation this evening, Regina and I decided on a fun little game to play at yoga on Wednesday night when we are both finally together again. Don't worry, dear Diary, it's not a kinky game; you can get your head out of the gutter now.

We thought it would be fun and interesting to go to yoga and pretend that we weren't friends... or lovers. We won't have seen each other in a while and it would be a challenge to try to pretend like we were indifferent about each other's presence.

I'm not really sure how this concept materialized in the phone conversation. I think it was Regina who was kind of wondering out loud what it would be like to see each other with fresh eyes. Then the notion morphed into this little plan where we would pretend to be apathetic about each other.

We both thought it would be exciting to feel all that pent up romance for each other and not be able to act or dive into it, like that same buzz kids feel on Christmas eve. There are presents under the tree but you can't open them until the next day. (My dad was always the biggest proponent of delayed gratification).

Hopefully our little activity of feigning apathy will not end in some kind of catastrophic explosion of hurt feelings. But we thought it was worth the risk and vowed to always try new things in our relationship so it will never turn stale.

It's late now and I'm typing while wearing my corset. I'm going to tie my ankles together to sleep tonight. I told Regina about it and it seemed to arouse her. We agreed that at exactly 11pm, we would both masturbate together. Even though we would be in different locations, it was a way to connect. Nighty night.

--- WEDNESDAY APRIL 11 --- Strangers all over again

Good morning Diary. Are you a male or female? Never mind. That was a stupid question. You are a female.

I had such a great sleep!! I just came from the shower. Regina and I had a great sex last night. How do I know that, because she texted me this morning and said she did the 11 o'clock thing just like I did.

Today is the big day we finally get to be with each other again since she will no longer be on mommy duty for a while! I'm really excited to show up to yoga and NOT give her a hug. She said she is excited about it too. I'm going to treat her just like any other woman in class. Of course, my heart is probably going to be racing with excitement underneath the blasé façade. Who would have ever thought that pretending not to be lovers with someone would be hot? Does anyone else do that? We must be freaks!

At lunch, we Skyped for a few minutes. She looked so cute. It was really fun seeing her smiling beautiful face!

Dear Diary, don't tell her this but I was scrutinizing her face during the video call. She has this little way her nostrils flare out at the sides whenever she is smiling. Her eyes are so full of life and excitement. It's easy to see there is something exciting and curious behind her eyes, which radiate a playful, inquisitive, and slightly mischievous energy. God only knows what she sees on my end.

After work, it was finally time for yoga. I had been literally counting the minutes! I walked up each step toward the class with ever more anticipation. When I arrived in class, I quickly scanned the people in the room. Regina hadn't arrived yet.

I put out my mat and started stretching. A few moments later, a new girl walks in. Actually, it was Regina incognito. Hahahahha. She was dressed like a totally different person. Instead of her usual yoga pants and tank top, she wore cobalt blue short shorts and a navy boyfriend tee, and get this… charcoal thigh high leg warmers! Her hair was done in a loose off-center braid that fell to the front of her right shoulder. Even though she is 38, the outfit completely worked on her. The effect felt classy and stylish in a whole different way then her usual self. Clearly, she was taking this whole "stranger" concept to a level I had never expected. I was dressed as my usual self. Boring. I wish had been more creative like her.

She placed her mat about 5 women away from me, never giving me eye contact. I tried to ignore her. But the truth is, every time I thought I could get away with it, I stole glances at her. Maybe she did the same to me, but I really got the sense that she was COMPLETELY in character and never broke to spy on me.

There was this secretive energy between us that felt really fun and devious. Well, at least, it felt that way to me.

Every once-in-a-while, our teacher initiates partnering up. (There are a whole bunch of yoga poses that are done with partners). So today, of all days, it was "partner" day. We had to pair up.

The woman next to me asked to be my partner. Regina asked someone behind her to pair up. So there we were, stretching and doing these intimate poses with real strangers. I wished I could have been partnered with Regina, but that's not the way the dice rolled in our little game.

The woman I was working with was pleasant enough, but I had absolutely no connection to her and will probably forget her face by bedtime. We were going through the motions. I kept thinking how sexual all these poses would have been if I were with Regina.

In spying on Regina, it seemed she had a bigger connection to her partner, an athletic-looking woman I had never seen in class before. They seemed to be having fun and an awful lot of eye contact and smiles, all while intertwining their bodies in various ways.

Okay, I admit it. I became a bit jealous. I kept thinking that Regina's natural charisma wasn't for me alone. Maybe she was capable of charming others like she had with me. At first, I thought there was a unique energy between us. But the more I watched her with this new yoga partner, the more I thought that maybe Regina simply shines her light on whomever is present. It's kind unnerving to think that I'm not special in that way. It's threatening to think that she could find someone else to connect with so easily.

But there was no reason to be jealous. It must have been just a bad head trip I was playing on myself. Maybe I was reading into their connection. Perhaps Regina was merely friendly in a polite way to make the other woman feel relaxed. Perhaps her seeming connection to this woman was merely a superficial part of our little game in an attempt to heighten our stranger experience. Well, if that were the case, Regina sure was doing a great job of playing buddy-buddy with her partner.

Just when I had almost had enough, the teacher called for us to go back to our individual mats… and not a moment too soon. I was really starting to get resentful and hurt. What a stupid game.

We did our warm down and brief meditation. When class was wrapping up Regina stepped to the drinking fountain and I found myself right next to Regina's partner. I couldn't help myself by probing the woman with, "How'd you like the partner yoga?" "It was great," commented the woman who introduced herself as Nancy. She continued, "It's always easier when you have a little history together." I felt my stomach sink like a rock, especially when I took note of Nancy's sporty appearance, "Oh, you two have a history?"

Just then, Regina walked up. Nancy pulled her over to meet me. "This is my sister-in-law, Regina." Regina was clearly sensing that I was flummoxed for some reason. "Hello, Regina," I said, "I've seen you around class quite a bit."

"Regina is a wonderful person to know," said Nancy before continuing to Regina with, "Technically, I'm not really your sister-in-law any more since you are divorced from my brother, right." Regina laughed, then said, "Anyway, maybe Nancy has a point. Would you care to join me for some soup around the corner? We could get to know each other." Nancy endorsed, "Great idea. Then you can be partners next time if I'm not there." Regina and I smiled at each other with a secret wink.

I was so relieved that Regina's ex-sister-in-law was… just her ex sister-in-law! Sheesh.

Regina and I both changed out of our yoga clothes at the studio. When Regina emerged from the bathroom, I almost had a heart attack at how she looked! She was wearing the new Ugg booties I got her!! That was so fast! I didn't even expedite the shipping and she already had them.

With the shoes, she wore a camel pencil skirt that went to her knees. Tucked into it was a crispy white blouse with a standup collar. And the coup de grace, around her neck was that impossibly sexy brown leather slave collar (the 3-inch wide one that looks like it was cut down from a high-end designer belt). The collar was a stunning accent to the outfit. Plus, it made me want to dominate her! Her hair was no longer in the side braid, but rather in a high ponytail. She looked super cosmopolitan... like Vogue NY.

Neither of us seemed to know how to exit the "stranger" game. I made the understated comment, "Cute outfit." She responded with, "Thanks, yours too." I was wearing a black turtleneck, black tights, and our brick red boots.

It was awkward because we stayed in character, and didn't know how to get out of the scene. It wasn't our regular game and I wasn't the mistress.

We went to the restaurant and sat at a booth. Even as the waitress took our order, I was conflicted about if I should break the "stranger" game or not. Regina seemed like she was completely fine as strangers. But I really wanted to be with *Regina* Regina. So I pulled a ruse.

I pretended to check my phone as if it had been vibrating. "Oh no," I worried aloud, "I have to go help a friend. Sorry but I'm going to have to leave." Regina, sat in confusion as I hastily disappeared out the front door. She looked so sad as I was walking out, kind of like a bomb just dropped on her.

Outside the restaurant, I waited about thirty seconds before racing back in as I called out, "Regina! So sorry I'm late." She perked up and a wry smile came upon her. I walked over and gave her a kiss right on the lips. "I missed you soooooooo much! Thanks for waiting for me!! I had some problems being stuck with a stranger. Long story." Regina was beaming and chuckling. We were back as ourselves.

I don't know why I felt compelled to exit our game that way instead of just telling her that we should be ourselves. But it seemed, kind of like our kinky game, that we had both thrown ourselves so deeply into character and into believing the circumstances that it would feel embarrassing and awkward to break character without some type of exit device. It would be like if you were watching a stage play and the actor all of the sudden broke character and said, "Can you excuse me for a couple minutes? I gotta move my car before the meter expires."

But if the play ends and you see the actor in the lobby, you would expect that he or she would have left the character on the stage to become a regular person again. Regina and I need that type of transition. Plus, it feels emotionally safer to know when we are in a character in the character's world. We won't be judged for acting strange because it is all part of a stage act.

So there I was in the restaurant with the real Regina. I went over to her side of the booth and slid next to her. It felt like we were both love-struck. We were very tactile, holding hands, playing with each other's hair, etc.

Just as in the play analogy, it feels okay to talk about everything once it has officially concluded. Our conversation went like this:

> **ME**
> *Thank God Nancy is your ex-sister-in-law. To be perfectly honest, I was jealous about your familiarity with her. I thought she was a virtual stranger to you and that you were flirting with her.*
>
> **REGINA**
> *I could sense something was going on with you.*
>
> **ME**
> *You were aware of me at yoga? I got the impression you totally shut me out as part of the game.*

REGINA
Are you kidding? I have Meg-dar. That's like radar. I'm telepathically tuned into you.

We both chuckled and then took a pause to eat and breathe. The conversation continued:

REGINA
Other than Nancy, did you think the game was sexy?

ME
It was so sexy!! I loved seeing you and not being able to jump on you. It was mental bondage. Your outfit was fantastic! You looked like a completely different girl!

REGINA
Different girl? But... you would never want that in the real world, right?

ME
God, no.

REGINA
Me neither.

ME
You know what?

REGINA
What?

ME
I have never done any kind of role-playing before in relationships. It's so fun!! I'm thrilled that you're cool with it.

REGINA
Cool with it? It's dreamy hot.

ME
Speaking of hot, your collar is driving me insane!! I really want to fuck with you in a dungeon.

Her eyes flirted with the fantasy. We snuggled close and I leaned my head on her shoulder. She took my head in her hand. Just then, a piercing voice interrupted, "Ms. Baker!"

Crap, it was Amanda, one of Regina's 5th grade students with her dad in tow. They busted over to our table. The conversation went like this:

AMANDA
Hi Ms. Baker!

REGINA
Hi Amanda. Hi Mr. Swenson. How are you two?

AMANDA
We're great. We just saw "Far Fetched".

ME
Oh, that's the movie about the toy dog who wants to be real, right?

MR. SWENSON
Yes. It was pretty clever. I give it 4 out of 5 stars.

REGINA
(After a smile of acknowledgement)
This is my dear friend, Meg.

Mr. Swenson looked like he was calculating the odds that we were merely "dear friends." Of course, he had a lot to work with since Regina and I had been practically drooling over each other. He also spent a decent amount of time staring at her leather collar.

MR. SWENSON
C'mon, Amanda. Let's let them get back to their dinner.

AMANDA
Okay. Bye Ms. Baker.
(She turned to exit but then swung back around)
Your collar is really pretty.

REGINA
Thank you, Amanda. See you in class.

MR. SWENSON
It was nice to meet you, Meg.

ME
Likewise. Have a good evening.

Regina gave a cute little wave as they left.

ME
Does that bother you?

REGINA
What?

ME
That your school half sees this half.

REGINA
No. It doesn't bother me. Better than running into me sloppy drunk in a bar.

ME
I mean, the fact that you're with me.

REGINA
In know what you meant. It doesn't bother me. Luckily, we live in the progressive state of California in the even more

progressive city of San Francisco. People can be themselves.

ME
Do you want to go home with me and play a different kind of game?

REGINA
Would you be cool if I slept over?

ME
That's very forward of you.

REGINA
You're right. Please don't tell that mean Mistress friend of yours. She has it out for me.

ME
No worries. We can go to my house and play cards or something. And yes, Ms. Baker, I'd love you to sleep over.

--- THURSDAY APRIL 12 --- You're fucking awesome

Insane! When we got to my house last night, we jumped into the game (the real game, not the stranger game) and kept it up until 6:45am when my alarm went off to get Regina up for school in time.

Here's what happened. We got back to my house and we were both feeling really connected to each other. I poured us each a glass of wine and we sat on the sofa. Regina was sitting with her legs crossed, favoring her new high heels toward me. She looked like such a femme fatale. I wanted to see her smoke a cigar to complete the image. Luckily, I happened to have one upstairs that my dad had given me a while back when I expressed interest.

Nobody in my family smokes. Neither Regina nor I smoke. But I still thought it would be hot to see her smoke a cigar. Normally, it would freak me out to smoke anything in my house. It is completely off limits! But my libido got the best of me and I threw caution to the wind. I wanted to see this femme fatale with that stogie between her lips.

Regina thought the idea sounded disgusting. I knew she thought that because she said, "No fucking way am I smoking a cigar." Hahaha, But with a little coaxing from my dimpled smile, she was sparking up five minutes later. She coughed a little at first, prompting a round of giggles, until I told her you're not supposed to inhale cigars. Keep in mind, we hadn't started the game yet and she was not being ordered by her mistress to smoke the cigar.

I stepped across the room to watch her smoke it. The image was every bit as perfect as I had envisioned: White blouse, heavy brown leather slave collar, pencil skirt with crossed legs, beautiful hair and the perfect self-righteous attitude she had suddenly assumed. She ignored me as I watched her, as if she was alone in the room. After savoring the sight for a while, I couldn't take it anymore from a distance. I needed to shut her down and take control. I wanted to own her sexually.

But just when I was about to get into action, she stunned me by puffing on the cigar and invoking the game with *"Can you believe how blue the sky is today?"*

I wondered, since she was the one who initiated the game, did she all of the sudden want to be dominant? She certainly looked the part in her femme fatale outfit.

But I wasn't in the mood to be submissive to my own freaking slave. It was time to jump into my bitch self and ask, "Yes, slave, exactly what did you want to say?" Slave Regina, in full game mode, shot back, "I have missed you terribly dear Mistress. I'm lost without your discipline."

Feeling more and more of the edginess of the game developing, I said, "And so you took it upon yourself to enter my world?" She nodded. I approached her quickly and grabbed her face firmly. "A nod is not a respectful answer." And I slapped her face briskly, causing her to involuntarily let out a little scream. After recovering, she looked at me deeply in the eyes and pleaded, "I crave you, Mistress."

"No more chatter from you," I scolded sharply. Then I continued with, "Stand up." She stood obediently. I reached up her skirt and removed her panties, then hiked up her skirt to allow full access to her pussy and stunning ass. Handing the edges of the skirt to her hands, I had her hold her own skirt up for me. I sat on the sofa and told her, "Pretend I am a man in a high-end strip club and give me a lap dance. When the bouncers aren't watching, kissing and fondling is okay." "Thank you, Mistress," she beamed with flames of lust in her eyes.

Straddling me, she put part of her weight across my thighs as I sat. Slowly, she gyrated and started caressing her tits. She wasn't doing it as a mere gesture; from her core she was emotionally immersed in and connected to the scene. We were both really warming up.

After a while, she reached over with both hands and started playing with my breasts. First her hands were over my turtleneck, but soon she had slipped her hands up my shirt. I paused briefly to undo my bra. When her warm hands hit the raw skin of my breasts, it was unbelievable.

She was slowly riding my thighs while playing with my breasts in perfect rhythm. A moment later, I was treated to her lips contacting mine in a loose mouth kiss that rambled and rolled from my face to my ears to my mouth to my neck. I put my middle finger between her legs from the back as she continued her lap dance. My fingers gently traced the moisture of her pussy. Once my fingers were completely wet, I slowly stuck my middle finger up inside her. That caused her to make these yummy moaning sounds as I started thrusting my middle finger in and out.

I slid my body down the sofa between her legs so that my mouth was right at her clit as she clutched the back of the couch, kneeling on the cushions over my face. With my finger still penetrating her, I tenderly massaged her clit with my tongue.

Gauging her reactions carefully, I would alternate licking with pushing my tongue into her vagina alongside my finger. She was a flaming mess of erotic frenzy, moaning and jerking and borderline crying. Sensing she was extremely close, I thrust into her harder and deeper with my finger. She was starting to tremble from over stimulation combined with her thighs weakening from the thrusting in the lap dance. She exploded into a painfully sexy moan with a very strained utterance of, "I love you, Mistress. I love you."

The smoke had cleared, I told her to go clean up, compose herself, change into some of my jammies upstairs and then call me when she was nice and calm. "Yes, Mistress." She complied with relaxed joy in her voice.

A while later, she called me up to the bedroom. I hugged her warmly to make a nice connection for a moment. Then I told her, "Your outfit tonight was quite dominant and audacious for a slave. To deepen your understanding of me, we need to switch perspectives. I want you to chain me spread-eagled, face down on the bed with each of my arms and legs secured to the bedpost so that there is no way for me to escape. You will use your creativity and intuition to get me to come by any means possible, gesturing to my growing box of kink toys on the closet floor. I don't want to hear a peep from your mouth. Is that perfectly clear?"

She knelt down before me and clearly nodded silently in order to obey my command of silence. I put my hand on her throat as she knelt there. "Just because I will be restrained doesn't mean you are in control. You will always be my slave," I sternly reminded. Then I slapped her lovely cheek quite firmly. She took my hand and kissed the palm gently, assuring me that she was still my pet.

I knelt down to her level, looked straight in her eyes, and then indicated she should stand over me, which she did. "You may now execute my command."

She stared down at me for a moment, coming to grips with her new dominant authority. I stared back, ordering her with my eyes to take charge.

SLAP! She shocked me with a cold clap to my face. She did it with unflinching resolve and, being solidly in character, gave no hint of remorse. At first I was taken aback. She seemed to have moved too quickly and easily to the dominant mindset. It was almost instant, and especially out-of-place coming from and adorable girl in pajamas.

But then again, I did get the sense she was deeply invested in the slave role and wanted to please me to the strongest degree. If I ordered her to be dominant, she would be dominant. If I ordered her to lick my feet, she would do that just as obediently... with full passion to please me. Still, I can't believe she hauled off and slapped me in the face without apology.

Relationship experts say that sexual partners do to their mate what they like done to themselves. I thought this would be interesting to see what Regina would do to me sexually when given free reign. I thought perhaps I would discover some deeper ways to please her. But mostly, I wanted to feel her authority.

After the slap, she stared at me coldly for a moment before guiding me to standup. Once I was standing, she stripped me naked with clinical detachment, tossing my clothes on the floor in a pile. But she made me put back on our brick red boots, which really turned me on.

In the same detached expression, she directed me to lie on the bed. Then she went to my toy box in the closet and pulled out 4 lengths of heavy chain with which she chained my ankles and wrists to the corner bedposts. The cold steel felt intimidating on my wrists. The pressure of the chain through the leather on my boots was a delight.

Being facedown with my nude ass exposed, I felt really vulnerable as Regina's mistress. The possibilities of what could come were extremely arousing. There could be kisses, a massage, a whipping, or even something shoved up my ass. It was all at Regina's whim. I decided to completely give up control and go with the idea of being a bottom.

She rooted around in my underwear drawer and came up with my corset, which she put around my waist. She began lacing and cinching tighter than I have ever felt! She must have spent 10 minutes pulling and gathering until my torso was so constricted that only the shallowest of breathing was permitted.

I had created a monster. She wasn't done yet. She took her wide leather collar that she had been wearing and strapped it around my neck, cinching it to the tightest notch. Now who was the slave! The collar said it all. It was like Wonder Woman's lasso. Whoever is in its grasp is rendered completely helpless and submissive.

She found a knitted wool hat in my closet and pulled it over my head, all the way over my eyes. Then she disappeared for a couple minutes, presumably to go to the garage. When she returned, she had some duct tape and made dozens of runs around my head over the knitted hat. It was scary to feel completely blindfolded like that. There was no chance in hell I would ever be able to see a single thing. The compression of all the tape was so tight that I wouldn't even be able to open my eyelids if my life depended on it.

Next, she shoved my own dirty sock in my mouth (the ones I was wearing in my boots before she stripped me down). Continuing with the duct tape treatment by going around and around the back of my head over the knit cap and across my mouth, sealing in the sock. Only my nostrils were exposed. It was really frightening. There was literally no way for me to talk or end the game with "That was some kind of crazy day I had." Basically, I was fucked.

She straddled me, sitting over my ass, and then reached in front to play with my tits. It was wildly exciting to be so helpless and objectified under her. She kissed my neck and gently squeezed my nipples with little pulses of pressure. As I got more and more turned on, my breathing became more difficult; I couldn't get very much air through my nose, especially with the corset constriction.

She sat upright over my ass. With one hand, she began massaging my vulva. With the other hand, she was rubbing my back above the corset. I was really getting turned on, to say the least.

Again, she disappeared for a moment. When she returned, she straddled my corset, facing toward my feet. She played with my ass gently for a bit before I felt some lube being applied to my asshole. I felt a rounded, elongated object slowly entering me in the ass. (I would later find out it was the handle of my designer ice cream scoop that was inside a condom). She penetrated it really deep inside me with one hand as she played with my clit with her other hand. I was struggling to breathe against the corset and duct taped mouth and it was quite terrifying to be blindfolded and restrained at the same time. After the scoop handle was all the way inside me, she left it there and inserted a dormant vibrator up my pussy. With the exception of my nose, every orifice I had was either covered or filled.

She got off of me and knelt beside me on the bed. Because I was restrained, filled up and constricted in every way possible, any touch on my skin from Regina felt magnified by one hundred times. I could even feel her breath, even though her mouth was an arms length from my skin!

She began caressing me all over my whole body. It was a massage of the lightest touch imaginable. Her fingers felt like cotton balls gently rolling across my pores. Ever so gradually over the course of 15 minutes, she delivered more pressure until it had turned into a full massage. She was working my muscles and knots. Sometimes I would feel her elbows doing the craft and sometimes it was her fingertips. She massaged in slow, rhythmic strokes and circles. Intermittently, I could feel her chin digging my knots and could feel her hot breath on my skin. I loved imagining what I must have looked like to Regina. I was floating in sensuality, lost in swirling thoughts of passion that had me exiting the physical body to an altered state of sexual intoxication.

I felt her warm left hand leave massage duty on my back while the right hand continued. In one smooth and controlled move she pinched my nose closed so that I couldn't breathe at all! My whole being burst into a state of alarm. I was petrified. How long would she cut off my breathing? After about thirty seconds, I was starting to lose my breath. I started squirming and fighting the restraints and vocalizing in grunts for her to stop. But she kept my nose sealed. I started really freaking out! I was thrashing violently against the chains and becoming blinded with desperation. Even so, I felt outside of myself and surfing the buzz of a sexual drug. Everything was turning white and I burst into full panic mode!

Just as I felt like I might black out, she released my nose. I sucked in all the air I could from my nose but it wasn't enough. I needed more air! Regina instantly picked up on this. She grabbed some scissors from my nightstand and cut in the duct tape to release my mouth and remove the sock gag. Thank God! I gasped and gasped while she rubbed me tenderly to calm me down.

After a good two minutes, I was in a better place, coming off the sex drug and back to myself in our game. Just then, she got the duct tape and re-taped my mouth shut again! Fuck. I wanted to see. I wanted to be unrestrained! I was terrified.

But Regina took this shit seriously. She turned on the vibrator that had been shoved up my pussy, causing me to yelp from the surprise. It felt amazing. Instantly, the restraints felt good again. Being tightly blindfolded was adding to the sensation. She played with the ice cream scoop in my ass while the vibrator ran in my pussy. Just when I was about to erupt with a volcanic orgasm, she left me for a moment.

SMACK!!! I felt a leather belt hit my ass... the same ass that had been stuffed with the ice cream scoop. SMACK!! SMACK!! She continued. The blows were steady and firm.

After about 20 hits, my ass was starting to sting and burn like crazy. I was unable to tell her to stop. I was unable to hold my hands in protection over my butt. I was exposed. But she kept at it. Finally, I couldn't take it anymore. I started to whimper and cry. It was involuntary. Tears were flowing through into the knit cap over my eyes.

Finally, she stopped. She gave me a hug against my tied up body. The contact of her flannel pajamas against my skin felt splendid.

Slowly, she pulled out the vibrator and the condom-covered ice cream scoop. Then she unchained my ankles and gestured for me to pull my legs up to support my ass up high (a bondage version of downward dog). My arms were still chained as she crawled under my pussy and began the most serious cunnilingus in the world. Her warm tongue against my clit felt like fireworks. I have never sensed such direct and powerful stimulation. She moved her tongue sensually and expertly with tremendous awareness of what I was experiencing, reading my every moan and quiver to maximize the effect.

Finally, I blasted into orgasm!! It had a strong start and just kept growing. My whole body was quaking and throbbing. I couldn't breathe well due to the corset and duct tape, but it added to the sensation to be so constricted. It felt like I was in some swirling kaleidoscope of orgasm, steaminess, and flashes of Regina controlling me. I was living the Helmut Newton themes. It wasn't multiple orgasms as much as it was a continuous orgasmic wave pushing me along.

After what seemed like several minutes, I closed my legs over Regina's face to indicate that I was completely spent and couldn't take it another second!! She quickly read my hint and stopped.

Next, she went to my head and carefully cut away the duct tape from my eyes and mouth. Then she pulled off the whole knit cap with the tape on it. Surprisingly, none of the tape had adhered to my hair and she got me clear without pulling a single strand.

The second my mouth was free to breathe easily, I gasped in as much air as I could. But I was still constrained by the ultra-tight corset. Regina, very in touch with my needs, quickly unlaced and removed the corset. She licked my middle back where the corset had made imprints into my skin. She took off her collar that I had been forced to wear. And at last, she unchained my wrists and set me completely free.

When I was able to pull my aching body up off the bed, I saw Regina kneeling in a very submissive pose at the foot of the bed. Her head was down and she had put the collar back on herself. It clashed quite a bit with her pajamas, but the meaning was clear. She was silent, just staring at the floor with her hands behind her back.

Rather than jump right over to her to express my profound appreciation for all she had given me, I left the bed and headed straight for the shower. She stayed motionless kneeling with her head down at the foot of my bed.

The warm water felt incredible against my tortured skin. It felt so good to feel the blood rushing to all the places that had been constricted. I rubbed my wrists and ankles in the heated water and let the spray wash away the pain and tension of the session. I lathered my head with chamomile shampoo and then held my face directly under the showerhead for a lingering rinse off. There wasn't a cell in my body that wasn't relaxed, if not completely spent.

After the shower, I put on my thick terrycloth robe and headed back to Regina… who was still kneeling at the foot of the bed. Even though she had made the mess, I decided to clean up after her. I put on a mellow playlist and picked up all the bondage gear and straightened up the room a bit, kicking up the room's heater so we would be nice and cozy.

Gravity pulled me to the inviting bed and I lied down with a giant sigh of relaxation. "Look at me," I softly spoke to Regina. She raised her head slowly to meet my command. Reaching out my arms in a beckoning gesture, I invited her to come lay on top of me, which she did. We hugged quietly and very gently. "You are welcome to speak again," I whispered into her ear. "Thank you, Kind Mistress," she responded softly. We began kissing on the lips ever so soothingly. We were kissing with slow, moist pecks and looking straight into each other's telling eyes.

And then the strangest thing happened. I started to cry. At first, Regina responded by kissing each tear. But then I started to cry more and more. Just as my orgasm had grown steadily, so was my crying. It went from a soft whimper to really heavy tears. And then it was like the floodgates had broken.

Regina did her best to try to console me. She has a beautiful maternal nature that felt so loving and comforting. But I still couldn't stop crying. In fact, it got worse and worse until I was an all out mess! What was going on with me? Why was I so inconsolable?

Regina seemed a little scared by it all but kept reassuring me that it was okay to let it all out. "We have complete trust, Mistress. We have complete love for each other. We are okay." She began sweetly caressing me and kissing my neck and ear with pure tenderness. My whole body was quivering from the crying. This has never happened in my entire life.

She took my hand and began gently sucking on my thumb while applying pressure to a spot on my palm. Believe it or not, it started to have a calming effect on me. I was gradually coming down from the emotions. After a few minutes, we were able to lie calmly on the bed next to each other as my heart rate slowed.

I was embarrassed by the crying episode and voiced it to my slave. "It's not like me to breakdown so fully. Thank you for not judging me." Regina reassured me, "It was a release for you, Mistress. It was a much-needed release. I worship you for being able to share that with me."

In fact, she was right. There was clearly something that had been triggered from deep inside me. Perhaps the shame I have felt about my kink for my entire life was finally unclogged and allowed to flow openly. Perhaps the tears came from allowing myself to completely submit to my fears of being with a woman. My emotional collapse could also been have been from feeling profound love for the first time. It could have been prompted by the direct pain and fear of feeling helpless and being terrified for my life. Whatever the root was, my gushing out clearly needed to happen. I literally felt cleansed. I felt whole and unashamed.

To complete my connection, I wanted to have the real Regina there with me. "That was some kind of crazy day I had," I said softly to her.

Her eyes instantly warmed and I could see Regina, the schoolteacher, mom, and lover was with me again. We stared at each other for a moment, before smiles grew on our faces. Regina let out an involuntary giggle. Then so did I. The dark tone had given way to giddiness as we both started and couldn't stop. It was hilarious!

It was the feeling of getting off the rollercoaster after having endured sheer terror. I hit shuffle on my Pandora and the classic song "You're Fucken Awesome" by Spiderbait came on... so I cranked it up!

Next thing you know, we were dancing all over the bedroom together as we rocked out, she in her jammies, me in my robe. It was so carefree and silly. Regina jumped up on the bed and pretended she was the lead singer up on stage. As she rocked on, I opened my dresser drawer and started tossing panties to her up on the stage. She played it up like she was real rock star. Finally, I rushed the stage from the mosh pit and tackled her. We rolled around wrestling on the bed and cracking up.

As the song wound down, we lost steam and collapsed together on the bed. "Stay there, I'm going to draw a bath for us," I said. I started the water, then went downstairs to make a snack tray and pour some drinks, which I set by the tub before rejoining Regina.

She was lying face down on the bed and looked so cute in her pajamas. I sat by her and was immediately drawn to her adorable butt. I pulled down her pants. "Hey, you can't do that!" she let me know in a joking tone. "Wanna bet?" I shot back. Then I started spanking her playfully. "Hey!!! Stop it!!" she said with a giant grin, "You're not allowed to do that outside the game!!"

"Oh sorry," I responded, "I'll take it back." And I playfully licked her ass for a while. But soon, she started to actually relax... and was getting aroused by me licking her. But she broke it off with, "Let's get in the tub." So there we went, two girls in the bathtub together.

I sat on one end and my soulmate sat on the other. In a completely automatic action, I grabbed her right foot and began to massage it under the water. As I rubbed her foot, I kept thinking how incredible it was to be with a woman, especially this woman!! God forbid if we ever broke up, I'm pretty sure I don't ever see myself being with guys anymore. I've crossed to the other team. Yes, I did. Then again, maybe I was always on this team and am merely awakening to that fact.

Our bath was lovely. We had a sweet time talking about life, sharing stories, and dreams. When we finally got out of the water it was after 1am! Yikes! Time flies with love this hot. But it was a school night. We figured we'd better get some sleep or we would be a wreck in the morning.

After we were dry and warm, we crawled into bed without pajamas. Her hot body felt amazing next to my skin. We took a few minutes kissing and caressing before settling down. We were spooning and just about asleep when I suddenly got really turned on with an idea.

Regina, out of it, seemed surprised when I said, "Can you believe how blue the sky is today?" Never mind the fact that it was night. I got up and went to my toy box. "I need to chain you down for the night," I let her know matter-of-factly. I grabbed one length of heavy chain and chained her wrists together at the top of the bed. I put my leather thigh high boots on her and then chained her ankles together at the foot of the bed. She was tied in a long, straight line from one end of the bed to the other. I kissed her nipples, mouth, neck, and ears for a little while. She seemed to really enjoy it.

Then I lied next to her on my back and started playing with myself. Slowly, I was getting more and more turned on until I climaxed in a quiet little orgasm. I landed one sweet peck on her lips, turned away from her, and went to sleep. It was kind of selfish, but I really didn't feel like getting her off. Good night.

We mostly slept straight through but there were a couple times she woke me when struggling against the chains, trying to get some relief from being stuck in the same position for hours. I remember we were both in a dead sleep when the 6:45 alarm went off. It was a brutal awakening. Right away, I unchained her and ended the game with, "That was some kind of crazy day I had." She instantly climbed on top of me and kissed me sweetly. The leather of her boots against my thighs felt naughty because we were in bed with her shoes on.

I made us coffee and she dashed off to her day.

--- FRIDAY APRIL 13 --- Finding our balance

That's right. It's Friday the 13th! However, no meteors hit the earth and no evil spells seemed to have been cast upon my world. The day was pretty standard, just our usual texting gushy messages to each other. But at 3:12pm there was a strange occurrence. Regina called me and asked if there was anyway I could pick up Tucker from school and let him hang out with me until she got home after 5pm.

It wasn't her day to pick up Tucker. Why would she ask me instead of picking him up herself?

But she explained that her ex-husband Alex was out of commission due to a giant migraine and Regina would have no transportation until her car was out of the shop at 4:30pm.

Naturally, I really wanted to come to the rescue. But, I had a really important client stopping by my office at 4:00. Wanting to give it my all to help them out, I decided to bust a move over to Tucker's school and pick him up, then get back to the office before the client arrived. Regina was so grateful! She sent Tucker's school an email to explain the situation (that I'm not a creepy kidsnatcher).

When I arrived, Tucker seemed super excited to see me, having gotten advanced notice from the office. At first I figured he was merely excited from the novelty of something new. But as we drove, his bubbling chattiness really made me think he was delighted that I was the person picking him up, not just the novelty of change in routine.

We got back to my office and I introduced him around, explaining that he would be sitting in on my meeting with the client. Not surprisingly, everyone thought it would be a bonus for the mood. I agreed. A kid with a big smile can handily neutralize tension in a room full of egos.

Before the client arrived, I was trying hard to put on a one-woman show for Tucker. I felt responsible for making him feel comfortable in the foreign environment he had suddenly been tossed into.

Our first task was to printout paper shadow puppets from the silhouettes of our hands made in the copy machine. Next it was time to raid the fridge for leftover birthday cakes. Then we hooked a bunch of rubber bands together and stretched them across the arms of a chair to make a giant slingshot for shooting wadded paper at my coworkers. Some jokers actually fought back with flying cardboard coasters. Tucker and everyone in the office were getting a kick out of it all.

When the clients showed up, we went in my office and closed the door. I explained that Tucker was my intern. And of course, they played along.

Having Tucker there worked great. They ended up signing a whole new extension to their ad campaign with us, granted I didn't contribute much to the meeting and my boss did the heavy lifting. But the client booked work at our firm for tens of thousands of dollars. It was probably the easiest sale we have ever done. Thanks, Tucker.

After the meeting, Pete (my coworker buddy) showed Regina into my office. She had arrived at the tail end of the client meeting, waiting politely until we had finished. When she entered, her presence felt like sunshine in Scotland. She hugged Tucker, then me. After our hug, we stared at each other for a moment, flirting back and forth with our gazes. It must have been pretty obvious because Pete joked, "Clearly not strangers are we?" Being an observant gay man, he was easily able to see that we had something deep going on between us.

She asked Tucker if he had fun. He asked if I could pick him up from school on Monday too! Regina and I both laughed. As they headed out across the office, they were attacked by a deluge of cardboard coasters from the evil worker drones. Regina screamed/laughed and raced to the exit with Tucker.

After Regina and Tucker left, Pete remarked covering his ears with his hands, "Oww! They're too loud!" Confused, I asked, "What's too loud? " Pete continued, "The wedding bells I'm hearing for you two! She's freaking adorable! You kill me... pretending all this time you were miss straight girl."

I couldn't believe we were that obvious. Pete made it seem like I dove into her pants or something. Really, wedding bells?

Once I got off work, Regina invited me over to her place for a casual dinner with Tucker before his dad would finally arrive for pickup. Of course, I was delighted to say, "Yes." It feels wonderful to have a close friend ask me over. It's a validation of the friendship and makes me feel loved and significant.

What to wear? I decided on a short blue cotton skirt, white scoop neck tee with 3/4 sleeves, and black strappy sandals with a casual heel.

When I arrived, Tucker greeted me at the door with a playful mood. He was eager to show me a new Lego space station he had built and whisked me toward his room. As we breezed by the kitchen, I caught a glimpse of my love in an apron at the stove. She was cooking onions and didn't bother to pause to formally greet me. I played it coy with a simple, "Hey, Regina." She smiled, returning the "Hey."

Tucker spent about 15 minutes showcasing every single detail of his space station. I was thinking, "Enough already, kid. I really need to go flirt with your mom." But he eventually was forced to finish as Regina called us to the table for garden burgers with grilled onions.

Dinner was great. All three of us told stories and joked around. Things suddenly got a little dicey when Tucker surprised the table with, "Did you know my mom has a lover?" "Oh, really?" I responded anxiously, "Who is it?"

Regina looked really nervous and started to blush! I was quite eager to learn the answer from Tucker. In a split second, my mind was racing through possible scenarios that Tucker was referring too. Though I doubted Regina really had a lover, my eyes were locked on to Tucker's mouth to see the words of truth the moment they escaped his lips.

And then they came… "She's in love with Brock. She wants him to knock on her door and sweep her away," spouted Tucker. "Oh, really?" I pressed while trying to contain my flaring jealousy. I turned to Regina and coldly pushed, "I've never heard of this, Brock." Regina was composing her answer in her brain when Tucker jumped in with, "He's the rich businessman on her soap opera. Every girl on the show is crazy about him." Phew!! Well! At least that was some kind of relief… I guessed. But even though it was only a soap character, I still had thoughts racing. I excused myself to the bathroom.

Once in the bathroom, I texted Regina as fast as my thumbs could fly. Here's the text conversation:

> **ME**
> *"WTFFFFFF? Are you straight?"*
>
> **REGINA**
> *Haha!! You might be over thinking it!! Let's talk after Tux's dad picks him up. I'M IN LOVE WITH YOU!*
>
> **ME**
> *Ok. Coming out now. Fuck.*

When I rejoined them at the table, I led with, "Did you guys know today is Friday the 13th? They smiled and we all talked about the validity of superstitions and whether we have any. Of course, Regina and I were trying to have a different conversation via our eye contact. But it wasn't really working and seemed to satisfy neither of our emotional questions for each other.

We bounced along several topics of conversation until the end of dinner. Afterward, Regina poured me a cognac and we sat in the living room by the piano. I asked if she would play me a song, but she demurred and insisted that she was a sucky piano player, only keeping the piano for Tucker. But he boasted that she was a fabulous player. With that, I urged Regina to play. But she flat out refused with, "How about them Giants?" Which basically means, the case is closed.

Luckily, Alex showed up to pick up Tucker. Regina introduced me as her "dear friend, Meg." Fair enough. Alex was not like I expected. I think I had been expecting one of those rich business types, clean cut, type A, who abuses substances and women in direct contradiction to their clean cut appearance. But Alex, on the other hand, was artistic looking and had the air of a Robert Downey, Jr. His goatee and intensely focused eyes pulsated his Scorpio vibe. He was quite handsome and charming. It's easy to see why Regina was initially attracted to him.

Tucker seemed to be drawn to him as they joked around and teased each other. But their rapport was nothing close the bond I had seen between Tucker and his mom. Surprisingly, Alex was flirting with me… at least that was the vibe he gave off. Like drugs and alcohol, sex was probably another one of the weapons in his coping quiver. In reading Regina, I could tell that she picked up on his flirting with me. I'm sure she has seen that side of him a hundred times during their relationship. Between the two of them, the air was cool but taut. There was a subtext of bad history mixed with the love that once was.

Tucker grabbed his stuff, hugged Regina and I, and off they went.

Before I could draw a sip of cognac to help change gears, Regina dove right in to the Brock thing. The conversation went like this:

> **REGINA**
> *He's just a guy on TV. It's stupid.*

ME
But he's a guy! Are you attracted to guys? It makes me wonder if we can be in this for the long haul?

REGINA
What the hell? The whole point of this relationship is that we both finally realized that we are neither straight nor gay. Our sexual identity is kink. It is about fitting together.

ME
Well, yeah.

REGINA
Don't you ever fantasize about some other parallel life that has nothing to do with reality?

ME
But he's a man. I'm not a man.

REGINA
Don't you think living that life in a mansion and having more money than God would be fun? Wouldn't it feel good for a guy to lavish you with expensive gifts and take you on vacations to Monaco? It's just a stupid fantasy.

ME
I'm putting all of myself into this relationship. Since I met you, I haven't fantasized about wanting a different life... or man. When we met, I finally felt like my true self had been realized beyond any other needs.

REGINA
Me too! The TV show is escapism for me. It's just a way to unwind. You can't read that much into it. If I fantasize about living in an 18th century French Chateau, that doesn't mean I really want that in real life.

ME

Can't you see how it's confusing for me?

REGINA
We can't be the thought police! If you read a novel, I'm not going to be offended if you have feelings for the protagonist, even if it's a dude. It's a fucking character. You know who you are to me. You know how I adore you! I want to be your slave and have you piss in my face. What more could I possibly do to prove that I'm crazy about you and devoted to our relationship?

In fact, she was right. No matter how great Brock is, I'm the one who is tying up Regina. I'm the one whose feet she licks. I'm the one who spanks her until she cries. I'm the one she trusted with Tucker today.

We stared at each other as I released my doubts and jealousy. I dropped to my knees in a heartfelt submissive manner and hugged her legs softly. "I'm sorry, Regina. I feel so good about our relationship that it seems precarious at times. How can two people have it this good? It makes me think there is another shoe that will drop at some point."

Regina stroked my hair softly for a while, accepting my apology. "Stay on your knees", she commanded in an emotionless monotone. I remained posed in the submissive position… as her slave. It felt sexy and dark to acquiesce to her command. Even though it was not in the context of the game, it felt healthy to submit to her.

She went to the piano, taking a seat on the bench. After a contemplative pause, her fingers pressed the keys and she started to play a song. The music flowed as if it being played by a master talent. The song was full and rich modern classical music in the vein of a Philip Glass composition. There was no melody at all. It was just a swirling, rolling, melding of musical waves. It was the audio version of starling murmurations… you know, when thousands of birds flock together to create memorizing black patterns in the sky. That was Regina's music. It was especially intoxicating as I knelt before her.

After about two minutes, BLAM! She stopped cold. The abrupt silence felt like a jump into an icy lake. She looked at me to gauge my satisfaction. Her look was cute, kind of like she was an embarrassed teenager after performing at the school talent show. I told her it was amazing. She deflected my compliment, then rose from the piano bench, took my hands and raised me to my feet.

It was delightful that she felt comfortable enough with me to share her playing. In fact, it was her song. She made it up on the spot and said she had never played it before… basically just freely jamming. That was her style and she lamented that she never learned to play proper piano.

Feeling much closer, we put our hands around each other's waists, pulling in close. We kissed and kissed in an amazing connection. It was really getting me moist. I swear, if I were a guy I would want to take my dick out and bend her over the piano!

But then, she spoke quietly… "Can you believe how blue the sky was today?" Before I could answer, she continued, "I'm here to serve you, Mistress." My ears welcomed this sentence; especially since a moment earlier I was in a submissive position. But I was definitely in the mood to top her.

Popping into mistress mode, I demanded she find her homemade leather (haut-couture) collar and strap it onto herself tightly.

"Yes, Mistress," she eagerly responded before heading toward her room.

A moment later, she returned with the collar on, her head down and awaiting my next command. She had taken my request very seriously regarding the tightness of the collar. The skin on either side of it was puckered with redness. "You need to go outside and cut your self a switch from the ash tree that I will use to punish you. The thinner the stick, the more blows you must endure. If you choose a thicker stick, I will use fewer blows… but they will hurt 10 times as much," I explained coldly. Then I clarified it with, "In other words, choose the thinner one if you want more welts and whip tracks on your skin. Choose the heavier one if you prefer bruises instead. "Yes, Mistress. I understand," she answered solemnly.

I took a seat on the piano bench to wait. As I sat, she broke my moment of relaxation with, "Mistress, may I have permission to get a knife from the kitchen to cut the switch?" After thinking just a beat, I granted her request with a condition attached... "First, you must bring me our boots and put them on me."

She went to her room to fetch the boots. When she returned, she helped me into the boots with the skill of a shoe salesgirl from Barney's. It felt special and important to have an attendant who provided such excellent service to me.

Once I was in the boots, she remained kneeling at my feet. Clearly turned on, she hesitantly asked permission to lick my boots, which I denied. She seemed surprised at the denial and groveled, "I understand Mistress. Please forgive me for asking so selfishly."

It was mind-bogglingly hot to see how deep and how quickly she had fallen into the game. Regular Regina was a thousand miles a way. The slave Regina was completely mired in the present.

If I would have told her to walk to the 7-11 store completely naked, I'm positive she would have thrown herself into it without the slightest thought of the legality or dangers involved. The teacher Regina was somebody completely different. But of course, as a responsible slave owner, I would never subject her to anything in the game that could be detrimental in real life. Plus, we have rules about that.

Unlike Regina, I am able to be deeply engrossed in the game while still keeping a toe on the ground in the real world. Do you know how dolphins sleep? They literally turn off half their brain and let it sleep while the other half remains just lucid enough to maintain function and watch for dangers. Isn't that the coolest? That's kind of how I am in the game. But that doesn't mean I'm not profoundly engaged in our scenes.

"Bring me that switch," I blasted. Terrified and eager to make up for the overindulgence on the boots, she immediately grabbed a knife from the kitchen and headed out the back door to the ash tree.

The Helmut Newton book called out to me as I sat on the piano bench. I began thumbing through it while the slave went about her task outdoors.

It must have been 10 minutes before she returned. That seemed like an excessive amount of time just to cut a branch from a tree. Was she indecisive about the weight of the switch? Was she having difficulty cutting the branch? Either way, it was grounds for punishment.

Finally, she returned, holding not one but two switches in her hands. One was the diameter of a pencil. It would really bite when whipped! The other was the thickness of the fat end of a pool cue. That hunk of wood looked dangerous. She was a brave woman!

"You brought me two. How indecisive of you. So I shall use both." But here's the crazy part… she had literally whittled the bark off the top six inches of each stick to reveal a perfectly smooth, white handle that gave it both functionality and a fine aesthetic. Clearly, she was aiming to protect the delicate hand of her mistress. It was her choice to leave the business-end of each stick covered in bark. That's because in her mind, she is not worthy of something fine and clean. Yep, she took the task seriously and wanted to please me.

I took the sticks from her hand and set them on the piano. Then I held her close and kissed her softly on her lips and neck. She purred in delight at being able to connect with me in a loving manner.

Embracing her with one hand, I caressed her hair and ear with my other hand. She relished it in the way that felt like when an opera singer delivers a show-stopper of a song and has to stand there soaking up an interruption of two standing ovations before returning to the performance. There is nothing to do but bask in the warmth when someone is adoring you.

And to clinch the feeling, I couldn't help myself from whispering in her ear, "Regina, I'm in love with you." But she heard it in the context of the game, not real life, because she quietly responded, "I'm in love with you too, Mistress."

Acting as a responsible Mistress, I needed to know how painful these switches would be against the flesh. It wouldn't be cool to start blasting Regina with multiple blows without knowing what harm could be done and the severity of the blow each switch would yield.

I gave her a rather unconventional order. I reached in my purse and pulled out some handcuffs, which I held up for her. "You need to handcuff me to the piano leg so that I'm bent over, then pull up my skirt and give me three solid blows with each stick on opposite cheeks. I need to gauge the severity of the blows each stick delivers, do you understand?" "Yes, Mistress," she quickly answered, "May I have the freedom to warm you up a bit once you are handcuffed so that you will be in the right frame of mind for the test?"

Thinking about it, this seems pretty important because the pain threshold in a sexually-charged scene is much higher than in a cold real-world situation. So I let her know, "Yes. You may prepare me as you wish, but for no more than 15 minutes; you are not permitted to touch my pussy." "Yes, Mistress," she replied sincerely.

She took the handcuffs and locked my wrists around the bottom of the piano leg, causing my ass to be high. Then she quietly disappeared. It felt strange to be alone and in a submissive position. I felt vulnerable because I was the one who was supposed to be in charge. I never gave her permission to leave me alone and restrained. What was she up to? How dare she leave me.

Just as I was thinking about how insubordinate she was, she

reappeared wearing her leather opera gloves that go all the way to her shoulders. "Sorry, for leaving you, dear Mistress. I thought you would enjoy being caressed by the leather of my gloves.

In fact, she was right. I got a great glimpse of her loveliness in the gloves, which had the immediate effect of getting my juices flowing. She looked super sexy!

She raised my skirt over my back and slid my panties off. Using two fingers, she delicately traced circular patterns all over my butt, letting her hands glide over every contour of my behind with a touch so light that her leather-clad fingers felt dandelion fuzz.

She removed her thick collar and strapped it very firmly around my neck. I felt owned and objectified. She disappeared once more and, about thirty seconds later, returned with a roll of duct tape. Knowing that she only had me for 15 minutes, she quickly tied my ankles together very tightly over the boots with the tape. She ripped off another length and put it over my mouth. This slave had some balls to be so aggressive with me, pushing her luck for when the tables would be turned again.

With her left hand, she began fondling my breasts, which were hanging straight down as a result of my bent over position. With her right hand, she grabbed the heavy stick that was an inch in diameter. BLAM! She hit me really fucking hard. It produced a deep ache that felt like a punch from a fist. BLAM! I screamed against the duct tape. BLAM! Another one. This stick was really painful. But I was encouraged to know that I had just one more blow to go. I think it hurts less when a finite number of blows are expected. Real torture would be to not to know how long one would have to endure such punishment. BLAM! Ouch!!! Damn that is hard!

She continued rubbing my breasts for a bit, using her other hand to rub out the pain from my left cheek.

All of the sudden, her gloved hand stopped the gentle caress of my breasts and turned to a more violent and sudden action of pinching my nose closed so that I couldn't breathe. The duct tape on my mouth was very secure and there was no air at all! It had the effect of immediately heightening the stakes, both sexually and adrenaline-wise.

She took the longer switch and tickled my butt by running it gently along my right cheek. The anticipation was palpable as I was waiting for gentle strokes to turn violent. I was getting near the end of my oxygen and I desperately needed to breathe! Then, in a split second, my ass was on fire! She whipped me 3 times very hard in the course of about a second. When the whipping stopped, my ass burned in a way that felt naughty and sexy. She released my nose and I struggled to catch my breath. Sensing that I was not getting enough air, she yanked off the duct tape from my mouth, "Ouch!"

Both sticks had their appeal, but the stinging one was more to my personal taste. The aching one seemed dangerous and dark. There's a place for that too.

As she was soothing my ass with the soft caress of her gloved fingers, I started to softly cry, which wasn't in character for me and I don't know what was going on. It felt like "happy tears" but it was mixed up with lots of different feelings of pain, inadequacy, and longing for cuddling. But honestly, I think the source was pain.

Regina put her cheek next to mine to comfort me. "You're ok, Mistress. You can be yourself in front of me," she reassured me. Then she uncuffed my wrists and pulled the tape from my ankles. She gently lifted me up to a standing position… where we fell into loving hug and a spell of soft kisses. When she sensed I was coming around, she knelt at my feet to resume her regular submissive role. I stroked her hair for a bit, her eyes gazing downward as a sign of acquiescence to my dominance.

I handcuffed her hands behind her back as she knelt there. Then I removed the collar from myself and strapped it briskly back on her Audrey Hepburn neck.

Without a word, I led her to the bedroom and had her lie on the bed, her hands still locked behind in the gloves. I cuddled in close to her and stroked her head for a bit with the intention of taking a nap together. As her head was resting on my chest, she seemed to be as full of bliss and content as humanly possible. I was too. It was hard to imagine a better feeling. Everything seemed heavenly, from the light on her skin to the peaceful room with no sound or music. There was no feeling of the outside world, no worries or concerns. The energy was beautiful! We dozed off and slept for a good hour like that.

Upon waking, we were still in touch with that warm and heavenly vibration. We kissed a couple times. But as I looked into her eyes, something started charging in me. It was my id waking up to seeing a beautiful woman in long, black gloves… handcuffed. She was mine, my object.

"Stand up!" I snapped at her. Eager to please, she stood immediately. I grabbed her nipples with each hand and scolded, "How dare you disobey me!"

She looked completely confused and nervous to have disappointed me. "What did I do, Mistress? I never meant to disobey you," she sheepishly responded. I reminded her of how I had asked for her to cut a single switch from the ash tree, but she took two! I expressed that it was very greedy of her and that she must face harsh punishment. In fact, she showed immediate remorse and seemed truly ashamed to have disobeyed me.

I kissed her softly, hugging her around her handcuffed arms. Of course, she purred under my affection. Something whisked me out of the game for a second and brought me into reality to say, "Regina Baker, I love you so much!" Regina, sensing that we had momentarily exited the game without the usual code, spoke as herself overflowing with commitment, "Oh, my God. I love you too."

It was a mini moment of delight, a brief intermission that popped out organically. Somehow, we both felt the boundaries of the game still solidly intact. It was like a commercial break in an HBO movie. You knew that the movie was going to resume again. But for that brief period, it was delightful. We rubbed noses and cheeks and stared into each other's eyes so closely that our eyelashes were whisking together.

It was time to get back to the movie. The game switched back on in a flash. "Don't ever disobey me again!" I threatened. Her eyes jolted sharply back into the game. I dragged her over to the wall, turning her to face it. On a side chair table, I noticed the Bettie Page postcard I had sent her. I grabbed it and placed the card between the wall and her nose, with her nose making contact with Bettie's stiff pointy bra. "Hold this postcard to the wall with your nose until I comeback," I demanded. "Yes, Mistress," she complied solemnly. I continued, "I'm going out for a bit. Don't drop that postcard or you are dead. Capiche?" "Yes, dear Mistress," she responded.

That "Dear Mistress" response inflamed me; it bordered on patronizing. I pounced on the long wispy branch she had cut and started whipping her ass as she stood with her nose holding the postcard. Between hits, I forcefully spoke through my gritted teeth, "Don't you dare try to soften me by referring to me as 'Dear' mistress. It's only *Yes*, Mistress or *No* Mistress. Are we clear!"

Her pelvis squirmed left and right to avoid the pain of the whipping... but her nose stayed glued to Bettie as she uttered under misery, "Yes, Mistress."

I whipped 10 more times for good measure, leaving her ass a fiery red. "Don't fucking move!" She was stoically trying to hold back tears while doing her very best to keep the postcard pushed against the wall.

On the way out the front door, I grabbed her keys out of her purse and pulled the door locked behind me.

Outside, I saw that the entire street parking was taken and I didn't want to lose my spot. I opted to get a Lyft ride. Lyft is a peer-to-peer taxi service that I depend on in the city for quick trips. It's cheap and has ultra-fast pickups, all done through my smartphone. I got picked up by a handsome Latino Coast Guardsman and told him to take me to my office. (He said he drives for Lyft to augment his low salary with the Coast Guard).

Before I had met Regina, I would have probably had sexual fantasies about some exotic romp in the back seat with him. But in this case, the thought was nowhere in my mind. All I could think about was that I had the beautiful gazelle of a woman facing the wall, handcuffed in opera gloves, and waiting patiently for me to return and have my way with her. The notion was a thousand times sexier than any fantasy I had thought about with a guy!

The driver pulled up at my office and I asked him to wait while I went it to grab something. The office was dark, but nobody would care if I let myself in.

When Tucker was with me at work, I was eyeing this roll of industrial quality pallet stretch wrap... basically heavy-duty Saran wrap. I thought it would be fun for bondage games with Regina.

I jumped back into the car with Coast Guard boy and told him to return to Regina's address. I have no idea what he thought about me holding this 3-foot roll of pallet wrap. Whatever.

He dropped me at Regina's curb and I headed in, kind of turned on about what I was planning.

I made a beeline for the bedroom. And there she was, still holding Bettie Page with her nose. Her ass was still pink and displayed tons of thin whip marks. "Very good job," I commended her for maintaining the postcard on the wall. "Release the card to turn and kiss me," I ordered. She did. It was a slow and fun kiss that felt more loving than dark. But then she interrupted the kiss with, "Mistress, may I please use the bathroom?" Rather than answering, I simply grabbed her by the collar and dragged her coldly to the toilet. As the seat touched her cheeks, she winced with a little yelp from contact with the whipping wounds. I stood and watched her as she peed. A slave like her is not worthy of privacy.

Her hands were still locked behind her back. Obviously, she wasn't going to be able to wipe herself. As her compassionate Mistress, I did the job myself. She was greatly embarrassed that I had to tend to her in such a way, "Please forgive me, Mistress." But I gave no response at all. When she was all set, I told her to go back to the bedroom. The real fun was about to begin!

First step, blind fold. It's amazing how taking away someone's sight instantly weakens them and makes them incredibly vulnerable. It suddenly makes one feel dependent and submissive, even if they are in loving and trusted hands.

I found a black scarf in her dresser and wrapped it several times around her head to more than cover her eyes. Her lips, the only real feature left in the clear, were thirsty with anticipation, wanting a kiss or a ball gag or anything at all. Really.

But instead of floating a gentle kiss onto them, I took my panties I had been wearing all day and crammed them deep into her mouth in a harsh motion. She was devouring the forceful treatment, showing so with an approving moan as she felt the pressure of the panties being crammed to the back of her throat.

Hoisting up the heavy roll of palette wrap, I started encircling her head many times, leaving just her nose exposed for breathing. Since the saran wrap roll was wide, I had to funnel the sheet down to a width that would that was only a few inches wide, which made it extra strong and tight around her eyes and mouth. The black blindfold was becoming less and less visible as the layers of wrap added up. Same with her mouth. I loved the idea that under all that wrap, my panties were still jammed in her mouth.

With her head in a complete state of sensory deprivation, I transferred my wrapping action to her torso. Her hands were locked behind her back in the gloves, so I just wrapped right over them and around her chest about a million times as tight as I could. I wanted to leave lower half completely exposed so she could walk and so I could play with her as I wished.

The aesthetic result was extremely pleasing! Regina's head was completely covered in heavy plastic except for her nose. Her torso was strictly bound under the wrap with so many layers that the definition of her arms and boobs was completely lost. She was a tight little package with only long legs and a perfect ass protruding.

For my own curiosity, I reached my hand down to gently touch her pussy. Sure enough, it was dripping wet! She was in heaven!

To taunt her a bit, I caressed her clit a little with my left hand while I pinched her nose with my right. With the lack of air, she started making terrified moans pretty quickly. She was struggling against the plastic wrap.

But I was just messing with her. Before she could really get worked up, I released her nose and pussy, and gave her a playful slap on the butt. "Don't worry. I'm not really a cruel Mistress," I ribbed.

From her closet, I found some really high black pumps. It's not something she would have normally worn, but perhaps she bought them for some swanky soiree at some point. Regardless, I wanted them on her feet. Lifting up her right foot, I had her slip into the shoe, but she started losing her balance and almost toppled over (she wasn't expecting to be tested on her balance and couldn't grab anything for stabilization because her arms were in bondage). I jumped up and held her from falling over. She regained her balance and I slipped her other foot into the second shoe. Her elongated legs looked ever more delightful sticking out of the plastic wrap.

I told her I was going downstairs. But I didn't think she could hear very well due to the plastic wrap and blindfold fabric over her ears. So

I moved my mouth right next to her ear and spoke loudly and clearly: "I'm going downstairs by the piano. You need to make your way there by yourself. Do you understand?" She nodded. "If you fall, I will no longer be your Mistress, do you understand?" I threatened, then hammered it home with, "YOU BETTER NOT FUCKING FALL!"

I headed out the room and down the stairs, stomping loudly so she would hear me abandoning her despite her covered ears. But then I tiptoed back upstairs to observe the slave in action.

Due to spinning her in the palette wrapping process, she had no idea which direction was anywhere. With no vision and limited hearing, she moved extremely cautiously as she began to try to navigate her way outside the bedroom. She would take a baby step forward, but before putting weight down, she tested to make sure it was solid footing. Once assured, she would land the foot and do the process again for the next foot.

After about 11 such steps, she encountered the wall between the bed and the dresser. She traced the wall to the right with her toe and used it as a guide to eventually get to the doorway.

Using the foot testing method, she finally figured out where the stairs were. Keep in mind, she was in 4 inch heels! Carefully, she was able to lower herself down on the first stair. She collected her balance and then went for another... then another. There was something so sexy about seeing her struggle with each step in such a precarious action. She looked really weak and vulnerable as she teetered to each step. I loved that she neither had vision nor use of her arms.

She managed to get to the bottom of the stairs. It was funny to watch her tap around with her foot to make sure she was, in fact, done with the stairs. Now she had to figure out a way to get to the piano. So again, she began trying to trace the wall with her foot in order to make her trek. Just to have fun, I turned the piano bench on its side and butted it perpendicular to the wall so that when she came upon it, she would think it was a corner.

It worked. She met the "corner" and began to follow the turn. But quickly she ran out of piano bench and stood, confused. Then I quietly lifted the bench away so that she was stuck without her bearings. When she went with her toe to find the wall again, she was lost.

I interrupted her confusion by appearing out of nowhere and hugging her. Even though her eyes and mouth were blocked, I could tell she was really happy to feel me. I hugged her dearly and let her know that she did a great job getting down the stairs.

Grabbing some nearby scissors, I cut away the palette wrap from her mouth and removed it all below her eyes, her torso still restrained. Her face was red from both the heat and compression. I pulled my panties out of her mouth, then gave her a brief kiss. "Baby, Are you okay?" I asked. "Yes," she replied, " I'm fine, Mistress. I'm really glad you are here with me. My mouth was starting to ache." I wouldn't usually refer to my slave as "Baby," but it just came out that way.

I assured her that she was in loving hands. We kissed for almost a minute, a burning warm kiss. My little package was a great kisser!

After an ample period of personal connection with each other, I turned cold and marched her to the piano bench that I had righted once again. I had her go to her knees and then lay her chest on the bench so that her ass was sticking off the end in a perfectly exposed position. Once again retrieving the wispy switch, I began whipping her ass in slow and gentle swats that wouldn't even hurt a baby. It was merely a way to let her know that I had the whip in hand. She welcomed it with sighs of approval.

After maybe thirty strokes, I slowly increased the magnitude, but stuck to the steady metronome-like cadence. Soon her ass was getting redder and her cute little sighs were transforming into moans. Same tempo, I really started going with the whip. She was starting to wriggle and squirm on the piano bench. Soon, I was scaring myself as her ass started to get dangerously red and welted. But she was still onboard for whatever I would give.

I stuck the whip in her mouth to hold for me. Of course, she complied, giving that classic "rose in the teeth" image. (By the way, where the hell did that ever come from and what is it supposed to mean?).

To soothe her wounds, I took some tissues out of a box on the end table and dragged them across her reddened ass as lightly as if a cloud were kissing her skin. At the realization that the torture may have been over, she enthusiastically spoke in garbled words around the whip in her mouth, "Mistress, I love you so much! I love you so much! Thank you! Thank You! Thank you! I love you!" I kept the tissue treatment going for long enough for her to calm way down and slow her breathing and excitement. She was in pure bliss.

When she was good and relaxed, I surprised her with a vibrator, placing it lightly on her clit. Apparently, it was just what she needed. She quickly got into a gentle thrusting rhythm and did the best she could to reciprocate with the vibrator. (I mean, her hands were still cuffed and she was face down on the piano bench... the poor girl).

Not even a minute later, she was lighting up in a big time climax. All the energy of the evening was bursting out in ten seconds of violent thrashing and moaning!

And then she just deflated like a rag doll, dropping the stick from her teeth. I really wanted the real Regina back ASAP so I sweetly said, "That was some kind of crazy day I had." After a giant pause, she softly sighed a few times as she collected herself and then let out with, "Oh, baby. I feel like a bus hit me. Can we take a bath together and be close?" Of course, I was eager to do the same. I quickly untied her and hugged her sweetly.

I drew a hot bubble bath and put her right into it. Then I went and made a plate of cheeses, kiwis, and olives to accompany a fresh green veggie juice. She was really grateful and started munching right away as I slipped into the other end of the tub with her. I began rubbing her feet... which caused her eyes to close and head to take rest on the end of the tub. There was no music, just lovely silence.

After about five minutes of rubbing her feet, she finally spoke with her eyes still closed: "I'm getting my period." I asked if she was feeling that way during the scene, but she said that the scene must have masked the symptoms. It just hit her like a ton of bricks. I continued rubbing her feet, staring at her loveliness. A few minutes later, she was sound asleep. I mean, REALLY sound asleep, completely spent!

I didn't know if I should wake her or not, but after about twenty minutes, I gently woke her and dragged her to bed where she hit the pillow and continued right on sleeping. It was 2am. Time flies when you're riding the emotional rollercoaster of kinky passion. Come to think of it, my period is due in the next day or so also. It's funny how we're in sync.

--- SATURDAY APRIL 14 --- A new game goes public

At morning, we woke up together around 9:30, completely relaxed to the core. Regina made us coffee and a poached egg plate and served us in bed where we talked about our jobs, old boyfriends, Tucker, family and life. We shared details of how it felt to each of us when we played "the game." Both of us agreed that the feeling, whether playing the dominant or submissive, felt tingly, rushing, vibrant, ethereal and otherwise beyond description.

It was luxurious to be so relaxed and free with each other. Our relationship felt like old friends, even though we didn't have the 10-year history that it usually takes to cultivate that kind of bond.

After a while one thing led to another and we made out with some kissing and loving. It was really vanilla and delightful.

Today was the big day she would come to dinner at my parents to meet my family. We decided to watch a movie and then catch the afternoon yoga class. It would feel great to hit the yoga mat after such a sunny morning together.

For our mid-morning film fair, we decided to watch "Imagine Me & You" (2005), pulled from a blogger's list of top 10 lesbian flix. We wanted to explore our newfound world.

The film didn't disappoint. It's the story of two female friends who gradually become lovers, interrupting the straight marriage plans for one of the girls. It's a really sweet movie and had a nice effect on us. I spent the majority of the movie rubbing Regina's feet, much to her great satisfaction.

After the movie, I pulled her Helmut Newton book from the piano and we sat in bed comparing our thoughts on the photos… which ones we liked best, which ones were the kinkiest, who looked the hottest. Regina's favorite photograph was the one of director David Lynch holding the throat of his stunning model of a wife, Isabella Rossellini. They were standing up, both fully clothed. But the photo was overflowing with steam! His hand is holding her delicate throat with her head back as she anticipates the darkness of her lover. Her heavy eye shadow accents the mood of sultry danger.

Both Regina and I thought it was the sexiest picture in the book. The S&M implications were strong and implied and the sexuality of the two completely transcends their sexual orientation and/or gender.

Suddenly there was a knock on the door. Regina went down to answer it. Low and behold it was Victoria! She asked if Regina's name was Regina and was delighted to learn it was. How on Earth did Victoria know I was at Regina's? But even more confusing was the question of how she found Regina's address! Victoria launched into an enthusiastic monologue:

> **VICTORIA**
> *Oh my God, you're as pretty as Meg says! You may think this is weird, but one time Meg described where you live on this block and I remembered it! Three years ago, I lived at number 450 just a few houses down. So when I was driving by just now and saw Meg's car, I knew this had to be you! And look at you! No wonder she's in love!!*

REGINA
And you must be Victoria.

As Regina was blushing and trying figure out this person, I joined them at the door and greeted Victoria. She continued:

VICTORIA
Don't mind me. I won't stay. But when I saw the car, I just couldn't wait to meet you!

Meg, may I have a word with Regina in private?

We both looked at each other in fear. What was Victoria's deal? What was she going to say? But Regina gave a sheepish nod and Victoria seized the opportunity by taking Regina's arm and leading her out the door to the sidewalk. Feeling awkward, I closed the door and waited inside, wondering if Victoria was going to say something annoying.

A minute later, Regina entered alone, saying Victoria said to tell me "bye" and that she had to get going. I quickly pounced on Regina with, "What did she say?" Regina told me that Victoria looked at her for a long time with an extremely serious face and finally said, "Nobody's ever made Meg this happy." Regina felt really touched. I concurred, "Well, she's right." Regina lit up a warm smile and said, "I feel the same about you."

Later, we both went to yoga in boots. Regina wore our brick boots with a casual skirt and I wore my thigh high boots with my jeans tucked in. Even though my boots were high, the look was bohemian casual with the contrast of an earthy oversize sweater. We rode her electric Vespa to class with me on the back. We were feeling very close to each other and laughing at the occasional ogling from people en route.

As we got off the bike and headed to class, our natural instinct was to hold hands. But right as we were about to enter the room, we suddenly became self-conscious of our handholding and separated. Regina said,

"Screw it," and took my hand back so that we entered holding hands. The funny thing was, nobody gave the slightest reaction about us entering as a couple. I think we looked cute. Who wouldn't want to be seen in such a joyful state of romance?

Class felt amazing, despite the fact that we were both a little crampy from our in-sync periods. It's so great that we both have yoga in common, a practice that could keep us healthy and trim our whole lives.

After class, we changed back into our regular clothes and waited in the hallway to signup for the next 6-week session. But the signup lady wasn't going to be there for a half hour, so we sat on the stairs to wait.

As we were talking, Regina was mindlessly tracing the stitching on my thigh-highs with her finger, the type of action people usually do when doodling on a post-it. She was cute as could be and her finger tracing was turning me on.

After conversing a bit about yoga, Regina was timidly trying to get into another topic that was on her mind. The conversation went like this:

> **REGINA**
> *Did you ever want to... um...*
>
> **ME**
> *What?*
>
> **REGINA**
> *I don't know. Forget it.*
>
> **ME**
> *Hey. You can't do that! Did I ever want to what?*
>
> **REGINA**
> *It's nothing.*

ME
Regina, c'mon.

REGINA
Fine. I think it would be fun to start a new game.

ME
Instead of the one we play now?

REGINA
No… in addition to it. I love our game!! This would be another version for when we are in a different mood. You know… sometimes you want to play volleyball and sometimes you want to do yoga.

ME
I really don't have the urge to play volleyball, but tell me more.

REGINA
Ok. You know how I like to be tied up?

ME
What? You like to be tied up? That's some freaky shit.

REGINA
Ha ha.

ME
Sorry. Go on.

REGINA
Sometimes, I think it would be fun to be tied up by you… and not the Mistress.

ME
I don't think I could be mean to you as myself and yourself.

REGINA
I wouldn't want you to be mean. We would save that for "The Game."

ME
Ok. What would this new game look like?

REGINA
It would be fun if you, Meg, had the right to tie me up in everyday life. It would be more playful. We wouldn't have to start the game or end the game with the code phases.

ME
I'm listening.

REGINA
What if, whenever the mood strikes you, you tie me up, spank me or whatever? But it would be in the spirit of fun. We could have dinner and talk or watch a movie together while I'm tied up. I could be around the house in bondage. It's just like "The Game" but it is in the spirit of playfulness and being ourselves. It wouldn't have to be so sexual.

ME
Mmm hmm. What would the rules be?

REGINA
Just three rules:

1) Only you could decide when to tie me up or untie me. I would never be able to initiate it or end it.

2) When I'm tied up, we act like ourselves and do regular things at home and have regular conversations. The only thing that would be off limits is talk about Tucker. It would feel weird to be tied up and talking about Tucker.

ME
Can I spank you or whip you? Can I fuck you?

REGINA
There's not much I could do to stop you if I'm restrained.

ME
And what's the last rule?

REGINA
The third rule is: If I'm tied up, you need to help me avoid real life trouble... like being late to work or missing an urgent phone call because I'm tied up.

ME
You've certainly thought this all through already.

What would you get out of this new game that the old game can't provide?

REGINA
It would give me that feeling of being your toy without having to have sex... like for my period. It would feel good to have you be in control in daily platonic life. I know this sounds weird.

ME
Platonic life?

REGINA
Whatever. You know what I mean.

ME
Can I tie you up in public?

REGINA
I'll let you be the judge of that. If it feels safe and fun, then

sure.

ME
Maybe we could be at a party and joke with people that you're the designated driver and we did that so you won't drink.

REGINA
Ooooooo. Yeah!

ME
This sounds fun!!

REGINA
You're cool with it all?

ME
It might be really fun to have you as my little tied up pet.

REGINA
But I would still be me.

ME
I got that. And of course, your Mistress can still initiate the darker game at will, right?

REGINA
She sure better!

All kinds of fun ideas started darting through my mind about having Regina under restraint in daily life. It would be everything I ever dreamed about in a partner. She would be available for me at every moment. For the first time in my life, it would be full acknowledgement of my kinky sexual orientation to my partner. This would be the end of shame around the subject! We could both live freely and be our complete and natural selves around each other. Awesome!

I extended my hand to Regina to shake on the deal. With some deep and happy eye contact, we sealed the arrangement with a firm business shake. If nothing else, this contract was further proof that I own Regina. I love owning my lover. That has never happened in my life!

After yoga, we each returned to our respective homes for a little chill time before getting ready for the big dinner at my parent's house. To be honest, I was a little nervous about how they all would react to Regina…well, more specifically, how they would react to me being with a girl. I was thinking it was going to be fun to introduce Jenna and her husband Mark to my newfound gayness. Hopefully their brains wouldn't melt.

At 6pm, I called Regina to see if she was ready for me to pick her up. She was, so I headed over. When she met me at the door, she was wearing a cute off white striped tunic with leggings and our brick boots. It played nicely off my purple turtleneck, jeans, and high clogs. (Even though it was sunny and bright, the air still felt breezy and cool.)

Seeing her quickly turned me horny. We were supposed to be heading out for a 6:30 dinner, but I couldn't help needing a little relief. I barged into Regina's house with a "Wait here a second" and went straight to her laundry closet for a length of the cotton clothesline I had seen on a shelf previously. I returned with the clothesline and quickly tied Regina's hands behind her back (to her utter delight). "Boy", she remarked, "You're not wasting any time with my request!" "No I'm not," I shot back. "The thing is," I continued, " Rather than being normal, I really feel the need to be mean to you. Is that cool?" She sent me a warm smile with "I'm yours, however you need me."

I told her go get her vibrator. She quickly dashed off. It looked hot to see her dressed up for a dinner party with her hands bound behind her as she walked out of the kitchen. A moment later, she returned and handed me the requested device. I set it on the table and began hugging and kissing her all over.

It's so hot that she couldn't hug back. I don't know why that is such a turn on for me. I guess it really feels like I am taking advantage of her. Her mouth, on the other hand, was fully capable and engaged. We kissed like lovers who hadn't seen each other in weeks, ravishing each others' necks and lips as if we were starring in a French arthouse film. Once I was overcome with passion, I shoved her away and told her to go face the wall.

It was strange; I felt like I was the Mistress and probably even carried that tone. But Regina didn't respond with the usual, "Yes, Mistress" protocol. In fact, she seemed like regular Regina. And there was an odd little conversation about it as I took the vibrator and laid on the kitchen floor staring at her:

> **REGINA**
> *Are you going to get yourself off while I just stand here?*
>
> **ME**
> *I was thinking about it, yeah.*
>
> **REGINA**
> *That's kind of perverted, don't cha think?*
>
> **ME**
> *Just be quiet and stand there so we can get going to my parents' house.*
>
> **REGINA**
> *You're such a pervert. Go ahead and jerk off to me. I'll just stand here facing the wall as you objectify me. Nice.*
>
> **ME**
> *I don't know if I can do this without "The Game." I just want to fuck you up and torture you.*
>
> **REGINA**
> *I'm sorry. I'll shut up. Except for one last thing...*
>
> **ME**

What?

REGINA
I have to tell you that you look amazing and I'm really turned on by you.

ME
Yeah, well I love you, Regina.

REGINA
I love you too.

BZZZZZZZZZZZ. The vibrator took over my headspace. As I lay there on the floor, I couldn't stop appreciating Regina. From her body to her style to her energy, everything was pulling me in. This was the real thing. I loved seeing the back of her head as she faced the wall! It was such a submissive position… and she was doing it just for me!! Sooo hot!!

But as I was getting close, she left the wall and knelt down to kiss me lovingly all over as I continued with the vibrator. We both seemed to be super turned on. The kisses were driven by passion more than lust. This type of energy would have never been expressed within the darkness and power imbalance of "the game".

Before I knew it, I was unleashing my pent up sexuality that had been building pressure since I was a small girl. Never did I expect to have my kink so perfectly expressed with a partner. It was different than the Mistress game. This was just about being myself and admitting that I adore bondage, either seeing it or doing it.

After I came, Regina continued to kiss me tenderly, speaking sweetly with loving comments.

Just before I was back to my relaxed self, I stood up and gently helped Regina to her feet (it's hard to stand up on your own when your arms are tied behind your back). Hugging her from behind, I slowly kissed her neck and told her how much she meant to me. I put the vibrator on her (from my rear hugging position) and she was extremely welcoming of it as the device easily penetrated the fabric of her leggings and panties.

While my orgasm was a blast of relief, hers came on more like a slow burn, ultimately ending in soft moans of fondness and fidelity. Afterward, we kissed a bit more. This new game, the lighter version, was still confusing, but it showed great promise as a whole other type of satisfaction in the relationship.

"Come on, we gotta get going," I said. "Aren't you going to untie my arms?" Regina wondered aloud? "No, I wasn't planning on it. You have to ride in the car like that," I responded with a wink. "Are you serious? What if someone outside sees me?" she said with a twinge of fear in her voice. "Tough, they will have to deal with it." She continued her protest; "You are not to take me to your parents' like this!" "Don't worry," I responded, "I'm not crazy."

The more I thought about her public bondage, the more I over thought it. I figured it wouldn't be so great if she was walking on the sidewalk to my car with her hands tied when, God forbid, she runs into a student of hers or someone else she knows. I decided to throw a coat over her shoulders like a shawl to hide the fact that her arms were bound. "Ok, that should do it. Let's go," I encouraged her.

The coat across her shoulders seemed to do the trick. It emboldened her, a cape for a superhero. As we walked out her door and headed out, part of me really wanted to run into someone she knew! It would be a titillating secret that only Regina and I would know that she was tied up in public. Of course, that would suck if some acquaintance tried to shake her hand! Whatever, we made it to the car without incident.

She took her seat on the passenger side and I leaned across her to buckle her seatbelt. But I took a quick interruption to bite her tit playfully as I was bent across her. She started cracking up as I bit the other one too. As we drove down the street, she let out a big, bright comment: "Fuck, you're great!!" Then I pinched her nipple, causing her to squirm and giggle to get away.

We arrived at my parents' house. Jenna and Mark's car was already there, meaning we could make a grand entrance. A light bulb went off in my head; my little toy was really going to have to enter with her hands tied up!

She totally protested and got really vocal about not wanting to enter like that. But the thing is, she was full of it. I could tell by the giddy tone of her protest that she actually wanted to enter like that! Manipulative little faker!

At the doorstep, we both stood there making funny eyes with each other in anticipation of how this was all going to go down.

I opened the door and lead Regina in with "Hi Guys! We're here." My parents, Mark, and Jenna were all sitting in the living room with cocktails and hors d'oeuvres. They immediately stood to greet us and all eyes jumped to Regina to check out what the lezbo looks like. "Hey, everyone. This is my girlfriend, Regina," I happily boasted. I think I used the word "girlfriend" both to make a statement and to get a rise out of them.

Mark went to shake her hand, but I quickly shut him down with, "She can't shake your hand because her hands are tied up!" Regina flashed a playful smile and displayed her bound hands behind her back. Then she said in a giggly tone, "Meg was eager to get here and told me that if I didn't stop messing with my hair she would tie up my hands for two hours! Of course, I didn't believe her… and here we are!"

Everyone laughed and continued greeting each other. My dad lightheartedly urged, "C'mon, Meg. You can untie her now. I think she learned her lesson." But I set him straight: "Dad, if I do that, she will never trust my true intentions again! This girl needs to know that when I say something, I mean it." My mom chimed in with, "Yep, that's Meg for you."

She whispered knowingly to Regina, "If you want be friends with

Meg, I'm afraid you will have to get used to these types of antics from her." Regina delivered a sly response: "Don't worry. I'll have plenty of opportunity to get my revenge!" Mark and Jenna just didn't know what to make of the whole scene. Mark shifted gears with, "How about a Merlot for you both?" Both Regina and I spoke at the same moment, "Perfect. Thanks."

He poured the wine and didn't know how Regina was going to drink it. I took both glasses and said "cheers" to everyone, clinking glasses on behalf of Regina too. Then I literally held the glass to her lips so she could drink. The others were really getting a kick out of it. Even though it was all fun and games, both Regina and I knew that we were secretly turned on that I was the boss and that she was tied up in public. It had only been several hours since she told me of her desire to play this new game... and here she was, tied up in real life... meeting my family for the first time! Ask and ye shall receive. Life's too short to be shy.

As the evening went along, my family and Regina had the usual banter of getting to know someone. Obviously, I had to feed Regina each bite. Mark and Jenna kept bringing up their church activities. Perhaps they were just probing to gauge Regina's level of religiousness or perhaps there were feeling "Holier than thou" about having such righteous lives.

But Regina, in all her adorableness, was never phased at all. She spoke freely about being a progressive vegetarian and had no problem holding her own in the conversation. I always felt that my sister felt superior to me because she is going to be saved and I will be burning in hell. But Regina's style and personality completely disarmed that argument and she just came across as... well... extremely charismatic, smart, and non judgmental of the others. Even being tied up, she carried the room to a wonderful and fun level.

Dinner was over and my mom was serving dessert: chocolate lava cake, which was perfect for a couple of chocoholic girls like us. I figured Regina had "suffered" enough with the whole bondage thing. "Time's up. What do you think, should I untie her now?" I brought up to the table. "Maybe you should leave her like that forever," Mark joked to the amusement of the table. "Good idea," I agreed. But before everyone could wonder just how long I was going to carry this bit, I said, "I'm pretty sure she has learned her lesson."

I untied her. She immediately threw her arms around my neck in a loose hug and looked in my eyes with a devious smile: "You've got a bit of a dark streak I'd better watch out for." Everyone laughed. "Don't worry, Regina, as long as you follow my rules, you'll be fine." Again, laughs from the table.

Regina continued, "Now that I am free to move about, I'd like to give you all the welcome hugs I missed earlier." She went around the table, giving each person a sincere hug and greeting. It was super endearing and cute. My "girlfriend" had handily won over my family. She sat back down, took a bite of her lava cake and dropped a bomb that had been the elephant in the room: "So what do you guys feel about your daughter having fallen for me, a woman?"

An awkward vibe plowed into the room like a Mac truck hitting a snow bank. No one knew what to say or had the courage to say it.

Finally, my mom started, "Sweetheart, love is love. If it works for you two and you're happy, then we are thrilled for you both." The others echoed the same sentiment. They seemed pretty genuine in their support. People are generally touched by the joy seen in a new romantic relationship. I think my family was just surprised that I would end up with a girl, rather than judging it. Even Mark and Jenna seemed sincere in their live-and-let-live remarks.

The energy in the room was truly elevated. In fact, my own judgment of my family's potential judgment may have been misunderstood all these years. It gave me a feeling that Regina was the one.

She stood from the table and excused herself for the restroom, joking that it would have been difficult to do that while tied up.

While she was in the loo, the family almost suffocated me in praise for finding Regina and being in a relationship with her. She had more than won them over. There was some innuendo about how "maybe that's why none of my past relationships with other *guys* never worked out." Of course, reading between the lines, it's apparent they were referring to the fact that I must have been gay all along. Whatever. I didn't take it personally. Sexuality is extremely complex and has many layers. Mine is particularly so. And maybe they were right.

That was also the time they were asking about Tucker and how all that stuff works. I think they felt it was odd that I'm dating a mom. But she's not just a mom. That's only one big part of her. She is also many other things. And let's face it, she is a hot mom!

Regina returned from the bathroom and whispered in my ear, "Sorry, I had to go get myself off." She winked at me in the cutest way possible. We finished dinner and wrapped up the evening, everyone having had a fantastic time.

When we were at the car, Jenna came running out and indicated Regina should roll down her window. Jenna held up the piece of rope and ribbed, "Don't forget your rope! You never know when Regina is going to be in trouble again." Regina took the rope and responded with, "You're right. You never know with me!" Then Jenna continued, "Oh, and I love your boots. They're so cute!" Regina responded with, "Actually, they're Meg's. I'm just borrowing them." Jenna looked at me and complimented, "Meg, you have good taste." And we drove off.

If it weren't for Regina's presence, I would have taken the boot compliment as the completely sarcastic and pejorative remarks of a prude. My past had been filled with comments of Jenna putting down my boots as too sexual or slutty... even Doc Martens'! Boots have always been my biggest fetish, so the comments were especially effective at making me feel like a freak.

But the comment to Regina was for real. Jenna seemed genuinely taken by the palpable romantic chemistry between Regina and I. Secretly, I bet she and Mark yearned for such a deep and sincere romantic connection, especially one that manifested fully in just a month. Unfortunately, I'm afraid they both settled for each other out of fear of releasing their full sexuality and passion on another human being. It's like bungee jumping. Some people are too afraid to let loose, therefore missing out on an experience of a lifetime. Jenna and Mark would be so much happier if they felt free enough to take a cock in the ass or be whipped and humiliated for an hour.

Regardless, Jenna's perception of me seems to have shifted seismically in the course of a single dinner... thanks to Regina... and the fact that the two of us are able to have such an honest relationship that others dream of. Kink is a big part of that. The trust in our scene play is immensely powerful. That foundation informs and supports the rest of the relationship.

After arriving home from the dinner, we decided to sleep at my place. I could have strapped Regina down to the kitchen table for the night, but I was more in the mood to cuddle. We hung out in bed talking for about an hour, meandering across conversations from flirting to politics. Regina fell asleep with her head on my chest. Sweet.

--- SUNDAY APRIL 15 --- Things suddenly get real

Dear Diary, I hope you are not lonely. Even though you can't hug me, I know you care about me too. I really appreciate you being there for me. Thanks for not judging me!

Regina left shortly after coffee this morning. She had some papers to grade and needed to do a bunch of errands. We decided to rendezvous for a casual dinner back here. I needed the day too, both for my own headspace and for paying bills, and of course, finishing my taxes! Regina had already done hers a month ago. But I usually get an extension. It's free. Why not take the time since there is no penalty and it takes the stress off? I put on some Pandora and got into the zone. The sun was shining on my arm at the table. I felt so in love.

After messing with the taxes for about two hours, I ended up taking a nap by falling asleep on the couch to a Rykarda Parasol song (Her music is so sultry and mysterious). The sleep felt amazing... until... Blare! Blare! The stupid phone started ringing. It was my mom.

She called to say how much she enjoyed the evening last night and how much the whole family enjoyed meeting Regina. She went on and on about how it was great to see me so happy with someone.

But with my mom, she's never going to leave it as a happy conversation without imposing her views. She has to give me her advice. Sure enough, she started with, "Do you mind if I share some concerns with you?" Of course I do. I didn't want to hear anything negative coming out of her. Welcome to my childhood with her. She had an opinion about everything. Her advice made sense sometimes, but other times it felt preachy. Intangible things like love operate independently of her well-meaning logic.

For example, I'm 26 years old and she still sends me articles in the mail about how to do things better in my life. She'll send me an article about how bad caffeine is, or how to avoid being mugged as a single woman at night. I really don't need that crap. All it does is aggravate me and make me rely on my own wisdom even more.

My mom wouldn't be done until she has an opportunity to dispense her advice. I figured she was going to tell me how hard life is going to be as a gay person. Gay people are discriminated against, etc. But instead, she surprised me with a lengthy sermon about how our age difference will end up being a big problem.

Regina is 12 years older than me. Big whoop, right? To my mom it sure is. For twenty minutes I listened to her address about the problems with our age difference: *"You won't be able to relate to the same music or cultural references because you both grew up a dozen years apart. Regina's friends will be much older than you and you will feel awkward when you are out socially together. People may even think she's your mom. When you are 40, she is going to be 52. She will be in menopause while you are still in your prime. Your own friends are much younger and will wonder why you are with someone so much older. Your friends and her friends won't be on the same* *wavelength. Her hair will be grey while yours is still red. She has a child, but what if you want one of your own and she has already been there and done that? When her son is 20 he could have kids and make you a grandma before your 40th birthday. When you are 70, Regina is going to be 82 years old. 82!"*

Jeeeze!!! I'm freaking 26 and she already has me at the retirement home. WTF! I didn't even want to dignify my mom's monologue with an answer. A twelve year difference is nothing. Look at Jay-Z and Beyonce. Or Celine Dion and René Angélil with a whopping 26 year difference. Ellen DeGeneres and Portia de Rossi: 15 years. Humphrey Bogart and Lauren Bacall: 25 years! If Regina were 12 years older than me as a man, I bet my mom wouldn't have said jack. I politely let my mom know, "Thanks, I got it covered."

I was all worked up. I decided to go for a little roller blade along the Ocean Beach esplanade to clear my head. After a good 45 minutes of seagulls and sea breeze, I was finally forgetting all about that phone call, especially after I saw a pod of dolphins poking along by the surfers.

On the way home, I picked up some groceries to prepare for dinner with Regina. Strangely, I found myself seeking foods that were high in anti-oxidants like blueberries, kidney beans, artichokes and pecans. Without even realizing it, I think I was shopping for foods that would help Regina preserve her youth longer. Fuck. That is really messed up!! My mom's comments had poisoned me. At 38, Regina looks better most women could ever hope to. What the hell is wrong with me? I am not going to be poisoned by my mom's well-meaning nonsense.

After a shower, I got ready for Regina, assisted by a scotch on the rocks. As the clocked ticked closer to her arrival time, I found myself getting kinkier and kinkier thoughts about having a badass S&M scene with her. I wanted to dominate and humiliate her. I wanted to torture her and be cruel. I needed to play the "weather" game again.

But when she finally showed up, I opened the door to find the sweetest smile on a woman whose energy felt like radiating sunlight. "Hey, Baby," I welcomed. We hugged and kissed tenderly. Her lips were telling me that she loved me more than anything in the world. How could this divine creature contain even an ounce of kink? People from her school and neighborhood would be stunned if they found out that she adored sexual pain and high leather boots. Our delicate kiss took a sharp turn when she bit my bottom lip; I recoiled with a quick scream. Clearly, she was not the sweet daisy I was enjoying a moment earlier. She asked for it! "Can you believe how blue the sky is today?" I shot out with a cold smirk.

Bang! Just like that, she was entranced as my slave. "Yes, Mistress," she responded as her face instantly transformed into the darker personality. Her eyes cast downward and she knelt before me with her head down. "Get up," I ordered. "How dare you presume to be my slave without the proper attire," I censured. "You need to go upstairs and find my corset. Even though it maybe a little big for you, it will cinch down to your size if you pull the lacing as tight as you can. Understood?" I pushed. "Yes, Mistress," she submitted. "Dress like a slave… and you'd better not forget your heavy leather collar," I continued. "Yes, Mistress," she agreed and disappeared toward my bedroom.

While she was gone, I pondered the upcoming scene and how I would like it to unfold. When she returned, she looked like a living Helmut Newton photo in my corset, her long gloves, and thigh boots. The corset strongly accented her striking figure.

For a millisecond, my head took a recess from the game and said in my mom's voice, "Meg. She is a 38 year old woman, 12 years older than you!" But my mind quickly jumped back into the Mistress's body and I realized that whatever minor wrinkles or aging effects Regina may have or would develop, she is smoking hot! Her age is a turn on to me. She is a powerful, beautiful and fully alive woman. Anybody on Earth would agree.

I walked right up to Regina, just an inch from her face, grabbed her jaw overbearingly and stared into her eyes. Then something took over and I sternly articulated, "You need to prove your love to me. You need to chain me down and hurt me. You need to fuck with me until I cry... until I have nothing left... until I am nothing but a pathetic mess. No safewords. No ending the game. No stopping until you achieve your goal. Understood?"

"Yes, Mistress," she responded flatly. She pulled my hand from her jaw, stared callously in my eyes, then slapped my face with full intent. Her instant switch shocked me!! The slap hurt! Heartlessly, she dumped on me with, "You are pathetic, Mistress. You think you're so tough, don't you?" Her words had the effect of completely taking away my power. She grabbed my wrist and dragged me to the kitchen post where she locked my arms around it with the handcuffs that she had brought downstairs with her after changing. I'm assuming she had thought the handcuffs would be on her wrists instead. But things moved rapidly and I suddenly found myself handcuffed to the post and under the control of my own slave.

Before I even knew what was happening, she had grabbed the plastic bag the artichokes had been in and whipped it over my head, pulling the plastic tight to cut off my air. It wasn't erotic, it was just fucking scary!! I couldn't breathe at all. I shook my head and writhed around in vain trying to escape the baggie. She wasn't letting up. Completely desperate and freaked, I tried kicking her violently with all my might and tried to reverse headbutt her, but she was able to easily avoid my desperate flailing.

Just when I was about to black out, she yanked off the baggie! I heaved for air in giant gasps. "Pathetic," she dispassionately said to herself. As I struggled to gain my breath, I wondered... "Was this really Regina? Was she still my slave? Was I still the mistress in charge?" She had either taken my orders very seriously or something had snapped in her.

With my hands locked around the post, my back was to her. She fondled my breasts from behind, kissing my neck and nibbling on my ears. Gradually, her hands lowered to my waist and her fingers undid my belt and unbuttoned my pants. She pulled them all the way to the floor, taking my panties along too.

Her gloved hand caressed my ass for a while, which had the effect of making me super moist. She pulled off her right glove, then shoved her index finger into my mouth forcefully for me to suck. She seemed to really appreciate how I sucked it like a cock. With her other hand, she continued fondling my tits, sometimes pinching the nipples. Her bare hand went back to my ass to caress it. SLAP!! She broke the tone with a solid spank. Then another... and more and more. She was spanking my ass as hard as humanly possible.

At first, I was digging it, but the more she went along, the more the pain turned from sexual to actual. I was aching and moaning and begging her to stop, telling her I'm sorry and trying anything at all to get her to quit spanking.

Then, she did. All was quiet. A moment later, I felt her middle finger on my clit. She started working me with a magic touch. Suddenly, my eyes widened with a start! She had shoved her middle finger all the way up my ass! While playing with my breasts, she started fucking my ass hard with her finger. It was super hot! I mumbled something like, "Oh my God, that feels soooo good." But it must have pissed her off. She instantly stop playing with me and spoke harshly, "Did I say you could fucking talk?" With her gloved hand, she shoved the other glove deep into the back of my throat. Because it was a shoulder-length glove, it more than filled every bit of my mouth.

She dashed to the sink, took of her other glove and washed her hands. A moment later, she returned with duct tape. She wet the back of my hair by my neck with water from her hands, then strapped the tape around my mouth and neck with several passes to secure the glove in my mouth. (I figured she had wet my hair so the tape would come off later without sticking).

Her forcefulness and ultra cold demeanor was a real turn on that I hadn't expected from the sweet little Regina slave. She took the belt from my pants and started whipping my ass. It's a heavy leather belt and it really smarted, especially since my ass was still on fire from the spanking. She got into a tight 1-second rhythm with the blows. My ass was starting to burn big time. She kept at it. After a couple minutes, I was getting near the end of my pain threshold. She was perceptive enough to know this, so she pulled back up my pants and buttoned them. She ran to my room and came back with my vibrator, which she shoved into my pants, parking it right on my clit.

With the vibrator running on me, my pain threshold expanded. She continued whipping me over my pants. Surprisingly, my ass was so sore that the pants didn't seem to give much insulation from the blows. She really got into it.

After a while, she switched to whipping my back! It felt like the classic whip scene from an African slave movie. By that point, I was convinced she was going to be directing a lot more pain onto me. Sure enough, she whipped my back until I started screaming against the glove that was gagging my mouth. My cotton top was no match for the leather belt, which hurt sharply more on my back than it did on my butt. Occasionally, the vibrator would help me turn the pain into sexual fuel. She whipped and whipped. I was in real pain and started panicking. Regina didn't seem to care one bit that I started crying, screaming, and shaking my head with "No!"

She continued the assault on my back until I was an absolute wreck, bawling like a baby as I fought against the handcuffs. I was outside of myself with pain and completely terrified that something had snapped in Regina and that she was going insane.

In my whole life, I had never been so out of control with my emotions. It was difficult to breathe with the gag, leaving only my nostrils for all the air I needed. My wrists were getting scraped up from fighting against the handcuffs and she kept whipping me. I was literally flailing to and fro to try to escape each next blow.

Transformed into a bundle of nerves, I was completely freaking out. But all of the sudden, I heard a sound I couldn't believe! Regina spoke in her normal friendly voice, "That was some kind of crazy day I had." The whipping stopped. "Hey, Baby," she reassured me, "It's me. I'm here with you. You're ok." She quickly uncuffed me and led me to my bed. We laid down in a loose hug, looking at each other's faces. A flood of emotion hit me and waves of weeping came through me. Regina somehow felt the same thing and began crying deeply, but quietly as if in solidarity.

After what seemed like ten minutes of this deep weeping, we finally began coming back to earth. Regina licked my tears and kissed my eyes. We kissed and shared the intimacy of each other's faces for the longest time.

Out of nowhere, she changed gears with, "Can you believe how blue the sky is today?" I couldn't believe I was hearing this and that we were back in the game already. Can't a girl get a break for a damn minute? Slave Regina spoke in a loving and nervous voice: "Mistress? Did I disappoint you by overstepping my bounds? I was really concerned about you, Mistress." This was a comforting tone for me to hear at that moment. "No, Sweet slave," I reassured her, "You did beautifully. Thank you for following my orders so obediently." I kissed her on the lips and ended the game with, "You are perfect for me. But I need to go now. That was some kind of crazy day I had." And we went back to ourselves.

"Regina, my back is on fire. Do you think you can rub some lotion on it for me?" I asked. "Sure," she said, "and you might need another scotch to take the edge off. Be right back."

She came back and pampered me. Seriously, I was in real pain. (Even now, my back feels like the worst sunburn imaginable). I was too agonized to make dinner for us so Regina stepped up to the plate, bringing me a tray in bed. After dinner, she spoonfed me ice cream. Later, she took my hand and gave it a massage. After a minute or two, she blew my mind by cavalierly saying, "Would you move in with Tucker and I?"

Wow!! Talk about out of the blue! Here's this woman I'd only known a month, a female love interest when I always thought I was straight! It's only been a month! It all should seem like a big heavy decision.

But for me, in that moment that followed such a heavy scene, the answer came quickly and without any concern or dread: "Yes, Regina. I want to. I want to spend the rest of my life with you!" Her eyes puddled up. "Really?" she asked, cutely crinkling her nose in genuine disbelief. I think she was expecting me to say no or get into a dramatic scene about it. She continued, "Tucker is crazy about you! We can have our own kind of family." That sounded perfect to me.

Who moves in after just a month of dating? But then again, people get married after a night in Las Vegas, so who the hell knows?

Even the mention of living with Tucker didn't throw me off. Sure, I would be sharing Regina with him, but being a part of a family is something that really appeals to me. When Tucker came to the office, I felt I would love to be more involved with him. He's such a great kid. Though… that may change when he's going through the emotional roller coaster of puberty. Just joking. I would really love to be around him in Regina's world.

Regina applied more lotion to my aching back and butt and we continued the conversation as follows:

> **ME**
> *How do we know we are not just in the honeymoon phase of dating?*
>
> **REGINA**
> *My gut tells me this is it. I've never had such validation of my feelings for someone.*
>
> **ME**
> *Same here. What will you tell Tucker?*
>
> **REGINA**
> *I'll tell him that I fell in love with you. He's fully aware about same sex couples. This is San Francisco. Several of his friends at school have two dads or two moms.*

ME
Don't you think he'll be jealous that I enter the picture to share part of his mom with him?

REGINA
I've seen the way he is around you. He's really rooting for us as couple. I think he is craving it. I can tell he thinks you are a positive force.

ME
What about kink?

REGINA
What about it? If we were vanilla, we wouldn't be having sex in front of him.

ME
You're right.
(a moment passed as we both contemplated moving in together. Then...)
That lotion feels so good on my skin. Thanks for taking care of me.

REGINA
Of course.

ME
What was it like for you to dominate and hurt me?

REGINA
It was really hard. I could never do that in real life! When I was whipping your back, it felt like skydiving or walking on fire. I had major adrenaline driving me. I knew you needed something dark.

ME
I think I wanted to see if you would really hurt me. I needed to feel a scary bond with you.

REGINA
I loved seeing my Mistress weeping. It was beautiful. I loved seeing her terrified. It was a trust and intimacy that I have never experienced in my life. I love you so much.

ME
I want you to hurt me again sometime. I want Regina, not the slave, to hurt me... to make me beg for mercy.

REGINA
I don't think I could do that. It would be too hard outside of the game. I wouldn't want to mix real feelings into making you suffer. We need our rules.

ME
Ok. I guess your Mistress will have to force you to do it on occasion.

REGINA
She'd better watch out. No telling what she will unleash! Next time I see her, I want to sass off. Maybe she'll have to teach me a harsh lesson.

ME
I bet she will.

REGINA
When do you want to move in?

ME
I can't believe this is happening! What about June 1st. I can sublet my place out.

REGINA
You don't mind giving up your space? I do think it would be best for Tucker to keep the consistency at my house.

ME
I don't mind. Where will he sleep, still with you?

REGINA
He'll sleep in his own room. That change is long over due. He's nine years old. We've only been doing it out of convenience and keeping each other company.

ME
Ok. He might like his own space now.
(She nodded and we stared at each other, excited by the thought of our new future together.)
Why don't you go brush your teeth and wash your face. You are going to have to spend the entire night in bed hogtied by some belts.

REGINA
A requirement from my Mistress?

ME
No. Just from me. I want to make sure you don't wander off.

Regina looked and me with such passion in her eyes that the feelings sent us into a long French kiss.

She's tied up right now in a tight hogtie as I write this. I can hear her faint moans as she struggles against the leather belts that are holding her wrists and ankles together. Oh, and she has a ball gag in place just for good measure. Don't sympathize with her; my back is still killing me.

--- MONDAY APRIL 16 --- Sexy sleep

Last night at 3am, I awoke to the sounds of Regina moaning softly and struggling against the ball gag. Something was wrong. I removed the gag to ask her about it. Her jaw was aching terribly due to having been locked in an open position so long from the gag. I had thought that the ball was narrow enough that it wouldn't be an issue. But she really seemed in a lot of pain. Once the gag was out, she stretched her jaw up and down several times and let out sighs of relief.

She was still hogtied facedown with her arms behind her back secured to her crossed legs. I checked her feet and hands to see if they were cold. If so, that would mean she was not getting enough circulation. But her hands and feet felt perfectly warm… which meant, she was going to have to continue sleeping in bondage. We kissed for a moment. She thanked me for removing the gag. Then I caressed her ass a long time with soft, steady strokes until she fell asleep about 15 minutes later.

We both slept until the alarm went off. It was a school day. We were both really happy and cuddly. She snuggled me with her head and I softly massaged her all over. After a while, I slipped my hand between her tied up legs and gently played with her clitoris, occasionally dipping into the well of lubricant she was creating by being turned on.

What started out as a simple connection of touching had soon become an erotic undertaking. Watching her getting aroused was getting me aroused too. I ended up playing with myself with one hand while playing with her with the other. We were completely in sync in our arousal, kissing in between breathing and feeling immense closeness. Then at the same time, we both escaped into orgasm together, flowing in waves, as opposed to the explosive releases of other times. Our final releases were mellow, but profound and bled off to a form of complete relaxation.

Longing for the closeness of her embrace, I untied Regina, tossing the belts on the floor. She rolled over on her back and her arms came around me as if starving for touch. As I lied on top of her, we hugged and kissed in silence for minutes upon minutes. Her nighttime ordeal was over and we were finally able to press against each other without restraint. She started giggling at the mere idea of being free, talking about how that position was really miserable for so long. I was giggling too. There was a giddy air between us as we both joked about how bad she was going to feel during the day from having such a rough night of sleep.

She hopped in the shower and I used the opportunity to make us both a strong cup of joe. When I returned, she was still in the shower, looking as radiant as ever with her wet hair and soapy body. I took the liberty of slipping into the shower with her. After a quick, soapy kiss, I slid down to my knees so my head was at her waist level. I gently hugged her thighs and rested my head on her tummy. She looked down at me lovingly and stroked my head as the warm water streamed all over us. There was something in her look, in her face, that told me we were complete together. There was an energy from her that let me know we had found each other forever. She continued to stroke my head as I softly hugged her thighs and saw all the potential I had ever craved in a love.

--- WEDNESDAY APRIL 18 --- The mundane week

So far the week had been pretty typical. I went out to lunch with Pete for some girl talk. He was so happy that I had found Regina.

She and I haven't seen each other since Monday morning. She's been super busy catching up on her daily life… and soap opera she records. I still think that is so funny! Of all people, she is the last person I would think would be hooked on a soap! I've been busy in my job too. We picked up a new client, a national insurance carrier at the same time as preparing for a commercial shoot in Golden Gate Park for Toyota.

Oh, to celebrate Tucker's move to his own bed on Monday night, Regina and I decided to sleep on the phone together. It was sweet. We literally had the phones by our pillows on speakerphone. It was like she was right next to me. We talked about what it would be like living together and tried to work out the mechanics of it all. Would we merge our finances? Would we merge our laundry? Who would control the Pandora? What kind of personal space would each of us have? Who cooks and who cleans up? They were all real things that needed to be considered. It also made everything seem more real and solid to be thinking about the mundane details of living together.

Eventually, we fell asleep on the phone together. In the morning I was awakened by the alarm going off on her side. We said a quick goodbye and that was it. When people sign up for the *unlimited minutes* calling plan, I doubt the phone company considered someone will keep the connection opened all night during sleep!

Regina texted me that she had picked up Tucker after school. She said she was going to talk with him about me moving in. Gulp. That's scary. It seems unfair to burden and impose the parents' romantic interests onto kids. I would normally think it is a terrible idea to have a love interest move in so quickly. But in our case, we both sincerely feel that this is it. Tucker will have the benefit of being adored by both of us. I will always make sure they will have lots of their very own personal time together. I feel that Tucker will really thrive being around the energy that Regina and I create together. In fact, we all will. Each leg of the triangle will balance the other. Still, I bet it will be quite a transition to Tucker that such a big change is coming to his life. It will be big for all of us.

--- THURSDAY APRIL 19 --- Changing bedrooms

Regina talked to Tucker last night. She filled me in on the details today on her break at school. She said Tucker seemed thrilled that I would be moving in. She thinks Tucker is very in tune with everything and had expected this might happen. I agree. Even though things happened very quickly, it seemed like he was acutely aware of how fast things were moving and how much Regina and I are crazy for each other.

Tucker asked where I was going to sleep. She broke the news to him that she and I would be sleeping together. He said he was fine with that, but added that he would still like to sleep with Regina sometimes. That sounds good to me. It's nice that they have that closeness. Childhood is so short that I don't fault them for wanting to stretch it out as long as they can. In just a few short years, he will probably be hanging out with his buddies and embarrassed to have mom around too much. Kids!

Regina and I decided I should hang on to my place for three months as we test the waters of living together. It could either be a lifeboat or a private sex den. Seriously, we both doubted it would have to be a lifeboat out of a bad relationship. We know in our hearts we are made for each other. It's really exciting to think about sharing a life with her and Tucker.

Since the upcoming weekend was a Tucker weekend, I offered a suggestion for a really fun weekend. There is a new laser tag facility opening in Santa Rosa and I thought we could try it out and stay the night on the north coast. Tucker could bring his crazy buddy Jason and they could run around in the waves together, then try out the new laser tag place. Regina was all over the idea. I booked Saturday night at the Whale Watch Inn on the Sonoma coast. I'd been there before and it has a private beach cove that feels like a remote beach in a romantic movie. Sometimes you can see whales cruising by!

--- FRIDAY APRIL 20 --- Feeling on track

Not much to report, other than I feel really happy about life. I feel even more positive that moving in with Regina is the right thing to do. She told me she feels the same way.

Today I masturbated to the thought of when Regina was whipping my back. It was really terrifying to see her so engaged in the character that she was not going to let up until her task was complete.

I asked Regina what she thought about dominating me. But she said she never has. She was only whipping me in obeying orders from her Mistress. She said she wouldn't have initiated that on her own. When I asked her if she has a dominant side, she pleaded for me to understand that she only wants to be owned by me. She wants to be my slave. She wants to serve me and be abused by me.

--- SUNDAY APRIL 22 --- Bonding with friends

Yesterday morning I picked up Regina, Tucker, and his friend Jason for the drive up the coast. We busted a move straight up to the North Bay. I thought it would be fun to stop by Bodega Bay so the boys could run around on the giant cliffs of the Bodega Head overlooking the rocky coast. We spent about two hours there and everyone had a blast. The boys had plenty of energy to burn after having been trapped in the car so long.

While the boys were climbing a giant tree, Regina and I sat on the cliff looking for whales. Wouldn't you know, we weren't sitting there 5 minutes when we saw 3 whales just a couple hundred feet away. They were spouting and breaching. Awesome.

Making sure the boys were out of site, we kissed a bit. It was our first intimate contact since Monday morning. Regina has a kiss that touches me to the core. The sun was on us. There were whales. A giant fog bank that looked like a solid wall was approaching from the ocean. The kids were in bliss. Seagulls were everywhere. The universe was telling us we are on track to a celebrating great life together.

After Bodega Head, we stopped for lunch and then went up the coast to the Whale Watch Inn. The boys were so excited at the sight of the pristine cove below the balcony. It turns out our room was the same one Lucile Ball stayed in the 1980's.

We all got ready for the beach as quickly as possible. But Jason (Mr. Hyper) flew down the rickety cliff-dangling stairs and was in the water unsupervised before we had even gotten to the sand ourselves! Crazy monkey.

The sun was still blasting down, but just off shore was that same heavy fog bank. It was 72 degrees, so the kids were fine playing in the water (54 degrees). But when that fog would roll in, there were going to be some freezing boys. Tucker and Jason had a skimboard and must have played with that for an hour and half while Regina and I walked along the cove checking out the sea life and tide pools.

It seemed natural to be holding hands with Regina, but for some reason, we refrained from that. It felt like maybe it would have been too gay for a family outing. I know that sounds stupid, but there was something holding us back from being our regular selves. It may have been easier if we had already been living together and Jason and his parents were already aware that two girlfriends live together with Tucker. It's stupid how stigmatized that still is in society. The sad fact is, there's shame around the subject.

But it's ok. Regina and I both felt the truth of our bond, even without holding hands. When she was bent over looking at a starfish, I pinched her ass! She got mad and started throwing stinky old seaweed all over me. A rogue wave came and knocked us both on our butts as we laughed our heads off.

Just like that, the fog bank smothered the shore. The boys came running over, shivering and practically blue. We threw towels around them and raced up to the room. We had them jump right into the shower with their trunks on so they could warm up. They were rocking out to Jason's iPod that was plugged into some little speakers. While they were in the shower, Regina used the opportunity to shock me yet again. The conversation went like this:

> **REGINA**
> *I'd be ok with the Mistress having Victoria over while I am in bondage or submission.*
>
> **ME**
> *What? Where did that come from?*
>
> **REGINA**
> *I think it would be more humiliating to me. I've been getting turned on about it lately.*
>
> **ME**
> *We had a big issue about that whole thing. Has something changed?*
>
> **REGINA**
> *I feel safe with you. I trust you and I trust you with her.*

ME
You didn't before?

REGINA
I might have been scared you would like her more or see something in her that I don't have. It would still kill me if you ever had anything with her, but if she were just your friend who happened to be over while I was being tortured or neglected in bondage, I might find it pretty hot. But Victoria could never know. You could just tell her I was away. I know you would never make fun of me with her.

ME
Wow. I'm stunned.

REGINA
Would you want to do that?

ME
It would be hot to have my secret pet locked away while I entertained a guest.

REGINA
The whole idea is degrading to me, you two enjoying yourselves while I'm helplessly suffering.

ME
It's pretty degrading. But you deserve that kind of treatment.

We stared at each other with huge gleams of lust in our eyes. With a relationship like this, our sexual relationship could shift and grow forever. We definitely made the right choice to be together. I feel like this same arrangement in a man/woman couple would have ended up with the guy screwing Victoria too. It would have gotten messed up really fast. But in this case, it's all about my connection to Regina. The concept was so intriguing that I could barely function the rest of the evening as we went to dinner with the boys. That Regina is my dream.

Later in the evening, we thought it would be fun to show the boys Alfred Hitchcock's "The Birds," which was shot in Bodega Bay. Even though the effects were really dopey, the movie still scared the crap out of the boys. They both agreed it was the scariest movie they'd ever seen.

After the night at the inn, we headed back south, making sure to stop at the laser tag place in Santa Rosa. It was an absolute blast!! Regina, the little vegetarian, turned into a hardcore, competitive commando! It was us against the boys… and we actually won!!! Ha.

The whole trip was a great bonding and acquainting experience (especially for Tucker, Regina, and I) as we tried on our new roles together. After I dropped them off home, Regina called me later to say that Tucker literally said, "It's going to be so great living with Meg." My heart melted.

--- MONDAY APRIL 23 --- Blue Monday

Hello Diary, It's Earth Day! Hello Earth. Thanks for making Regina. Being back in the grind on Monday was a bit of a let down after such a magical weekend trip. Regina said Tucker slept late and had a crying meltdown while getting ready for school. She said she even had a hard time herself.

--- TUESDAY APRIL 24 to MONDAY APRIL 30 --- All in the mind

This week was filled with all kinds of talk and preparations for the big move. We both kept at our jobs and personal tasks and really didn't make the time to be together much. We both knew that soon we could see each other everyday. Also, it seemed like we were organically each trying to get our heads around who we are as individuals and what it was going to mean to be permanently together.

We showed up to yoga separately on Thursday night. When we got there, I kissed her on the lips and then immediately said, "Can you believe how blue the sky is today?" During all of the yoga class, the game was on. She was submissive and withdrawn. I loved seeing her like that and watching how the others reacted to her sudden change of personality. They must have figured she was really moody. Our mats were far from each other in the room. During the entire class, there was this conspicuous sexual anticipation between us.

When class was over, I held her chin firmly and said, "That was some kind of crazy day I had." She came back to reality, but it took a few seconds for the transition. It was the first time the Mistress had called the game into action without demanding anything of her. It was hot. Nothing happened, but it was so sexual. She stared at me deeply from 5 inches away and then softly uttered, "You're fucking sexy." SLAP!!! She slapped my face and stormed out coldly. Wow. This relationship clearly had layers!! I love this woman!!

--- TUESDAY MAY 1 --- Move-in Day

Since I was planning on keeping my place for a while, I didn't see the need to some go storming into Regina's place with all my belongings. Instead, I was only moving with three big boxes of clothes, my computer, all my shoes, my pillow, makeup and bathroom stuff. As I showed up with the first box, Regina gave me a cheek kiss and said, "Welcome to our new life!"

Tucker was super psyched. Before I was barely across the threshold, he proudly showed me a painting he had made in school saying, "This is to hang in the bedroom. I made it for you." It was a watercolor of the three of us sitting on the stoop in front of the house. The image was crudely painted, but it was really sweet! I loved it. I gushed about it to Tucker and he was delighted at my reaction.

I carried the box to Regina's room, our room. She showed me how she had cleaned out an entire dresser for me to use. She had also removed all her clothes from the closet, saying that she moved her stuff down to the hall closet in order to make more room for me. While that was thoughtful, I felt guilty for kicking her clothes out of her own room. I wanted to share the dresser with her. I told her that it would feel better to me to split the space in the drawers vertically so that half a drawer was hers and half was mine. That way we could get dressed in the same room. Our folded sweaters could be right next to each other's. It seems sexier that way. My panties could be next to hers. We were in this thing together. She thought my logic was adorable and agreed to the concept.

After my stuff was all in place, I still felt like a foreigner. What was my hang out spot? What did I do now? What's the "family" nighttime routine? If I want to disappear for a while to read, would Regina or Tucker be hurt? It WAS her house and it still felt like it. I guess I needed time to adjust to all this.

But Regina knew just what to do, taking charge by saying, "Would you mind helping Tucker with his Math while I start dinner?" And that was all it took. Tucker's math was challenging me to recall my long forgotten lessons. It primed the pump for us to start figuring out our place together. While I was helping Tucker, Regina lightened the mood by flashing me a boob when he wasn't looking. And that's how it went. It was going to be ok. We would find our balance in this new life.

--- WEDNESDAY MAY 2 --- Dinner Guest

When I got home from work, Regina was home grading papers and drinking some French table wine. Tucker was picked up after school by his dad per the usual schedule. She poured me some wine and remarked, "I didn't see you leave the house today. You look fantastic!" I was wearing a camel colored A-line skirt, a black top and our brick red boots. Before I knew what was happening, she knelt at my feet saying, "I love you so much!" Solemnly, she began to lick my boots very slowly and sensually. The sight of this beautiful grown woman licking my boots was unbelievable. It made me want to hurt and control her. I immediately invoked the game with, "Can you believe how blue the sky is today?" And just like that, she was slave Regina.

"Go put on the corset and my thigh boots," I ordered. She quickly complied. When she returned, I led her to the bedroom where I placed her on the bedroom coffee table on her back, spreading her legs up against the table legs. I chained each leg tightly to a table a leg, then chained her wrists tightly to the other legs. Her waist looked freakishly waspish in the corset, which she had laced quite tightly. It had the effect of making her a bit short of breath. I forced a bit gag in her mouth, strapping it firmly behind her neck. She was chained there, looking up at the ceiling. I found a black t-shirt in our dresser and pulled it callously over her head to both blind her and keep her gorgeous face from distracting me.

"You're lucky we are on the same page tonight," I said, "I'm having a dinner guest here tonight in 15 minutes." Regina was dead silent. I sat with my wine, staring at this impossibly beautiful girlfriend.

DING-DONG. The guest arrived. It was my dear friend Victoria. When she asked about Regina's whereabouts I responded with, "She had to be somewhere else tonight. Sorry."

Victoria jumped right in with, "That's pathetic! I was looking forward to hanging with you both tonight." I reassured her with, "Don't worry, we will have plenty of times to do that from now on."

I went about preparing and serving dinner, while completely obsessed with thoughts of Regina the whole time. Victoria really seemed to be enjoying the time with me (since I had been busy with Regina so much lately). At one point, Victoria got a call from one of her suitors. Who calls instead of texting these days anyway? She excused herself for a moment and went outside to speak privately, which afforded me the opportunity to check on Regina.

The silly girl hadn't moved an inch since the last time I saw her. She was tied to the bedroom coffee table exactly as I had left her. Slipping back the top of the corset, I sucked and licked her nipples for a bit, causing her to sigh with delight. Taking over her breasts with my hands, I fondled her softly and began kissing her mouth through the black t-shirt. It wasn't much of a kiss since the gag and fabric was blocking her mouth, but that restriction made the kiss all the more erotic... forbidden.

Once we were both worked up, I thought I had better get back to Victoria and left little miss helpless alone again. Good timing too. Victoria had just finished her call when I got back to the kitchen.

We had one of the best visits we had had in a long time. She was asking me all kinds of questions about Regina, our lives together, our kink, etc. I answered what I could, but teased her with vague answers about our sex life. She loved that I have finally found my sexual match. It turns out the guy on her phone call was a promising prospect, handsome and a good job. But he is a recovering alcoholic with 14 years of sobriety. At that point, it's hard to think someone would still be considered an alcoholic, but I guess it just take one single drink until their life crashes and burns again. I believe it. I've seen sober people bomb out after a long time. Victoria said the guy is super fun and works in tech sales. How great would it be for Victoria to finally find a great, steady guy?

After she eventually took off after dinner, I was anxious to get back to Regina.

I went to Regina and thought I would play with her just a little more. I unchained her feet from the table legs, then folded her thighs against her chest and secured them to her chest by running the chain behind her knees and to her neck. Basically, she was in a ball lying on her back with her ass in a vulnerable position. After first giving her a gentle ass massage, I spanked her over and over with my bare hand, occasionally switching to finger fucking her and playing with her clit. She was eating it up!

In order to overwhelm the slave with sensation, I put a condom on a small cucumber and shoved it in her ass, where it stayed as I continued the spanking and rubbing her pussy. She was moaning and writhing in an unbelievable expression of ecstasy, finally blowing up in passion, shaking and bouncing on the table.

I unchained her legs from the ball position and then lowered myself over her face, her arms still chained. There was nothing like my slave Regina's magic tongue. Her entire soul was entering me. In short order, I was burning into orgasm.

Finally coming down, I freed her and ended the game. We collapsed. Slowly coming back to reality, I hit the remote and we watched an ancient rerun of *Friends*, both of us too flattened to speak until the episode ended. We gave little kisses and casually shared about our experiences of the evening. She told me the Victoria aspect really helped make her feel anxious and worthless (In S&M, that's a good thing). I brought her dinner in bed. As she ate it, I massaged her feet.

--- THURSAY MAY 3 --- Color everywhere

When we awoke in the morning, I threw open the drapes to discover a miracle! The entire street was exploding in vibrant fuchsia bougainvillea flowers! They usually don't come until June, but somehow they came early! The bougainvilleas of San Francisco are the most beautiful flowers in the world. On block after block, the flowers creep up the fronts of the houses and outline the windows in joy. Yep. Summertime had come early. Regina Baker brought color into my life!!

I always thought I was meant to be with a guy. I thought I wanted that male counter part. Cock. But I never clicked with guys. Suddenly, I see why.

With Regina, I find myself being honest in the relationship. I find I'm more settled into my own self. I feel no shame, free from being a sexual outsider my whole life. It feels whole and wholesome and fun to be with her. She's a mommy. I can be part of a family... another thing I didn't know I wanted. But now I do! Regina and I have found each other. We fit. She's adorable. I'm in love with my best friend. She's a woman. I'm smiling.

Thanks for listening, Diary. I love owning Regina.

Printed in Great Britain
by Amazon

58685973R00165